McGarr and the P.M. of Belgrave Square

McGarr and the P.M. of Belgrave Square

Bartholomew Gill

THE VIKING PRESS　　　　**NEW YORK**

First published in 1983 by The Viking Press
40 West 23rd Street, New York, N. Y. 10010

Published simultaneously in Canada by
Penguin Books Canada Limited

LIBRARY OF CONGRESS CATALOGING IN PUBLICATION DATA

McGarrity, Mark (Bartholomew Gill, pseudonym) 1943–
    McGarr and the P.M. of Belgrave Square.
    I. Title.
PS3563.A296M28   1983   813'.54   83-47876
ISBN 0-670-46430-9

Printed in the United States of America
Set in Caledonia

For Max, collaborator

McGarr and the P.M. of Belgrave Square

1

Dubh-Linn. Black Pool. With the renewed burning of coal, its cloud was a mauve and smoky soup that not even a steady drizzle could dispel. It crept under doors and windows, ringed lights in pubs, and coated the tongue with a sordid taste, both bitter and sweet, like the char of burning flesh. Here by the Liffey it blotted out streetlamps, dampened any noise, made the brief days even shorter. Now at half four the spring light was failing and thin, as though winter had returned. Beams from Technical Bureau klieg lights cut crisp cones from the early evening air.

It was the expression on the face of the corpse that struck McGarr. The head was thrown back and the shoulders turned slightly to the side. The man had a long face and a bony, aquiline nose. His mouth was open and his eyes—pale blue, like his suit—were staring up in shock or dismay that he would be found like that. From the ditch the foul water, now crimson, had seeped through the wool of his expensive, tailored suit. The dampness had reached the lapels and the silk handkerchief that was precisely inserted in the pocket.

"One shot from what I can see, Chief. Low. The groin area. Something like a soft-nosed slug. It's . . ." Rubber boots to the hip, rubber gloves to the shoulder, the pathologist parted the leaves of the suitcoat.

Somebody swore. Most averted their heads before summoning their professionalism and forcing their eyes back.

McGarr's own again moved to the building which jutted from the rubble like a solitary, soot-blackened tooth in an old mouth. Having lost the support of contiguous structures, its walls sagged and heaved. Only the decoratively frosted, Victorian windows and a cast-iron façade, the capitals of which— *Craig & Son*, still gold-leafed—kept the long, narrow building from being an eyesore. Through the smog and drizzle he again saw the head of a cigarette, like a homing beacon, glow and then fade. The corner window, second floor, which looked out on the brick-strewn lot.

"Gone. The whole lower-middle anatomy. Base of the spine." The pathologist tossed the flap of the suit back over the wound and raised himself up.

"But was he shot here or just dumped here?" somebody asked.

From the pocket of his oilskin coat the pathologist drew out a torch, the beam of which he played into the vermilion, drizzle-spangled water. It was opaque, depthless, and thick. "Look for yourself, man. A pool of blood. If he's got any left, it's in his toes."

Yet again McGarr's eyes were drawn to the window and then back to the victim: Craig himself, he'd been told—a tall, stooped, old man with thinning hair, once blond. How old could he have been? Mid-seventies, perhaps, but fit. Care had been taken of him.

And his expression, as in *why*? Or, why *here*? Once more McGarr glanced up at the window that commanded a full view of the lot and this section of the quays, which now even commerce had passed by. The flats and shops that had been here when McGarr was a boy had become vacant, then used for storage. Following losses, they had been abandoned. Windows had been broken, panes had fallen in, and finally the structures had been demolished. Looking along the line of the quays, toward the seawall and Dublin Bay beyond, McGarr could see only a forest of ships' masts, winches, and derricks silhouetted darkly on the smoggy sky.

"I'll have to get him back." The pathologist climbed out of the ditch, the blood, like thin paint, flowing in feathered waves down the yellow boots.

The shot had been low. A poor aim? But then, why no second shot? Because the killer had been frightened off? Or because the killer had known? The slug.

And there were at least thirty paces to the only door that McGarr could see, an arched hatch in the garden wall behind the shop. Craig's shin, showing above a fallen sock, was narrow, blue bone. On an old man's bandy legs, would he have chosen to negotiate the ruin of the lot, had he not been brought here?

The expression. The window.

Strobe flashes, like purplish lightning, sprayed the shattered brick and the figures gathered on the rim of the depression. From a pocket of his raincoat McGarr dug out a Woodbine, which he lit. The tobacco tasted stale and harsh, like a quintessence of the foul, moiling air he was breathing, and he could remember in years past having come upon the shop and being surprised by its presence. Why had the antique dealer, Craig, remained here? Cheap rent? Space? Anonymity? Or had it been, as McGarr had noted before, the unwillingness of the elderly to abandon the locus of their lives?

He turned and began walking through the lot, picking his way through the mortared shards of the former buildings and around the puddled depressions. McGarr was a short, thickset man with a long face and clear, gray eyes. What little hair that remained was thin and red, and his baldness was concealed by a derby. Just forty-nine, McGarr was a chief superintendent of the Gárda Síochána, the Irish Police, and head of the Murder Squad.

He removed the cigarette from the corner of his mouth and looked down at it. Habit. He wondered what Craig's had been? A tall man joined him at the curb: O'Shaughnessy, his second-in-command.

"Just the wife on the premises itself," O'Shaughnessy said. "A cook, no less, and a maid/housekeeper come and go. The cook arrives at half seven, the maid a bit later. Both are usually gone by six. They claim they didn't see the corpse until this afternoon.

"Lights were on this morning when they got here, the 'Open' sign up. Thought maybe the victim had nipped out for this or that, but when he missed his dinner," by which O'Shaughnessy meant the noon meal, "they began to worry." He tilted his notepad so the glow of the streetlamp would strike the page: red, boiled face and a lantern jaw; six and a half feet, large frame; a countryman disguised in a Brown-Thomas suit. "The gardener's in the kip out back. Bernie's with him now."

From the street only the top of Craig's head, now lighted, was visible. And how to distinguish it from all the other round or semiround objects there? And then—now that McGarr had taken the cigarette from his mouth was the time to drop it; all day long he had not had one—anybody passing on foot would have walked in the road and most probably looked out on the quays and the river. A cul-de-sac, the street. No cars, no lorries unless by error, and people tended to acknowledge only the expected.

"In the window. Second floor. Corner room. It's the wife. Bernie says she was there when he got here, staring down."

From the crown of the road McGarr could see even less. Had Craig thrown open the door at the side of the garden wall, jumped down the four or five feet, and on his bandy, old legs tried to escape? A wasteland for two hundred yards. No progress, no hope of fleeing.

McGarr began walking toward the lighted front of the shop and loosened his fingers, letting the cigarette drop. Death, a banality. And the greater banality of death by cigarette. Not for the first time he asked himself why he smoked. Was it the need always to have something in his mouth? Was there any, say, nonpersonal justification for it?

Perhaps, for having spent nearly two decades on the Continent—first with Criminal Justice in France and later with Interpol in various Mediterranean countries—he knew that his compatriots smoked more than perhaps any other European people and smoked everywhere, it seemed: in theaters, buses, pubs, while on bicycles, in parks, shamelessly lighting up in areas where smoking was strictly prohibited.

Too much mammying, he punned—allowing his eyes to take in an exquisite, gold-inlaid, Louis XIV escritoire in the grated shop window—as infants. If it wasn't tobacco it was the drink or a cuppa or a sweet. Give us your lips. He thought of the couples—thousands of them all over the city—kissing at bus stops before parting on the last bus. The kiss, it was acceptable. The feel—it depended on how invisible the hands.

The city. McGarr thought of Blake's worm. Craig had not died in any howling storm. He wondered if he had even died at night or if there might even have been an element of drama in his death. Some staging. He thought of the wife and the window.

He stepped off the sidewalk and craned his head to look up at the cast-iron façade, the gold leafing, the frosted windows and neat painting. JEWELLERY, ANTIQUES, AUCTIONS OF ES-

TATES, ESTIMATES, all covered with a layer of dust and grime as identifiable under analysis as a fingerprint. CRAIG & SON. Singular.

And perhaps Dubliners preferred it like this, he thought—the dirt and the stench. Something memorable and tasty with each breath. The air at the brewery, at the bakery. It was said the former caused alcoholism in some, the latter ulcers in others. A constant sense of place, but not unlethal. And like most cities, Dublin had that feel of late—a grinding down. Attrition. A steady and inexorable life-loss, as though people provided the carnage that made the beast roar. Now at rush hour, its bellow was plain, even here by the river.

What had Craig's worm been? McGarr wondered. The booty he could see in the shop window? It was too early to know, and it was time for fog. His hand fell on the packet of Woodbines.

He stepped back on the sidewalk. "Who found him?"

"The maid, a crone. Upstairs from the kitchen window. Having her tea, so. But the missus . . ." O'Shaughnessy shook his head and doffed a plastic-shrouded, pearl-gray homburg as they entered the premises.

McGarr noted the sign, RING PLEASE. The imperative and an inversion, as though Craig had either been unused to the language or had employed an advertising technique. The subtle hook. But here where passersby were probably no more than a dozen a month? Why?

And not shills, the window pieces. The interior of the shop was filled with expensive and tasteful items: an Empire couch resplendently carved; a matched-grain Hepplewhite table that gathered fourteen chairs; rugs, tapestries, Venetian glass, silver gleaming under bare bulbs in rooms that led from both sides of a darkened corridor.

"What's missing?"

"Only a painting, as far as we can tell. Hughie's got a team on it now, going over the inventory. But there's this floor, the basement, and the one above the apartment, all filled with things."

Behind the door in the room that had functioned as Craig's office was a tall, ornate clock and a picture frame that was now empty save for a ragged bead of brightly colored canvas. McGarr had to squint to read the nameplate, which was tarnished as though never touched. It said, "L'Inondation à Port-Marly, Alfred Sisley, 1876," and McGarr tried but failed to reconstruct the illusion of the painting from what was left.

"Valuable?" O'Shaughnessy asked.

"I should imagine," said McGarr.

"Thousands?"

McGarr cocked his head. "Maybe more."

With his handkerchief McGarr grasped an edge and lifted it to examine the heavily embellished frame that wrapped the stretcher, obscuring all but the inner edge at the back.

"Would have been a job of work getting it out of that," O'Shaughnessy observed, "so whoever it was chose the easy way." He shook his head, as if to suggest that even criminals were not what they once were. "The frame alone must be worth something."

McGarr nodded. His wife, Noreen, would know. She had studied art in London and Paris and now managed her family's picture gallery in Dawson Street.

"Who knows about this?" McGarr meant the painting.

"Only the maid, I believe. She says she didn't discover it until after we arrived, and she's been in the kitchen since with the cook, but it's not as though there's much communication between them."

McGarr waited.

"Language barrier, it seems. But something's a bit off here, Peter, and I've yet to decide what."

McGarr turned and glanced around the office, saying

"Hughie" in both question and greeting to Ward, who was sitting at the desk. He was a recent and precocious addition to McGarr's staff.

"Chief," Ward replied, without looking up from a long ledger he was perusing. "It'll take days, maybe weeks." The safe—gold leafed CRAIG & SON—was unopened.

McGarr's eyes strayed out the door to the showrooms and the pieces he could see there, many of which were portable. But not like a rolled-up painting. No means? No time?

"What about the son?"

Said O'Shaughnessy, "An architect with a firm out in Rathfarnum. No attachments to the shop here that we know of. Lives out in Glencree, so we're told."

"*Craig?*" McGarr asked, questioning the name.

"From the North originally. That from the maid."

Her gnarled fingers, like a heap of old bones, were resting on the oilcloth of the kitchen table as McGarr entered. They jumped for the teapot. A ritual, a reflex. "Cream or lemon, sorr?"

McGarr only shook his head and looked down at the ring on her middle finger. It was topaz and set off by a rope weave of tiny diamonds.

"The mister gave me that." She screwed it back along the bone. "A kind man, a saint." She glanced up from it to the cook, who was cutting something at the other end of the kitchen. The click of the blade was intermittent and soft.

McGarr reached past her and parted the curtain. The window looked down on a rectangle of formal garden so particular in design that its contrast with the desolation of the area beyond the walls was nearly untoward. In an L, the street floor of the shop ran to an alley and a loading dock. In the field on that side Technical Bureau teams were still combing the rubble, but the corpse had been removed.

It was dark now, bleak and cold, the drizzle having turned to rain. It made the light in the hut at the end of the garden below seem yellow and warm.

"Can you tell me what happened to him?" she asked.

"Not yet, but you can help me." McGarr sat and eased his back into the chair. He folded his hands in his lap.

"I knew your mother. We were in service together. Leeson Street. Doctor Campbell. Coyne's the name. Rose Marie."

McGarr searched it back through the years. "Inchicore?" It was the working-class area where he had grown up.

"Where else with Coyne a busman all his life and that short."

"Railway Avenue?"

She nodded. "Right across from the works."

Sean, Kevin, Pat. McGarr now kept himself from asking after them, suspecting that the old woman would sooner turn her mind from the matter at hand. Then, she had something to tell him. The tea said as much. And the whisper.

"Still there?"

She caught her breath and inclined her head in both affirmation and lament.

She then reconsidered her hands, composing herself.

McGarr waited.

"I got here this morning at half eight. The usual. I let myself into the garden." She indicated a ring of keys that hung from the belt of her maid's uniform. "But to get into the house, I had to ring. Himself answered." Her eyes once more rested on the cook. "And browned off, I'm telling you, like his sort get. His lips—look at them—bloodless. And the nostrils flared out.

"Says he in his language, which I take on the carom, if you know what I mean, 'How d'ye think I'm to cook down here at the door?' Says I, 'How d'ye think I'm to clean down here in the garden?' Says he, 'Some changes will be made around here,' as if he was something more than just pots and pans and the seventh of them that's come in one window and out the other in me time.

"Well, boy . . ." She raised a hand, as though to touch McGarr's sleeve. "I'm not one to truck with a slagger, and I let him feel the weight of me tongue. One word to the mister, just one, mind . . ." She glanced up. Her eyes were milky from age, the hazel having soured to a deep, dead brown. A tear now formed in the corner of one. Her brow furrowed. "Who could have done that to the poor man, Peter, and why? He was so kind, so gentle. I never heard him even raise his voice."

Still McGarr waited.

"To tell you the truth, the way things is around here I didn't know who to turn to with me the only one on the place capable. It's gotten so I do all the orderin' here, and I don't mean just the groceries. Him"—she meant the cook—"I could do well without, except the missus, being French herself, is partial to their food, don't you know.

"The gardener, poor soul, has got the failing. When I went by his kip this morning, the odor of drink off the place was enough to fell a bullock.

"The son—well, he lives out in Glencree and hasn't been by here in over a week, except for what I saw on me way to work, but I'll get to that.

"And the missus"—her eyes blinked and she touched a hanky to her nose—"have you talked to her, Peter?" There were caution and concern in the question, although it did not require a reply, and in Rose Marie Coyne's face, which was bony but well structured, McGarr read a competence that rather denied her tone.

It was the gossipy familiarity of the Dublin streets, the whisper behind the hand, the advice given—take it or leave it—in passing. It was the vacant and fickle concern of being, for the moment she was with you, all her world, only to have her upon the turn of a heel direct herself to more efficacious cosmogonies.

And why now the tone? She had something to tell him.

Gripping the teacup in both hands, she raised it to the wrinkle of her upper lip. "Quiet, I'd say. Reserved." Her old eyes appeared over the rim. "And then it's not as though she really speaks the language." Another sip. "After the fourteen years that I've been with them, and my having heard, mind you, that she'd been with the mister and living here since a girl.

"And then she never goes out. Never. Times are she prowls the hall, pacing like a cat. A big, rangy gait. You can hear her step everywhere. Smoking them cigarettes of hers, and her eyes, when she looks at you . . . You'll see.

"And fist-tight? Janie Mack!" she exclaimed. "It's a sales slip for everything. Every penny accounted for, from a box of stationery to a Mont Blanc fountain pen costing half a bleedin' fortune just to write one letter. As if I couldn't have walked away with the shop come day, go day these fourteen years. And all the while lavishing every class of thing on herself.

"Not that the mister wasn't fair to me—the dear, dead man." Her eyes closed, as she sipped from the cup. "If there was kindness, if there was gentleness in this world, if there was love"—her fingers grazed the back of McGarr's hand—"then it was his for her, though, to be honest, I could never understand it.

"A big wreck of a woman. No mother, if the truth be known, nor no wife, and her in there, in that studio of hers for hours with them men and the partner—"

McGarr canted his head.

"Yes, *partner*, though silent in every way, if you ken me meaning. Rock, he calls himself, though it's spelled Ar, oh, see, haitch, ee. French, like herself, and him the worst of them. Flowers, always flowers, and with her he was more than the mister himself, babblin' away at her in their language, but she—to do her justice—hardly saying two words. Opens the door to that studio as much as to say, 'Oh, it's you,' then she walks away from the door, like he's a trial that she has to bear. Then she sits staring out the window, smoking until he leaves.

"She likes the flowers, though, I know so myself. 'Fresh water, please, Rose Marie.' Or, 'The blue vase with the red roses,' or 'The green with the yellow.' She studies them for hours, or I'll go in there and find she's painted them—slap-dash but a bang-up job nonetheless. Great form. She has a talent for it, so.

"Or many's the time I'll be working about the place at half ten or eleven of a morning, and I'll hear the studio door open and out he'll pop—Roche himself—striding down the hall, like the cat who just et the canary.

"More tea, Peter?"

McGarr had not touched his cup.

The spout rang on the lip of her cup. With the right hand she quelled the shake that had begun in the left, and her old eyes moved to McGarr's. "He was there in the studio when I knocked on the door to tell her about the mister." The pot thumped on the table, and she settled herself back into her chair. Her hands resumed their gnarled pose.

"These curtains, you see—I had parted them to look out. The gardener, like I said, is a bit off. But harmless. Harmless, now. That was the way of the mister, you know, and I was to check on the lad, especially like now in the cold, just to see if he was right. But it's getting so the stairs . . ."

She drew in a breath and let it out slowly. She turned her head to the side and the window, and a newly formed tear in the corner of her eye broke, tracking through a wrinkle toward her neck. "Him sitting there, mouth open. His legs. The suit. I thought it was some trick of the windows, and maybe he was down below in the shop or out in the garden. Me eyes . . .

"And then it was late—half three or so—and the light. I mean, what would he be doing sitting *there?*

"I'd been down in the shop most of the day. Standing orders. If for any reason the mister couldn't be here, I was to take off me cap, put something over the uniform, and open up. But I should have known right off how it was, Peter. I blame meself.

"First. The lights was on when I got here. Blazin', they was. I could see them from down the corner where the bus let me off. And the 'Ring Please' sign hung out in the front, like we were conducting trade, though the door was locked. And the mister hadn't missed a day in years. Years and years. Punctual he was and strong for all his age."

Her mouth pursed, emphasizing the furrows in her upper lip. Her neck was a sack of folded skin. Although she'd probably never been pretty, Rose Marie Coyne had instead a certain resolve, and McGarr wondered if Craig had appreciated what he had in her—maid, housekeeper, shopkeeper. What else?

But the tone continued. She had something more to tell him.

"No assistants. No need. Not that we were lacking for custom, but there was little in off the street. Old clients. Dealer to dealer. That class of thing. And with inflation"— she paused, closed one eye, and nodded her head—"it all mounted up. It was like we were sitting on gold, but without the risk.

"But . . ." She blinked once. Long. "I saw him. I saw him and I went back down into the shop, hoping to find him there—the windows and all, like I said. Not seeing him there, I went along through the shop toward the loading dock, out into the garden, and then had the devil's own time with the rusty lock to the door in the garden wall. I found the key where it belongs, on the peg in the mortar beside the door. There's a kind of little hole there.

"Out in the lot I had to be careful of me ankles on the broken bricks. Says I, 'Mister Craig, sir—come up out of that. It's rare cold, and you'll catch—

"But I was only talking to meself, mind, for I knew there was more trouble on him than that. His face and neck were blue-like and his pose unchanging and unnatural. And all that blood.

"I turned on me heel and"—her hand reached out and touched McGarr's sleeve; it was what she had to tell him—"looking up, I saw her, the missus, standing full in the side window, staring down at us. I suppose"—she paused—"it had been the sound of me voice that roused her." The fingers moved off McGarr's sleeve. "Have you spoken to her, Peter?"

McGarr shook his head.

She again wrapped her hands around the teacup and raised it to her lips. Her eyes closed as she drank, and only when the cup rattled back into the saucer did she continue.

"A darlin', the mister. A gent who couldn't do enough for that woman. Always phoned when he was out, to ask how's the missus. If he asked to speak to her it was like he was talking to the wall. Silence and them eyes of hers lost someplace on the ceiling or out the window or staring down at one of her fags. I've never known a woman to smoke so much. Even the son has made mention of it.

"A fine, strapping lad with the look of his father, though it's wrong of me, I know, to tell you that there's reason to doubt that they were." Her eyes widened, and she leaned back in her seat so that McGarr had to ask.

"Were what?"

"Father and son. You see, about two months—maybe more—ago the son got this letter from Paris, France, addressed 'Henry Fontaine' with the Craig in brackets and the 'Henry' spelled with an *I*. I know about it meself, since wasn't I the one to fish it out of the box? Addressed to him here, it was, though, like I said, he lives out in Glencree.

"Says the letter, 'You've been left this here painting by a granduncle Fontaine who just died in France. Come get it.' But strange I'll tell you it was that him—Henry—in spite of fancying pictures like he does, took little interest in that part of the letter. No. It was the address that irked him, the name which was repeated on the inside. No mistake. Didn't I see him studying it meself?

"Well, sir—he went to the 'father,' and a hoolie broke out about that and what they'd been fighting over ever since the son went out and became what he wanted to be, an architect of a sort. No work to speak of.

"See, the 'father' wanted the 'son' to come into the business. Fierce, he had it. Words led to words, as they will. 'Damn you,' didn't I hear the father say with me own ears, 'you're no more me son than a bastard in the street, and you never were.' He left it like that, the 'father.' I'm not sure they ever spoke again, the one to the other.

"And the poor lad, what was he to do? He went to that mother of his. He stormed and raged, wanting her to tell him all, but what did he get from her? Nothing. Not a hint of who he really is, and whether it was a count or prince or jarvey who was his da. There's some to who such things matter.

"It was then he flew to Paris. Six weeks past. And I'm after wonderin' meself if she *is* his mother. Sure, he's got all her talent for drawing and such, but blond he is and pleasant, and she dark and—well, I suppose that's me own look-out.

"And then"—here there was a long pause, during which she

shifted uncomfortably in the chair, as though weighing some-thing—"I don't want to slag the lad, and I'm no tout, mind, but there's a traffic light at the corner about a half mile from here. As usual I had taken me seat this morning up top of the bus in front and had collected me gear and was waiting for the driver to start forward again, so I could pull the cord, when I saw him.

"The son. Stopped, he was, like us—across the intersection in his fine, new car, a present from the mother. German, it is. B-M—initials, you know. Everything's changed round now, and I don't know one thing from the other. But what's the use?"

The fingers gripped the edge of the table. The interview was over. "Do y'think I could go home now, Peter? This whole business . . .

"And, sure—this place can mind itself. It's not much for me now."

2

Standing, McGarr glanced up at the clock on the wall behind the maid. It read 3:45 and had stopped.

Said she, "Sure I'm too bent and broken to reach the bloody thing. That goes for the one in the hall and the sitting room, too. If you're wanting the time, you'll find it in the missus's studio, for she tends that one herself. Art de-core, it is. A present from Mister Roche last Christmas. She thinks the world of the ugly thing.

"The only other clock that works is the one down behind the door in the office. The mister takes . . . *took* care of that." She sighed. "And to think of all the lovely clocks there is in the shop and us having to look out windows and guess the time of day."

McGarr left the kitchen and stepped down a long, carpeted hall to the door of the studio. There he paused and listened. He could hear murmurs, a male voice speaking French. All he could catch was, ". . . but why Hector, of all people? Didn't you *realize?*" And then the voice was lowered.

McGarr grasped the knob, paused a moment, then opened the door.

The man—Roche, the partner, he assumed—was standing

in the middle of an expanse of polished flooring, his feet set wide. Seated below him on a low stool was a woman—Craig's wife, McGarr guessed—her back to the door.

In turning to McGarr, Roche presented his profile, which was sharp. The brow was sweeping and shielded deeply recessed eyes, the nose short and beaked, the chin definite and cleft. But there was something unfinished about his features. They were reddened and coarse, as though the poor work of an inept plastic surgeon. Not simply gray, his hair was harsh white and had been combed back to where it curled on his neck. Roche was a big man, but in spite of his structure his body seemed soft, paunchy, the surplus flesh having been trussed up with a vest. On his hands were steel-gray gloves, the color of his suit.

Muttering an apology, McGarr stepped into the room and closed the door. Approaching them, he handed each a card, holding onto the one he gave the woman in an attempt to collect her eyes, though she turned away.

McGarr then moved past them to the corner window, in which, earlier, he had seen the cigarette burning.

Arc lights had been placed at intervals, as the team from the Technical Bureau continued its search of the rubble-strewn lot, the flux of heavy air blueing the achromatic beams. Out in the road a diesel generator strained to provide power. Its high-pitched whine rattled the window.

The watery and crimson depression in which Craig had come to rest was placed centrally, as though composed, in a frame. McGarr wondered when the murder had occurred. Early morning? First light?

He remembered the maid's description of the blazing lights, the "Ring Please" sign, and Craig in his light-blue suit with the handkerchief carefully folded into the pocket. Had Craig been expecting somebody? When had Mrs. Craig herself arisen? How long had she been in the room?

McGarr turned to her.

Like Roche she was a big person, strongly constructed, her shoulders cupping her body as she sat cross-legged on the stool. Dark, her skin looked tanned or at least deeply sallowed, and her hair was a rich brown color, streaked with gray.

Her face was long and definitely Gallic—a bridged nose widening at the end, the bones of her face hollowing her cheeks. Her lips were full and well formed. Fifty-five or sixty—she could be no older—she wore a plain cotton dress in a lilac shade, a cardigan of the same color, and stockings to mid-calf. On her feet were heeled huaraches, a deep burgundy. In all, a handsome if somewhat mannish woman.

"Yes?" Roche asked. He waited, then, "Are you intending to question us?"

Her eyes remained fixed on the floor.

Spotlights fitted on braces lit the room, creating bursts of light around the paintings on the walls, on a drawing board and an easel. The rest of the room remained in deep shadow, except for the ceiling, which was a recessed oval. There three soft colored lights—pink, blue, and a delicate yellow—had been focused eccentrically so that the colors melded in a kind of fleur-de-lys at the center of the ceiling. Through it the smoke from her cigarette sifted.

The effect was distracting, and McGarr kept wanting to raise his head and peer into the flux.

"If you are, I must inform you that neither of us will consent to being interviewed without a solicitor present."

Still McGarr waited, back to the window, staring at the woman.

At length, in raising her cigarette, her eyes drifted toward McGarr, met his momentarily, and shied up into the colored light. They were dark eyes, darkly ringed, and in them had McGarr read fear? Not quite. It was something less immediate than that, and Rose Marie Coyne's words came to him, "like he's a trial that she has to bear." Roche, it was. And McGarr wondered in what way.

"May I ask your name?" he asked.

Neither answered.

"Your name, please."

Roche glanced down at the woman, but she did not respond.

"Please, what is your name?"

"Mine?" Roche asked.

McGarr only inclined his head and smiled slightly.

"Roche."

"And your relation to the deceased?"

"I was in business with William."

That Roche's English seemed to lack any readily identifiable accent was curious to McGarr. It had been his experience that the French, no matter how practiced, spoke English with at least some telling difference.

"Business?" McGarr queried in a soft voice.

"This business. Down in the shop."

"Partners?" McGarr asked.

Roche's expression hardened somewhat more. "Look here—I've already told you our position."

"Are you a solicitor?" McGarr asked.

"Do you mean—am I licensed to practice law? I'm not, but Louise would like me to remain with her, and I believe that is her right."

Roche's knowledge of the law was nearly as interesting to McGarr as his protective approach to the woman. "Madame?" McGarr asked.

The woman only drew on the cigarette, letting the smoke billow over the glossy floor.

He asked again, and when she still did not reply, he moved, as though he would walk away from the window, then turned suddenly and rapped his knuckles on the glass.

Startled, she glanced up.

Their eyes met again, and, raising a hand, McGarr touched the pane with the tips of his fingers. Once more he smiled.

She forced her eyes from his.

Of Roche, he inquired, "Would it be convenient for you to present yourself at Dublin Castle tomorrow morning? With counsel, of course." His voice was still scarcely more than a whisper. "North entrance. Ask for Inspector Ward."

Roche glanced down to his gloved hand and the card, which he fingered.

With deliberation, McGarr removed a Woodbine from its packet and held a match to its end. Turning back to the window and the continuing search below, he smoked nearly half of the cigarette before leaving the room.

Either or both of them, he decided, had spotted Craig's body before the maid had. Unlike the two other windows, which looked out mostly on the garden, the third and side window presented a vista and not merely of the desolation of the razed buildings of the area. It looked east and at dawn had offered the quays, the Liffey, the barrier walls lined with tankers, ships, and cranes, and Howth Head and the harbor beyond. McGarr did not for a moment believe that the woman who had established her reclusion in the room and was an artist had not looked out the window until she had heard the maid's voice, if indeed she had. Then why no response? Could she have seen more than just the corpse?

McGarr again thought of Rose Marie Coyne's words, her description of the wife's reticence and how she had been sheltered. By Craig. And now by Roche?

Why?

The gardener's face was a study in pain. His features were

inspissated, his lips swollen and galled. The skin was shiny and red and seemed as fragile and puffed as the surface of a blister.

Thirty-five or forty-five? McGarr could only guess. In the chill of the hutch—no more than a large toolshed, really—which was positioned against one wall of the garden, his slight body was quaking, his chest where the shirt front was open a dirt-ringed knob. His shoulders were narrow, his neck long and now stringy.

The ungainly insubstantiality of an alcoholic, McGarr thought. Dark hair wiry and matted, like old steel wool. Mustache a dash on the upper lip with several days' growth of beard compounding the dirt.

The eyes blinked as McGarr appeared in the door, which O'Shaughnessy had left open. From the hut a stench both sour and sweet, like rot, blotted through the deep shadows.

"Christ," he muttered, "not another of yous and without a little message. Yeh think I can sit here all night?"

Yet he was standing and unable to keep his feet from moving, as though performing a slight, spastic, and sorry dance. A drink he needed; doubtless the hair (or better the entire pelt) of the cur that was consuming him.

The odor was thick and cloying in the entry, as the maid had reported. Something unusual. Something sweet. "Whiskey?" McGarr asked.

The gardener's eyes, which he had kept lowered, now rose to McGarr's. A glassy, mottled blur. His tongue passed over the raw meat of his lips, and a hand tugged up his pants, which were loose. A belt cinched its filth in folds. "Is that a promise I'm hearing?" And yet there was timbre to his voice—the bravado of the barroom.

Curtin by name. Perhaps it was that in their malaise all drunks looked alike to him, yet McGarr could not dispel the notion that he had seen the man before.

"As certain as death, Mister Curtin. And count on it.

"Liam?"

"But, Chief—the memorandum from the Commissioner."

McGarr only turned to O'Shaughnessy, and the tall, older man lowered his head under the jamb of the hut and stepped out into the rain.

Like droppings, piles of dirty clothes were scattered about the worn linoleum. The pillow on which Curtin laid his head was the color of rust. A worn boot listed in the middle of the floor. Cobwebs matted a narrow window.

Curtin's eyes followed O'Shaughnessy out into the darkness.

There, McGarr had noted on his way through the garden, daffodils were in bloom, rhododendron bushes had budded, irises had just broken through the soil, their shafts pale yellow and tender. Rose bushes of several varieties were festooned with bright hips from last year's growth, but nowhere were tulips, so prized by Dubliners, in evidence. Only perennials, and poorly cared for at that. There were weeds among the bushes, and the pathways of a low, boxwood maze had been hacked down with a switch. Curtin was a gardener in name only, and McGarr wondered what his hold had been on Craig.

"Been here long?"

The man moved closer to the door, the better to watch for O'Shaughnessy's return. "A while."

"Which means?"

"Year. Two."

"Which is it, a year? Or two?"

"Two," pronounced "tow." It placed him. Dublin.

And where had McGarr seen him? It had been official, but in what regard? "Lovely spot this. A soft spot, I can see."

Curtin expelled breath through his lips. "You must be blind."

"And you've a green thumb for all your bricks."

"Not me. Cavan's me home."

"Is it? And mine." Lie for lie.

Slowly the head came around.

"Close the door."

"Close it yerself."

McGarr waited. The whites of Curtin's eyes looked like meshes of bloody twine. Finally a dirty hand shoved the door to.

"Last night. Let's hear it."

Curtin wrapped both hands under his arms. "You're not getting me for this. It's just like youse, ain't it? Easy to haul in me who's got nothing when them—"

"Who's them?"

Curtin's temper squawled. "Them who would've known him. Them who would've done somebody like him in. You think I would've stuck it out here, if—"

"If you could have chosen. Last night, I asked."

Curtin's face was angry, bloated, and babyish, and McGarr kept struggling to give it the proper name.

"A few jars. What's it to you?"

"Of cognac?" It was the sweetness that lay over the sour fust of the kip. McGarr reached for a Woodbine.

"Got one of them for me?"

Only the promise. McGarr struck a light to its end. "Where would you get cognac?"

Curtin opened the door again and peered out into the dark garden. "Where would you? A pub, an off-license. All me friends fancy it. A fad, it is."

"Like the drum. All your friends fancy that too, don't they? Wonders for the memory, the drum. No distractions, but you know that, so."

The head went down, the chin touching his chest. "There's to be no bottle, is there?"

"I've had no answers, have I? Here or there, it's all one to me.

"Name?"

"Curtin."

Perhaps it was only the suggestion in the name that was causing McGarr to think that he had seen the man before, but it lingered. "Which drum?"

"Port Laoise. Kid stuff. Lifting cars, that class of thing."

"When?"

"Ten. Fifteen years ago. Longer. I forget."

McGarr had been abroad then. "First name?"

"Tom."

"And the cognac?"

A hesitation, a breath drawn. "I know you're not going to believe this, but it was a present from the mister, and that's the God's honest truth, so it is."

"What would he be doing giving you a present like that? Hard work? Your birthday?"

He hunched the thin bones of his shoulders. "I swear. I didn't know then, I don't know now. I found it, is all. Here . . ." He pointed to the concrete slab that was the floor of the entry. "When I got back."

"Last night?"

He drew in a breath in affirmation.

"And you gave it a home?"

Curtin shook his head, disconsolate. "Truth is, I spilt the feckin' t'ing. Here . . ." Again the finger moved toward the slab, which was stained. "I'd taken a nip, just to be sure, and it—right out of me fingers." He held them up. They were filthy and shaking, but there was no gainsaying his concern. To Curtin it had been a tragedy.

"It broke?"

"No. I tried to snatch it up before it could spill more, but it was"—he turned over his right hand; the knuckles were scraped—"slimy with the stuff. It kept spilling out. Jasus.

"And I'd been doing good, real good—just the odd jar, until the mister—"

"Time?"

"I dunno. Midnight, maybe later. I'd gone round to a friend's for a nightcap. Hello, says I, me foot coming up against it in the dark. I got a taste of it, though." He shook his head.

"The bottle. Where is it now?"

Curtin pointed to a set-tub along the far wall of the hut.

In the shadows McGarr found a heavy green bottle, a cup, and an old undershirt, which Curtin had used, he supposed, to sop up the cognac and wring into the cup. Bottled in Segonzac. The tax stamp was French. A customs tag glued to the side said it had been purchased at the duty-free shop in Orly Airport.

The peg for the key was, as the maid had said, beside the low, arched door in the garden wall. But it was concealed—in a recess that was not readily visible.

Said O'Shaughnessy, "No forced entry anywhere that we can see. We've got the victim's prints in the office and the housekeeper's, the old woman Coyne's, on the desk phone, the leather border of the blotter, the desk itself. The front door of the shop. At least it stands to reason that they're hers."

"Inside or out?" McGarr asked.

"Both."

"And here." With the beam of a pocket torch O'Shaughnessy indicated the handle of the garden-wall door and the long metal slide that was its lock. "Craig's too, here and here." He played the light somewhat higher, where he had grasped the jamb as he had stepped—not jumped—down into the lot.

Said McGarr, "What about this Curtin?"

"An alias. We've no record for him, and we should."

"Tail him. Bernie for the moment." McGarr thought of the man's raw lips, his quaking hands, how he was feeling sorry for himself. "He'll go to ground tonight, I'd say." McGarr then raised the bottle into the light.

"Cognac," O'Shaughnessy observed.

McGarr turned the label to him.

"Flights?"

McGarr nodded. "Here and there. Craig himself. The son"; yet again the old woman's words came to him, "Six weeks or so past. The partner, Roche. The wife, though she's doubtful." Had he forgotten anybody? "The cook." French like the missus, like the painting.

"And records, if any—of sales, credit-card transactions. That class of thing.

"And who stands to gain? Who gets all of this?" His hand swept the four stories of lighted shop façade.

McGarr then handed O'Shaughnessy the bottle and inclined his head toward the garden-wall door and the activity that was continuing there.

"Nothing yet."

And there would be nothing. McGarr thought of the window—a frame for murder and the foreground of the lot below. Had it been a composition designed for the appreciation of one viewer and one alone, the woman whose dark and darkly ringed eyes had refused to meet his own?

He glanced up at the windows and the rain which was falling soft through the enveloping haze.

3

From McGarr's office in Dublin Castle, where he filed his preliminary report, to his house in Rathmines, the Gárda Rover probed the smog, denser here where there were flats and fires. In a quiet broken only by the staggered sequence of the wiper blades and the ticking of the clock on the dash, he passed across the Grand Canal, visible only as a phosphorescent shimmer beneath him. Seven o'clock was pealing, seemingly off in the distance, though the cathedral was only a few yards from the curb. As always the pubs were the brightest beacons in the mist.

They rose, like stars in a celestial gloom. Inside, McGarr knew, they would be bright, cheerful, and familiar, but he gave them only a passing notice. He had home on his mind, and, given the murder of William Craig, antique dealer, the supper hour might be difficult to keep in the days to come.

And it was the hour, he well knew, that his wife, Noreen, enjoyed best, when, after a day of business and people, she suddenly found herself alone in her own house, in her kitchen, preparing their supper. At such times she would put something lofty or exalted on the phonograph—the *Brandenburg* Concerto, the *New World* Symphony; tonight it was a voice as clear as freshly distilled poteen singing "When First I

Loved You, Maggie"—and she would hum along, perhaps even sing or take a drink, her step crisp from the fridge to the cutting board to the sink. Her approach to cooking was exacting, efficient, and sometimes even inspired, and lifting his nose as he placed his hat on the rack in the hall, McGarr detected the unmistakable aroma of poaching salmon and the beginnings of *sauce hollandaise*.

He debated briefly saving his query until after dinner, but the obbligato being raised in the kitchen convinced him otherwise. Nearly twenty years younger than McGarr, Noreen was a trim, well-formed woman with narrow ankles and copper-colored curls. Her bottle-green eyes were limpid and deep. She was intelligent, well educated, personable, and loving, but she had two salient flaws: she could not sing, nor had she the ear to know it.

Yet standing in the door to the kitchen and seeing her at the cooker, her head raised so that her curls were spanking on her shoulders as she struggled to appropriate the ecstatic clarity of the voice from the speakers in the den, McGarr did not have the heart to break into her fun directly and rather enviously wished he could more often be moved to such heights himself.

Approaching her, he took his pen from his jacket. She turned to him and blushed, having been discovered at her most unselfconscious. She closed her eyes as he kissed her lightly freckled cheek, but she continued the song nonetheless.

On the wrapper from the fishmonger, McGarr wrote, *"Flood at Port-Marly," Alfred Sisley—stolen.*

She stopped singing. "You're codding me. Here in Dublin?"

He added, the ink beading on the surface of the slick paper, *William Craig of Craig & Son—murdered.*

"No. Really?"

"Reputable firm?" McGarr asked, taking the handle of the pot, which she had released, and sliding it off the water beneath it. The water had begun to boil, and heat was death to a good *sauce hollandaise*.

"Quite. But, *murdered?*" She shook her head. "Why?"

McGarr shrugged. "Hard to tell yet, but perhaps for the painting. It's the only thing missing."

"From that horrible, old place down on the quays?" she asked.

He nodded, adding a pinch of nutmeg and stirring the wooden spoon through the butter and egg yolks in the pan.

"You'd think he'd have—"

"Did you know him?"

"Only by sight."

"Valuable?"

"The painting?" Noreen now reached for the wrapper on which McGarr had written the title. "I should say so. Remember my trip to London last year?"

McGarr nodded, though for him all her trips—buying and selling for her gallery—were similarly inconvenient and unpleasant, since he nearly always remained home alone.

"At Sotheby's a Sisley canvas . . ." She paused to think. "*La Seine à Bougival*, a minor work in every way when compared to his Port-Marly canvases, sold for something over one hundred and twenty thousand pounds sterling."

McGarr replaced the pan on the boiler, which was no longer bubbling, and stepped by her to make her access to spoon and handle that much easier.

In the pantry he poured himself a ball of malt, noting that she had begun to hum and now sing again. But as he drank—looking at the pantry window which the mist outside made nearly opaque—he heard her voice falter, then stop. The pot was taken from the burner and the gas ring turned off. He then heard her footsteps out of the kitchen to the den, where the music was stopped abruptly in mid-chorus. The bookcase ladder was rolled over the floor, and then silence ensued.

McGarr finished his drink, took off his jacket, and hung it behind the door, where he found a second apron. A proper *sauce hollandaise* required patience, technique, experience, and no little inspiration, and food and its preparation enthralled McGarr. He poured himself a second drink and advanced on the range.

McGarr rose early the next morning, even before the alarm had rung on the clock beside the bed.

The storm had broken and pale patches, the color of new grass, were chasing ragged, inky smears from the dawn sky. And the wind, driving up across Ireland from the southwest and the Gulf Stream, had changed. Ruffling the gauzy curtains of the bedroom on the second floor, it was welcome and warm. Noreen stirred briefly, and he gently tucked the covers around her, though there was little need.

Below him in the yard he could see trellises and pathways dividing mounds of deep, black earth, a testament to his careful gardening. He had been waiting for the day for a fortnight now and could tell from the westerly direction of the wind that all chance of frost had passed. From seed six weeks before he had planted the hardy crops—spinach, lettuce, and peas—but today he would dismantle the cold frame and transplant his flats of summer vegetables and flowers.

McGarr dressed accordingly—khakis and brogans—and from his closet he pulled out a soft, tan cap for the sun, which was pinking a line of lofty, fair-weather clouds to the north.

In the mirror in the bathroom, he asked himself why he felt so good on such little sleep and wondered if it was, as it had been for his forebears, the call of the earth. And had they shaved before going out to the fields, his people?

He thought back to the farm that was bisected by the Monaghan-Tyrone border, so that his people might carry two passports—the other British—if they were of a mind. He thought of his grandfather and his uncle, who had offered the farm to him, though his career as a policeman had been well begun, and he had refused: fair weather or foul, winter or spring, they *had* shaved, for it was a matter of pride which began with little things and then spread out over their holdings. Details. McGarr removed his shirt, his torso still muscular in spite of his years, and lathered up.

In the kitchen McGarr took the kettle from the hob, dashed the hot water over some tea leaves, and went out into the yard. There he lifted the paned glass panels from the cold frame on the side of his house. The warm wind was heady with the scent of myrtle, and he worked through the early morning, transplanting his flats of febrile slips.

Rathmines: Dublin's first suburb and once a stodgy place, prim and implacably middle class, it was now a bit tatty but at least an established setting, not tractlike and anonymous, and McGarr rather enjoyed the suggestion of decadence in Belgrave Square's twisted chimneys and sagging Georgian houses. Rathmines had been a bastion of what had been ugliest about British rule—the hatred of all things undeniably Irish, right down to the names of many of the streets, which were London surrogates—but the British had made a contribution too.

McGarr now glanced over the wall toward the central green and the propriety of pollarded lindens on a manicured lawn. In one house laced patterns of dim yellow light gave evidence of quiet lives within; in another loud, frenetic music blurred the dusty tympanum of sitting room windows even at seven in the morning, the medical students who lived there having partied the night long. It was the Square's diversity, he decided, that appealed to him, and the tolerance that obtained, one neighbor to the next.

From the cellar McGarr carried out two cartons of jam jars that he had put by against this day. Pressing two mallow root seeds every four inches into the soft soil of his raised beds, he then twisted a jar down over them. The glass would act as a miniature greenhouse and magnify the effect of the pale spring sun. When germination occurred and the shoots surfaced, he would remove the jar and select the larger of the two—the genetically superior sample—and discard the other. Choices.

In straightening up to collect the cartons, he wondered if the appeal of gardening was the attempt to exercise a godlike control over nature: how did his thinning of plants differ from, say, the murder of the day before?

While lifting the cartons, McGarr turned to find that he had been joined by a neighbor, a large Alsatian dog that was sitting in the open garden gate, awaiting him, its tail brushing over the flagstones. Species. Therein the difference lay. The dominant species had declared its own form of life inviolable, at least while the laws of society obtained, and all others were at man's disposal.

The dog, whose cold nose now nudged the back of McGarr's hand, was a case in point. In its seventh year with the Gárda Síochána's Canine Corps, it had padded by a sophisticated electronic monitor in an I.N.L.A. (Irish National Liberation Army) safehouse and triggered an explosive device. "Fortunately the incident resulted in no casualties," a newspaper article had read, but McGarr had known better.

The dog's trainer had come to him for help in keeping the injured animal from being put down. Its right front leg had nearly been blown off. "I wouldn't mind if it was just another dog, but this one's special, probably the best we've ever had. Of any given hundred Alsatians, only a handful can be trained for either crowd control or perimeter security or scenting, but rarely do you find one that's good at all. And he's docile, a big pet of a fellow. And, Chief . . ." There had been a pause while the man had waited for McGarr's eyes to meet his. "He's done the Gárda a great power of good." But for the dog several officers would have been killed in the blast.

Said the Commissioner himself, "It was just doing its job, what it was designed for—saving the lives of policemen. In that way it was well worth the roughly fifteen hundred man-hours we've put into its training, but no more." But the dog's many "colleagues," as it were, took up a collection, and by the time it had recovered, McGarr had found it a place to retire.

"But, Janie," Maisie Edgerton-Jones had said upon seeing the dog, which McGarr had made sit on her front step, like a well-bred, prospective boarder, "I thought you meant a *hound*. Didn't you say it was a scenting dog?"

He had, but he was not about to correct her on any point concerning the capabilities of field animals. It was a province of knowledge that she, a West Briton, reserved to herself and her kind.

"It must weigh seven stone."

"Eight and a half," said McGarr.

"And what—how much—will it eat?"

McGarr had already settled that. The dog was being retired with pension, a modest sum having been left over from the recovery fund and the Canine Corps having volunteered to supply its feed. "The first sack of kibble is in the car."

She shook her head. "I don't know, Inspector," she said hesitantly. "I'm old and . . . Oh, damn, you've left the gate open."

McGarr simply said "Watch"—a command—to the dog,

which spun around and limped quickly to the gate without passing into the street. Agile in spite of the injury, it reached the top of the wall in a bound and paced back and forth until McGarr called it back to his side.

He explained, "Once he transfers his loyalty—usually in two or three weeks—he'll not leave your property without you. Once placed on 'Watch,' nobody not invited by you will be allowed in. Any armed intruder will be disarmed. The force of his jaws on a wrist is over five hundred pounds per square inch, and he'll then control that person, making sure the intruder doesn't leave or make a move toward you or the weapon until you order otherwise."

By the time the dog trotted to McGarr's side—its broken gait a rapid, rhythmic shamble—the old woman, who admired discipline in lesser orders, was beaming down on the dog. "What's its name?"

McGarr consulted the pedigree papers. "G.S.159."

"How impersonal and inappropriate," she said, reaching down to pat the dog's wide, silver-streaked head. "A tested veteran should have a soldier's name. We'll call him Wellington," she decided, after the Dublin-born British hero.

And it was not long before Maisie Edgerton-Jones was singing the dog's praises. "Do you know the latch on my back door? It's a lever, and Welly can prise it down and let himself out. When he's hungry, he carries his bowl in and drops it at my feet. I sleep nights now, knowing that he's here. Any little sound and he's up patrolling."

McGarr did not think he should disabuse her of the notion, but the dog was nearly deaf as a result of the bomb blast. It had been that, not the leg injury, that had kept it from further duty with the Gárda.

The name Wellington, however, remained Maisie Edgerton-Jones's alone, for the transfer of loyalty proved both quicker and more general than anybody had expected, and the McGarrs were soon calling the dog The P.M. (or Prime Minister) of 87, 88, 89 Belgrave Square. Like clockwork each morning, the dog bumped the McGarrs' back door just as they were breakfasting and, as a pensioner and former cohort, was invited in and given a handout or two. Positioning itself like a sentinel in the doorway of the den, it would then follow them with its eyes until they left for work, sitting on the corner watching the car until it was out of sight.

After her shop closed and regardless of the weather, Noreen inevitably found the dog posted on the wall under the canopy of a mulberry bush, which both houses shared, awaiting her return, whence the procedure of the welcome, the entrance, and the several handouts was repeated.

At Rabbi Viner's—89 Belgrave Square—its routine an hour later every morning and evening was little different, much to the rabbi's dismay.

"Chief Superintendent," the rabbi had queried in definite Dublin tones, "how can we get shut of the brute?"

"Poison," said McGarr. He had again been out in his garden, the first turning after winter.

For a moment dark eyes had searched McGarr's face, fearing he had meant it. "Don't mistake me—it's not that I'm indisposed to the"—a pause—"beast. But it's just that—"

"You hadn't realized he came with the property," McGarr completed. " 'All found,' as it were."

That afternoon the dog had positioned itself equidistant between McGarr and Viner's side of the wall—over which the rabbi, a tall man, had spoken—as though to show no favoritism.

"And his preference in regard to comestibles?" McGarr asked.

"Oh, kosher . . ." Viner's jaw went up, showing his neck beneath his beard, as he barked a laugh at the bowers of

McGarr's mimosa tree. A fifth-generation Dubliner, Viner had a deep and abiding sense of humor. "Strictly kosher. But dogs, they're—"

"Unclean," said McGarr.

Viner had reassessed his neighbor: policeman and, what was worse, an Irish policeman—unintelligent, obtuse, and intolerant? McGarr judged that Viner himself was too intelligent to think in categories. The rabbi had just moved in.

Said McGarr, "I think we both have to realize that its *their*"—he punched his spade into deep, black, and stoneless soil that had been enriched by millennia of peat formation and the assiduous conditioning of the last owner, who had been another West Briton—"turf, and that we're both 'blow-ins' here."

Wellington's mistress's family had lived in Belgrave Square for nearly two hundred years and in the Pale since the English had begun their attempt to civilize the country during the reign of "The Queen" (Elizabeth I), or so McGarr had been informed on the first day that he had met Maisie Edgerton-Jones, years ago.

Her voice now startled him, as he clipped the hedge. "Oh, there you are, Wellington." Standing on a soda crate, she was peering over her side of the wall. "I should have guessed as much," she went on, seeming to mean, You Irish are so good with dogs; for some inexplicable reason they love you.

The dog, seeing her, only turned its large head, its ears pulling back in recognition, its tail beating a sustained tattoo on the grass. But it did not move, as much as to say: Not just yet. I'm yours but I'm after waiting for what might drop from the sky in the way of a treat—a pig's trotter, a sausage, some of them luvelly, smoked rashers they favor. The dog licked its chops. Why McGarr assumed the dog was Irish and not German he did not know. Or British.

He glanced up from the hedge and bid her good day.

"Lazy beds, Inspector?" she asked, inclining her head toward the mounds of earth that McGarr had formed down each run of his garden.

Actually, McGarr's method was an experiment—Chinese raised beds, which he had read about in a British periodical, and his early crops were thriving. The clumps of spinach—the leaves wide, glistening, and almost rubberoid—looked too real, like an artist's mock-up in an advertisement.

But he only chuckled, telling himself that nothing could alter his mood. And then—he glanced up at the long, haughty face, the nose that was thin and sharply bridged, the sweeping brow, the narrow chin—her consciousness of herself and her family had in effect made her embattled, when she was nothing more than a lonely old crone and perhaps more Irish in her approach to life than he himself: letting the dog off the leash, as though they lived out in some back bog; her seizing upon any change to gossip with the neighbors without seeming to stoop. Down at the local she sat at a lounge table that gave her purchase on the bar and ordered sherry, "From the wood." A command, no "Please."

"Did I say something comical?"

The dog's head turned to the open kitchen window, from which the aroma of sizzling rashers now wafted. Noreen was up, and the treat was imminent, along with McGarr's second pot of tea. "No, ma'am. It's just that we've been blessed with such a grand day, and I'm enjoying myself."

He saw the glint in her eye. "No work today then?" Her rates, her taxes.

"None. Not a jot. I thought I'd take the day in the hills."

She smiled. He was confirming her opinion of him: a Paddy—lazy and irresponsible in spite of what she had read in the papers, and there she had been all these years paying his salary.

The back door opened and Noreen stepped out. "Good morning, Maisie. Would you care for a cup of tea?"

The dog turned and moved with its broken gait to the stairs.

"Well . . ." She swung a wrist up to her eyes, as though some engagement had better claim on her time. "A small cup, perhaps."

"Business, is it?" McGarr rose from his haunches and the lower leaves of the hedge to help her over the wall.

"Aye." The Scots touch. "In town."

"The lad going with you?" McGarr meant the dog, which from time to time he would take for a romp in the park or out to the strand.

"In his retirement? Sure, the hills are more the place for him today. Someplace high and clear, like Glencree." Her eyes glinted. The steel was out and her mind sharp; she had already read the morning paper and deduced McGarr's itinerary. "Where'd you get that outfit, London?" she asked Noreen, who only smiled, although McGarr knew she had bought it in Grafton Street.

The old woman nodded knowingly, her eyes narrowing on the suit of brilliant, gas-blue satin that contrasted with Noreen's curls, which were a deep gold color in the full sun. Poised on the top step, her leg was svelte. Her mother's name had been Frenche, and, as a "hybrid," her familiarity was somewhat more acceptable to the old woman.

McGarr offered his hand.

"I've negotiated higher gates than this, mind."

"But as a paladin." McGarr was not about to let her off, good day or bad. "We're in another age now."

On the top of the wall she stopped and looked down at him, the roll of her nylons cuffing knobby knees. "Doubtless a recrudescence. Perhaps I should walk around." Precise diction, patrician tones.

The dog was already in the house, no doubt waiting patiently in the doorway of the den, its eyes on the fridge.

"Give us your mitt now. The day's too altogether green for the evocation of any bawdy pattern." He meant the Union Jack.

4

Under the caress of a warm, spring sun, the mostly treeless lines of the Wicklow Mountains were soft and flowing, like the body of a woman. Rounded in domes and cones that rose to over three thousand feet in places, the hills were a windy barren, brown and wild, of spongy peat bogs and moorlands. Now in spring the heath grass that had re-established itself on the occasional mountain trail was thin and bore in flashes of luminous green the print of every passing breeze.

And in spite of the clumps of yellow furze flowers and heather, pink and purple, that were sprinkled over the flanks of the bald hills, it was the overall barrenness of the area that appealed to McGarr. He slowed down to peruse the long vistas—of Dublin and its metropolis to the north, the bays and headlands to the east, and the forty or more miles of moorland to the south—and the several deep tarns and loughs. Through granite gaps they spilled into deep, narrow, and green valleys, their waters dark, tannin-rich, and turbulent.

The house had been placed on a ridge above the valley, just at the point where the newly forested hillside met the moorland of the mountain plateau beyond. From afar the diverging angles of the modern structure—at first seeming to be a cottage, only to become a compound of buildings as McGarr approached—blended with the landscape and seemed almost like a lower ledge of the granite outcropping that crowned the hill. Even the roof tiles had been selected to meld with the umber colors of the surrounding heath, and whereas individual elements—what McGarr guessed was a bedroom, a solarium which had been appended to one side—seemed harsh, the house as a whole appealed to him. He admired its strength and Henry Craig's daring.

It was windless here in the lee of the hill and the sun was hot. McGarr doffed his jacket and soft tan cap before approaching the door. Flies, the first of the season, had gathered on the white walls of new concrete, and the woman who opened the door remained in deep, interior shadows and was ly partially visible to McGarr.

In a foreign voice that sounded tired or weary or sad, she said only that Henry Craig had gone for a walk. The hand moved into the sunshine and indicated the heath that stretched, rolling and brown, for miles off to the southeast.

Squinting into the sunlight, McGarr also raised a hand to be given some bearing across the tractless expanse, only to hear the door click shut.

Opening the car door to let the P.M. out onto the gravel of the driveway, McGarr reached for the radio.

Said O'Shaughnessy from McGarr's Dublin Castle office, "Bernie's back from tailing Curtin, the gardener. I've put Delaney on him now, and I think he'll be needing the cover.

"Curtin waited for almost four hours after you left last night."

McGarr thought back. That would have made it half nine, an hour and a half before the pubs closed.

"And, fancy this—no pub, not him. He left by the back gate and proceeded down the alley to a bank of garages. Having keys, he opened a pair of doors there and left in a Mercedes registered to William Craig.

"He drove north first, over the Liffey and up the Malahide Road as far as Collins Avenue, then west as far as Finglas, where he nipped into an off-license, made a phone call, and bought twenty pounds' worth of petrol. He paid cash.

"Then back over the river by Kingsbridge and some messing about until he struck the Dundrum Road. He kept to the southerly route until Stepaside, where he parked the car. He walked through a residential neighborhood there, then doubled back, crossed the Enniskerry Road, and was let into a back door of the Silver Tassie."

"Who's the publican there again?"

"Briscoe, Enda Emmet."

McGarr now remembered. During the late forties and early fifties the man had been a leader of the then fairly inactive IRA.

McGarr looked up over the top of the car. The P.M., as though having reckoned their purpose, had surveyed the margin of the side-yard lawn and was now sitting beside a path that wound off through the gorse. Every so often it lifted its head, as though taking a long view across the moorland or scenting the air.

Briscoe—he would be an older fellow now, but why would Curtin have run to him? And in Craig's Mercedes and with money. Where would he have gotten that?

In any case, it had been a lapse of judgment by a drunk. And if the stakes were high enough for murder, then Curtin was now expendable. Only his having taken the Mercedes had kept that from occurring then, McGarr had little doubt.

"Lift him?"

McGarr batted at a fly that had entered the car. Craig, a Northern name. His own eyes now followed the dog's line of sight out across the heath, then swung to the compound of buildings.

A stream boiling through a small gap above the residence had been directed into a south-facing courtyard pool, around which several tables, lawn chairs, and lounges had been grouped. The courtyard itself had a curious shape, like half of a parallelogram, and was faced with French doors.

One opened and out stepped a tall, blond woman dressed in a white bikini, her skin tanned in a way that suggested a recent holiday. With an easy, practiced movement she insinuated her angular body into a lounge chair and raised a glass to her lips, then rested her head back against the webbing.

McGarr thought of the shop with its rooms of costly appurtenances, the painting, a Sisley, and now this house owned— could it have been built?—by the son, whom the maid had said was an architect "of a sort." Money. There was plenty here. And now the IRA.

"No," said McGarr. "Just keep an eye on him." Curtin, an alias. An irony? He wondered who had chosen the name. He thought of his garden and the winnowing of plants. "Anything on his prints?"

"Not yet, but give an ear to this. Hughie got onto the solicitor for the estate who owes us, sure. Says he, the will—Craig's will—for the whole kit: the shop on the quays and contents, the partnership with Roche, bank accounts, investments, a house in Glencree with some four hundred acres, was recently changed—come closer till I tell ya"—said the Gárda Superintendent, as though he were speaking into McGarr's ear and not a microphone—"changed from equal shares to mother and son, to the mother alone, the son being cut out without a farthing. Even the house that he designed and built himself but with the father's money now goes to the mother. About five weeks ago the change, which would make it a bit after his having returned from Paris.

"The original document was drawn up thirty-two years ago and updated in regard to real property every decade or so. Steady, substantial progress. Craig had a pile, so he did."

"Any reason for the change?"

"I reckon it was the argument. Craig mentioned to your man something about ungratefulness and the son's having been spoiled by the mother. His idea was that the son should have capitalized on the start that he himself had made. He said he had catered to the son's whims for far too long, that he had had a fair chance of making a go at what he'd been—the architecting—and, having gone bust, it was time to snatch up the reins of the business and work for what he'd someday get.

"When he refused, Craig did what he had to." O'Shaughnessy's sympathies were deeply conservative.

"The flights?" McGarr meant the inquiry into the airport records and the duty-free shop at Orly Airport.

"Nothing there yet, though I phoned Roche earlier and asked him to bring along his passport."

"Autopsy?"

The P.M., now noticing the woman, turned its body to keep the courtyard area in sight, as it scanned the heath.

"Apart from the wound, which was caused—get this—from an explosive bullet fired, it's assumed, from a nine-millimeter weapon, the body was only incidentally scarred, and the dental work is gold."

"All of it?"

"Yes. And skilled work. A root canal. Gold caps."

"Recent?"

"No, most of it quite old. Three decades. Four."

The gold dental work was yet another Continental touch: Irish dental work was mostly amalgam or cement, especially back then.

The scarring. "War record?"

"It's coming. Hughie found a passport among his personal

papers in the safe. Irish, though he was born in Strabane. Nineteen thirteen. Married the missus in forty-six. Her name is Fontaine, Louise. Birthplace, Saint-Cloud, outside of Paris. Nineteen twenty-five.

"McAnulty tells us that we've got gun oil in the center desk drawer, the one in the office. Lots of it, as though a handgun had been laying there for years and years.

"And the missus called."

"Whose?"

"Yours. She wants you to phone her at the National Gallery library, when you can. She'll be there till two."

There was a pause in which McGarr heard somebody speaking to O'Shaughnessy. Then, "Roche and his solicitor have arrived in the dayroom."

"Make excuses. Tea, coffee. Lunch, if necessary."

O'Shaughnessy knew the procedure. The long, distressing, bureaucratic wait. It wore on those not confident of an eternal reward.

The procedure. McGarr judged that Henry Craig had been the last to take the path from the house into the heath, and he merely pointed to it. The dog rose and came to his finger, his nose down into the fluffy grass, its gait broken as it moved forward from footstep to footstep, tracking Craig, the younger. The son but not the son.

One mile. Two, McGarr estimated, the path climbing Old-boley's promontory, dipping down, and then ascending the 1,825 feet of Prince William's Seat. More than once McGarr's hand moved to his jacket and the packet of Woodbines, but the P.M.'s pace was brisk, and the wind, which in gusts staggered him, was too pure to violate.

It was a place for verities—the roaring silences of the wind past his ears; the sea of brown and tumbling gorse, through which the path cleaved like a green part; the clouds, massed in yet another front overhead, which from time to time obscured the sun and made it almost cold. It was a setting that precluded any obscurity, any habitual response, and McGarr's mind, wandering like his footsteps, wound back on what he knew of the case thus far:

—that William Craig, the father, was dead, having been shot once in the lower abdomen and groin by some sort of fragmenting bullet. Why the low, single shot and why there beyond the garden wall near the back of the premises and in sight of the window in which he had seen the glowing eye of the cigarette? Craig had either tried to escape (though the position of his fingerprints on the jamb of the garden-wall door seemed to deny it) or had been brought there and executed—through the L at the rear of the building, then out into the garden, and then out through the low, arched door in the side of the garden wall. How many keys would that have required and what knowledge of the layout of the premises? Having started, say, from the office, at least one in the garden-wall door, the maid herself having had "the devil's own time with the rusty lock," and having "found the key where it belonged on the peg in the mortar beside the door." If Craig's killer had chased or taken him out through that door into the lot, then the killer had returned through the door and replaced the key on its hook. And the killer would either have had to know of the key's position, there in the recess, or have had the great good luck to have discovered it, just when it was required. Unless, of course, he had extracted the information from Craig himself.

—that when Rose Marie Coyne arrived at half eight, she had found all the shop lights on and the "Ring Please" sign hung out, though the front door to the shop itself was locked and she had to go round to the gate at the back of the garden near the hut and ring. The cook, not the gardener, whose hut was hard by the door, had answered. The gardener (in name only), Curtin (an alias, an irony?) had "the failing," as the maid had put it quaintly, which had been exacerbated by a bottle of cognac that had been placed on his doorstep the night before. The cognac had been purchased in the duty-free shop at Orly Airport. Both Roche, the partner, and the cook were "French, like the missus," and like the painting that had been stolen.

—that the day had gone on (perhaps unusually without Craig) but had continued nonetheless before the corpse had been spotted by the maid, who was sitting in a window that looked out on the lot obliquely. Nothing like the direct line of sight from the wife's studio, and "the missus standing full in the side window, staring down at us," when the maid had glanced up from the corpse. And Roche. "He was there in the studio when I knocked on the door to tell the missus." Who else?

—the son. "A fine strapping lad," who had also been called "a bastard in the street" and had "stormed and raged" before flying to Paris. For what? His birth records? "I'm not sure they ever spoke again. 'Father and son.'" And then the BMW, the son's, that she thought she saw from the window of the bus.

—and now Curtin and his IRA connection out at the Silver Tassie on the road to Enniskerry. And the son having been disinherited, about a month past.

When the trail descended into an abandoned granite quarry, McGarr was made to realize his good fortune in having taken the P.M. along. There the dog, lifting its nose into the wind like a deer, began air-scenting the desolate pit. Establishing a "corridor" downwind, it began ranging back and forth through the shards of the former excavation, advancing a few hundred feet with each pass until, out of McGarr's sight, he heard it begin to bark.

McGarr found the dog seated before a kind of cleft, where a large chunk of granite had become vaulted over another in falling, creating a large, dry interior space. At the farther end sat a young man—Craig?—who was staring out at the view presented there: a margin of buff strand fringing the shallow, ultramarine water of Killiney Bay; the imminence of Bray Head; near the deep shades of the horizon the ivory wedge of a trawler's bow bucking a heavy sea, its progress retarded and seemingly interminable.

Beneath the brim of a floppy hat, Craig's hair was blond, and the large features of his face were sharp and aquiline. Like the young woman in the bikini at the house, he was well tanned or perhaps naturally sallow, and the contrast with his blond hair was striking. From the length of his thighs, wrapped in jeans, McGarr judged that Craig was tall. Under heavy, hooded brows, lines, like webs, had gathered at the corners of his eyes.

"Grand day," said McGarr, sitting on a rock and looking out upon the view.

"You're the police?"

McGarr nodded. "Peter McGarr." He handed Craig a card. "Beautiful spot, this."

After a while, Craig said, "One of the most beautiful in the world."

"Think so?"

"I do. And, of course, I'm not the only one who's thought so."

"Really?" McGarr asked, turning to the young man, who, as though relieved to speak disinterestedly, told McGarr how as early as 1244 the English had expropriated Glencree, walling the wood and declaring the vast stands of primeval oak a Royal Park and preserve. "Its timbers were used to build Queen Eleanor's Castle in Haverford. In 1296 the king sent Eustace le Poer twelve fallow deer from his wood in 'Glincry,' but during the turmoil following the invasions of the Bruces in the fourteenth century, much of the timber was cut and the game hunted out."

Craig's face was an arrangement of large, conspicuous parts and a drooping eyelid that remained partially closed in what appeared to be an approximation of a wink. Its effect was disturbing, as though one eye affirmed while the other mockingly rejected the world that Craig saw.

It was one in which history mattered and was, as with so many other Irish, largely genealogy. Craig went on to speak of how Wicklow's deep glens and their forests of first-growth trees were described by the invading English as giving shelter to "wood kerne" and "all indisposed." It was a story that McGarr well knew: how the wild and barren Wicklow Mountains became "the seat and nursery of rebellion." Plans for the destruction of the glen forests were discussed, but the surest method—"And, of course, the most lucrative," said Craig—was put forward: establishing an iron works in each. "Bog ore was here, and the trees were felled for charcoal."

Only recently, McGarr mused silently, had more trees been planted. He could see some of them far off on the hillside near

Enniskerry—conifers which could be exploited as pulpwood within the lifetime of the owner and made for a monotonous, unvariegated forest. It was another age. McGarr searched for a Woodbine.

"Back there by the house," said Craig, "the Brits put through the 'Military Road'—a lovely way they have with their own words—after the rising of 1798. That gray stone edifice you passed was their barracks, which became in turn a reformatory, a workhouse, and a jail during the Troubles."

The sign that McGarr had read on the gate said RECONCILIATION CENTER, though the forbidding buildings, set beside a tumbling stream, seemed mostly abandoned. It made him feel somewhat more sanguine about his time-set. He drew on the cigarette and waited.

Eventually, Craig reached down for a pebble and tossed it over the precipice into the tumbling gorse valley below. "For some time I had had doubts about who I was—I *am*—and about two months ago I decided to do something about it. William Craig was"—he searched for another stone—"a quiet man, thoughtful and dispassionate, a gentleman in every way, but when I approached him about it, he said nothing but that we'd been *like* father and son for thirty-four years, and it was pointless to consider any other possibility.

"His reticence, his dispassion might have seemed to some a strength, but it was really a weakness, a mask. As my mother does in her solitude, he sought shelter in that persona, and it was"—he opened his hands, which were large and looked to McGarr curiously rough and calloused—"a delimitation, a failing."

McGarr recollected other, even rougher hands—Curtin's—and he was reminded of that other man's connection to the IRA crowd who hoisted jars at the Silver Tassie. "But you found that out in Paris?"

Craig's brow knitted in question.

"Why he needed a 'shelter,' as you say?"

He shook his head. "That, I think, will never be known. Now. In Paris I tried to find out about myself and who I am. It seems that I am not—I *was* not—William Craig's son. It could be that I am, rather, Pierre Roche's son, although that too isn't certain. My mother . . ." He turned to McGarr. "Have you spoken to her?"

It was the second time McGarr had been asked that question. Wife and mother, the inscrutable one. And witness. But no more than that? McGarr rather doubted it, but he would wait.

Craig was studying the back of a hand. "My mother was young during the war—late teens, early twenties. A beautiful woman then. A Parisian, an art student, a daughter of a noted family, and—I should imagine—a romantic, or at least the object of some . . . romantic attention.

"During the Occupation, one of her *admirers*—I don't want to make it more than I believe it was—was Pierre Roche, who was in the Resistance. But there were Germans, too. Working as she did at the Louvre, she met several of them. Shortly before Paris was liberated, Roche was picked up by the Gestapo and tortured and left for dead or dying.

"William Craig? He met my mother when, as an art historian, he was assigned to act as liaison officer between the museum and British forces who from time to time would recover art objects 'confiscated'—it was the word in vogue then—by the Nazis. Mother had only a minor post in the conservation department, but Craig was"—Henry Craig's chin, definite and cleft, came up—"kind, I should imagine. And he had money, something that was in short supply with her at the time. Roche was in hospital and would remain there for another year.

"When she found herself pregnant, Craig, as a gentleman who had been enjoying her favors"—Craig paused—"offered his name." He looked off.

After a while, he continued. "He—Craig—was mustered out there on the Continent, and he and she moved around some before returning to Ireland. The South not the North. He abhorred war and violence, from whatever source. A reaction to what he had experienced in France, I guess. And he preferred it here where it was peaceful. Then.

"As I said, he was nothing if not a gentle person, and I shall miss him very much."

"Even though he cut you off without a penny?"

"Maybe he didn't."

"I heard that he did."

"Don't believe it until you hear it in court."

"Rent free here?" McGarr meant the house.

The mocking eye now swung around and studied McGarr for several moments before Craig answered, "I'm moving out."

The eye was off-putting, and McGarr did not care for its gaze. "Greener pastures, or is it pride?"

"A little of both."

"Roche—how did he get here?"

"Ireland?"

McGarr nodded.

"After he recovered, he made contact with my mother. At her request William Craig took him in as a sort of partner. He'd been maimed, as you probably know, but he was an art expert of some repute, and he soon proved himself.

"They'd had a difficult time, Roche and my mother, caught between the Nazis and what the Nazis coveted. My mother's reaction was schizophrenic. She's been diagnosed that and recently. She withdrew into the little world of her art, while

Roche, it seems, learned more than pain and suffering from his experience. It hardened him, and much of the success of Craig & Son came by his hands."

McGarr thought back on them, foreshortened and stubby and wrapped in steel-gray gloves.

"And you learned all of this in Paris?"

"No. I actually learned little in Paris. When I got back I met Pierre at the airport. We went into the bar. He told me there."

"Does Roche work out of the shop?"

Craig shook his head. "The business has grown over the years. Branched out. The shop is only . . . an atavism, a throwback to their former endeavors."

"Branched out how?"

"Into the buying and selling of things—property, real estate, more recently container ships, tankers, wheat and soybean interests in Saskatchewan. Pulping and saw timber in Finland. Pierre has only just gotten back from Argentina, where we have antimony, tin, and some other mineral investments."

"William Craig let you in on all of that?"

"When he tried to have me enter the business."

"You had words. He called you a bastard."

Again the eye turned to McGarr, this time with a glint in it. "No. Oh, no—never. Not William. We spoke, we discussed, but we never argued.

"And then Pierre has kept me informed about the business."

"Why?"

"He's"—Craig thought for a moment—"a friend."

The wealth of the father's estate, the recent change in his will in favor of the wife, and the son's mention of her mental problem now occurred to McGarr. To test the son's reaction, he asked, "What happens after you get your mother declared incompetent?"

Craig said nothing.

"Roche have any family?"

Still nothing.

"Your mother's will—does it leave everything to you?" When Craig chose not to answer that either, McGarr went on. "Time. It complicates things though, doesn't it. Barring any unforeseen accident, it will take decades. Your mother's still fairly young, and Roche—he looks strong in spite of what happened to him.

"They get on?"

The eye met McGarr's, then looked away.

"Roche and your father, what about them?"

"You'd better ask him."

"Any business differences?"

"I'm after telling you what I know about the business."

"Trouble over your mother?"

Here Craig laughed. "Trouble?"

"Contention."

"*Sexual* contention?" Even at its fullest, the eye did not open more than half that of the other. "It seems you don't know much about Pierre Roche."

"Then who killed William Craig?"

"Whoever stole the Sisley. Impressionism has its devotees, Mister McGarr, people willing to pay high prices, especially for a hitherto unknown and potentially important piece like that. An East German, a Soviet museum—"

"Its certificate of authenticity, its provenance—where would your father have kept that?"

The eye closed briefly, seemingly contemptuous of both the allusion and the question. "Wouldn't it be better if the painting had no provenance?"

McGarr's brow furrowed.

"If it were . . . virginal, so to speak—a Sisley heretofore unknown to the art world."

McGarr stood and glanced behind him. The P.M. had positioned itself in the very center of the narrow gap that led out of the vault, and it rose with him.

"What time were you at the shop?"

"When?"

"Yesterday."

"I haven't been near the shop in over a week."

"You wouldn't have known about the painting unless you had. Since the murder all visitors and phone calls have been logged."

"Rose Marie. She told me when she phoned about William's death."

"When was that?"

"Two, I think. Maybe half two. I didn't check."

"And your car—she saw it from the bus on her way to work. In the neighborhood. Eight fifteen or so."

The long, irregular face turned to McGarr. "Rose Marie told you that?"

"A German car. A BMW. Two-door. Gray. A red pinstripe along the side. Not many of those about."

Craig seem puzzled. "I don't know what to say. She's an old woman and a bit off now compared to a few years ago."

"How do you mean?"

"She did virtually everything there then—cooked, managed the house, the shop, even went out and bought my mother's clothes, my own."

"Where were you yesterday morning? Early."

"Here—I mean, back at the house. In bed."

McGarr waited.

"Yes—with the woman there."

"And she is?"

"A friend."

"You have a passport?"

The eye with the drooping lid scanned the ocean horizon to the east. "Ask Lykke. She'll find it for you."

"William Craig—was he a political person?"

"How do you mean?"

"Was he involved in politics? Did he actively support any political party?"

Craig shook his head. "He was utterly uninterested in politics. He could not have cared less. I don't think he even voted."

McGarr glanced around the vault of rough stone and wondered why Craig had chosen the desolate vale when the heath on the ridges above it was so much more inviting and teeming with life now in spring. "Come here much?"

Craig did not answer.

"What shall I tell Lykke?"

"About what?"

"About you? When you'll return? What you're doing here?"

Craig looked off again. "Anything you like."

The woman, Lykke, had left the chaise longue, and McGarr again found himself knocking at what he supposed was the front door. Nor did it open much farther this time, though he could see that she had changed into white slacks and a brown tank top that was the color of the heath, the rooftop, and her eyes which regarded McGarr with no little suspicion. Her hair was straw colored and cut in short, stylish tufts.

"Yes?"

"Henry Craig said that you could show me his passport."

"And you are?"

"Peter McGarr, Gárda Síochána."

"You have documents to prove that?"

"Certainly." McGarr felt his back pocket, only to realize

that he had left his identification in the car, which he turned to.

The door to the house closed. When he returned, he had to ring again, and only after he fully displayed his Gárda card—holding it, as she directed, so the sun would not glare in the plastic cover—did she hand him the passport.

It said that Henry Craig had arrived at Orly on 17 April and was back in Dublin nine days later. Even before McGarr had fully closed the small green book, the woman was reaching for it.

He kept it in his hand.

"The night before last—you were with Henry Craig?"

"Of course."

McGarr wondered what that meant. "All night?"

She nodded.

"What time did he get up?"

"Is it of some moment?"

McGarr nodded.

"Then I'm not certain I can tell you. I go to bed late, he rises early, but I would have missed him had he arisen much before, say, five."

"You sleep together?"

There was a pause, as though she had to decide before she opened the door completely. Placing her hands on her hips, she stepped out into the sunlight: flaring shoulders, a narrow waist, the umber tank top making her breasts appear full and firm, the arch of her pectoral muscles obvious. The white slacks wrapped the roll of her hips and long, muscular thighs. She placed her feet in ballet's first position.

Like Henry Craig's, her features were irregular, her nose long and straight but set off at a slight angle that made what would otherwise have been a plain face interesting. Her jaw was square and dimpled, her cheekbones prominent, and her slight smile revealed a single dimple on the right side.

It grew somewhat fuller, her tan crinkling to crow's-feet around her eyes. They were the color of the stone that hung from a gold chain around her neck—dark topaz flecked with tiny golden chips. The stone had been cut in a parallelogram, like the gold ring on her finger and the design of the house.

"Beautiful day, isn't it?" Her teeth were wide, well spaced, and brilliantly white.

She turned and stepped back into the house. She closed the door.

How old could she be? McGarr wondered. Thirty-five? Forty? Not young in the usual sense of the term, in spite of her conditioning, and McGarr paused to consider what he had last seen—the way she had stepped into the house, the white, low-heeled shoes flicking out a bit before she set them down, the definition of the globes of her buttocks and the line of her calves crisp through the sheer of the white slacks, in a way that conveyed both strength and a certain femininity. An athlete? A dancer?

Turning to the car, he wondered what were the needs and preoccupations of such a woman, and he reflected upon the jewelry that she had been wearing. And the tan, which in Ireland could not have been produced by the pale spring sun alone.

5

His wife's preoccupation was more than evident to McGarr as he stepped into the library of the National Gallery, for she did not glance up from the long, yellow pad in her hands, though there was nobody else but the librarian in the small room. Spread on a table before her were half a dozen or so open volumes. A book trolley near the door carried others that dealt with impressionism in general and Alfred Sisley in particular.

Lowering the pad, she stared down at one of her shoes—gas blue, like the satin suit—swiveling it on the edge of its heel. It was a gesture characteristic of Noreen at her most absorbed and one of the several poses in which McGarr loved her best. It gave him an inkling of the depth of her passion and how completely she committed herself to those interests she chose to embrace. Her ardor burned no more intensely than at such quiet moments, and McGarr debated how best to intrude.

But she turned to him, as he approached.

"Busy, I see," he said.

"Of course. You're just in time." Her eyes were glassy, distant. "Look here."

Bending forward, she swept her hand over the reproductions of Sisley's paintings presented in the open books. "As you can see, his work is best when he balances his delicate brush against compositional strength and against the drama of moments when seasonal elements are either most fully established or in flux.

"Into the latter category fall the Port-Marly *L'Inondation* canvases, two of which were painted in 1873 and are mere sketches for the 1876 canvases that comprise some of the very best of Sisley's work." She pointed to the page, and McGarr noted the certain, confident timbre in her voice.

"Now, within the body of work painted while the village of Port-Marly was under various stages of flood and all called *L'Inondation à Port-Marly,* 1876, three canvases are undeniable masterpieces.

"This one, for instance." She pointed to a reproduction of a canvas that pictured a large, old village inn proudly confronting the challenge of the Seine. In the painting, the river has risen over its banks and inundated much of the ground floor. Two men in a punt are making inquiries at one of its windows. A door is agape, ushering in the torrent. And yet to McGarr the building seemed buoyant and implacable, as though used to spring freshets. "Exquisite, isn't it? It's almost as if"—she looked off, her hand following the line of her eyes—"that old inn comprises another and perhaps more heroic, because solitary, Venice.

"Sisley had a kind of Proustian talent, wouldn't you say? He touches, but gently, deep memories. We try to make sense of the scene. We call up from our memories some similar apprehension—who knows of what or where?—and we're flooded with recognition of a light or a vista that we've seen before but our conscious minds have not recorded. Perhaps we've never been to Port-Marly, perhaps we've never seen the inn, but it's *that*"—her hand came down on the page—"light and *that* vista."

Her hand then moved to McGarr's sleeve. "In such a way our appreciation is sensuous and active—it *thrills* us—not rational and academic."

Trying to suppress a smile, McGarr raised a finger and scratched an eyebrow, then glanced toward the librarian.

"Where was I?" she asked.

McGarr was not about to try to guess.

But again her hand came down on the volume. "Right. When this canvas was auctioned in 1900, it claimed forty-three thousand francs, then an unheard-of price for an impressionist piece. Ironically that was only a year after Sisley, who had been desperately poor throughout most of his painting career, had died of throat cancer. It ushered in the inflation in impressionist work. If for nothing else, that would make it an important painting, but it became part of the Camondo Collection and now hangs in the Louvre.

"*The Times-Sotheby Index* tells us that since 1950 all impressionist pieces have appreciated seventeen and a half times in value, while Sisley's canvases have risen eighteen and a half. A noted Sisley canvas might easily fetch a quarter of a million pounds sterling." She lowered the book and turned to him, finished with her report on her findings.

McGarr shook his head.

"What's wrong?"

He laughed and looked away uneasily. "I'm thick, I admit. But how does all of this . . ." Her eyes widened, and he raised his hands. ". . . *interesting as it is*—relate to the murder of William Craig?"

Her eyes grew yet wider until they appeared to burst with the realization that she had yet to conclude. "Oh, *yes*—simply this. That painting." She reached for the largest book on the table and picked it up. "The painting stolen from Craig is either the find of the decade and"—she shook the book—

"very much a motive for murder." She glanced up at the windows of the library, which presented a cloudless, spring sky, and added, "Or an . . . impossibility." It was as though she were trying the word for the first time.

"A what?"

"It's simple, really. Every recognized source from Sisley's contemporaries to Hector Langlois, who is the current Directeur of the Musée du Jeu de Paume in Paris and a renowned Sisley expert, declares that there were only two *L'Inondation à Port-Marly* canvases painted in 1873 and eight in 1876. No more, no less.

"This"—she brandished the book—"is a *catalogue raisonné* which Durand-Ruel, a Paris gallery that offered his work, published when they hung a retrospective show in 1959. It contains all the then-known works by the painter and the names of their owners. All the *L'Inondation* canvases were accounted for then, as"—her hand again swept the other books on the table—"they are now.

"Had there been a ninth or a tenth, I'm sure some mention would have been made of it. The name 'Craig' figures in none of the sales dating right back to when the pictures were painted. And then, where is the painting's provenance?" The safe in the office of Craig & Son had been opened, but no documentation of the painting's authenticity discovered.

"And then why did Craig hang it there in a dimly lighted, unventilated spot behind a door in a back office? I can tell you that if I owned such a painting I'd hang it someplace where it could be seen by customers who would recognize it for what it is and perhaps have the wherewithal to purchase paintings like it."

Noreen paused and again looked down at one of her shoes, twisting it on a heel.

"At the same time," she went on, "Sisley—like Monet but

somewhat later than 1876—did paint one scene at different moments, when a change in the quality of light had transformed the view presented. He suffered a paralysis of the face after painting out in the open during winter, but again, those series paintings are well documented.

"Still," she said, shaking her head, her lightly freckled brow furrowing, "Craig & Son's reputation is spotless, absolutely pristine. I don't think that they'd own anything that wasn't"— she looked off and tilted her head slightly, like a bird turning an ear to the ground—"right.

"And then there remains the larger question," which Mc-Garr completed. Why would somebody murder for an "impossibility," as she had put it.

He frowned. "Somehow I seem to think there's a proposition in all of this."

Now her hand came down on his wrist. "Don't you want to know which it is? Or more to the point, Chief Superintendent, don't you *have* to know which it is?"

Yes, McGarr thought, but there were more politic ways of discovering that than having one's wife take a direct part in an investigation, though now that her interest had been aroused he had little choice in the matter.

In spite of public policy, those who filled the higher ranks of the Gárda Síochána were, like most Irish men, staunchly conservative and profoundly sexist, and a wife's place in Ireland was still very much in the home. And Noreen was—well, she did not suffer mossbacks gladly.

McGarr debated how to go about it: through Phoenix Park and the Commissioner's office or through Tom McAnulty, who was Chief Superintendent of the Technical Bureau and with whom Noreen would have to work? Any expert, brought into an investigation as a consultant, had to be cleared by headquarters, but McGarr's disaffection from the bureaucrats in the Park was intense, and perhaps, Noreen being his wife, obviated the need to make a formal request.

"I'll phone McAnulty," he said, hoping he knew how much he was letting himself in for.

An hour or so later, Noreen set a large bag on the desk in the back office of Craig & Son. From it she removed a small, coiled ruler and a pair of magnifying half-glasses. Using the bezel of what she recognized as an early Georgian, musical, long-case clock as a mirror, she fitted the bows of the glasses over her ears. But when she held the ruler to the interior length of the stretcher—the interior frame to which the canvas was attached and in this case nearly obscured by a heavily ornamented, exterior frame—the small, dark man behind her stirred nervously.

McAnulty himself, and for all his concern for detail, baggy and unkempt, his head a spray of thick, brown hair matted like the bristles of a wet brush. In the manner of a trip hammer, a cigarette kept rising to his mouth and falling, the end now a brilliant coal in the shadowed room. Noreen knew why. He might actually learn something and have to say thank-you to a woman and one who—worse still—was a colleague's wife.

He now plunged his hands into his trouser pockets and turned his back to her, staring out the window as though he did not want to see what she might be doing. He knew well—although, she judged, he seldom thought of—what his own wife was doing. They had eight children, and she was pregnant again.

Noreen turned her attention to her work and the unusual, much-embellished frame that all but obscured the stretcher. It was a great, Victorian monstrosity which Noreen was rather surprised Craig had chosen to keep. She herself would have used it for kindling. All that remained unencumbered was the interior edge of the stretcher, which she now measured—24 inches; and the width—19⅝ inches. She double-checked, using the other two sides, and compared the dimensions to those in her notes, discovering that the stolen painting had been the same size as the *Inondation* canvas that was hanging in the Louvre.

A coincidence? Perhaps not. Many painters preferred to work with canvases of a definite size, and Sisley had favored smaller formats.

But then, Sisley had been poor at the time and had probably been forced to make up his own stretchers from whatever had been available—two, three, four at a time and all the same? It was possible but unlikely. And would he have measured them off with a square and cut them on a miter? In his art Sisley had certainly been fastidious, but she wondered if that concern could have extended to details as trivial as stretcher size.

She noted also that whoever had cut the painting off the stretcher had known exactly what he was doing. Either a combination of a straight edge and a mat knife or a special canvas cutter with a guide had been used to remove the painting from the frame.

She then bent back the flap of torn canvas—the painting had not been lined. It was the process of cementing any aging canvas of value to a linen liner and then restretching it. Most canvases of, say, eighty to one hundred years' vintage demanded such attention, and Craig & Son were renowned for their care in handling objets d'art.

When she reached out with the tips of her fingers and—careful of the door on one side and the clock on the other—lifted the empty frame off the wall, McAnulty turned and followed her every move. She carried it over to the desk and laid it flat on the blotter, sweeping her left arm as though to brush the Technical Bureau Chief away from the window and her light.

Moving slowly, he plunged a hand into a pocket of his rumpled suit and came up with a cigarette.

"Please don't smoke in here," she said, adjusting the half-glasses on the bridge of her thin, straight nose. "You'll alter my sample," as well as cloud my lenses and lungs, she thought, remembering how she had once heard the man say over a pint, "Kids. I love them. We can't have enough." She knew for a fact that he was never home. And here he was distracting her.

Again from her purse she drew a sterilized packet of glass slides and a small probe.

"What do you think you're going to do with that?"

"*Think?*" Her question was accompanied by a rapid flutter of eyelids and a slight flush that rose to her cheeks. "It's hardly a question of thought. It's a scientific investigation which will be followed by a report," she said, drawing the probe through the narrow gap between the stretcher and the frame, taking dust samples that she carefully deposited on one slide and then sealed with another. "You'll have it all in black-and-white."

"*Report,*" he scoffed, his complaint to her husband having been that only an expert acquainted with forensic investigation could produce a report that could weather judicial scrutiny. "The moment she touches that frame, I wash my hands of it. I'll not have my Bureau misrepresented." And yet here he was.

"Don't you have something to do?" she asked, though she kept working.

Dust. Any daily dusting of the painting over the years would have forced dust into the gaps between stretcher and frame and between the corner joints of the stretcher itself, and its composition would tell much about the painting's history—when and if it had been restored and perhaps where it had been hung. Every major urban area had its own specific mix of hydrocarbons, dirt, industrial and other fumes. The analysis of the dust could be fed into a computer to derive some clue to its background.

"I'm doing it."

"Which is?"

"Making sure that you don't make a"—he paused, searching, she realized, for a word that was not "balls"—"mess of that thing. You'll have it in bits, so you will, and then—"

"You can point the bloody finger. If you can't shut up, give over and get out."

"Orders, is it?"

"Yerrah, hump off," she said, in low, Dublin tones.

There was a pause, and then McAnulty asked, "What did you say?"

"Hump. Off."

Out of the corner of her eye, she saw his head go back. In his scheme of things ladies did not speak like that, and with her Norman background and art gallery on Dawson Street (pity, she thought, it hadn't been located on Dame Street), Noreen had always been very much the lady. His eyes ran down her gas-blue satin suit, reassessing her.

But the dust: at first she thought it was merely the difficulty of probing the juncture of stretcher and frame, given the enveloping shape of the latter, but she was now rather surprised at how little dust there was, even though the one edge of the stretcher that she could see appeared to be of requisite age.

And once more she wondered why the canvas had not been conserved. The impressionists had painted *en plein air*, using thick applications of paint taken straight from the tube, as opposed to following studio techniques that favored several applications of thinner paint which tended to age more uniformly. Craquelure—the tiny cracks that can be seen on the surface of any oil painting—was therefore more pronounced and required care.

Then, what was she now seeing? Where the knife blade had been drawn through the canvas, the paint on the surface had been shattered, and she noted a chip of white paint beneath the gray on the painted surface.

Glazing? She looked up beyond McAnulty and the bars of the window, out into the rubble-strewn lot.

"What is it?" he asked in a soft, conciliatory voice. "Find something?"

Glazing was the technique of applying a thin coat of a darker color over a ground of a lighter color to impart luminescence to the former; and, as far as she knew, of the impressionist painters, only Renoir, who in his youth had worked as a porcelain painter in a china works, had employed the technique. She thought of the later, lush canvases of Renoir—the portraits of women and girls—which were imbued with a sheen that he could not have obtained from a direct application of paint to canvas. But in Sisley's work?

It was possible, of course, Sisley having been trained in studio-painting techniques, but it seemed to her anomalous. Again she moved to her bag and extracted an envelope. She turned and stepped back to the rectangle of now lighter wallpaper, over which the painting had hung.

On the floor beneath it were paint chips that had sprayed off when the thief had drawn his knife through the canvas. She began gathering them into the envelope, wondering if the chief of staff at the laboratory of the National Gallery would allow her to use the analytical equipment there. Although she dealt with much of the conservation work that was required at her gallery, she had not had to analyze the composition of paint since her days as a student.

"Now what are you doing that for?" McAnulty queried. But

her eyes, flashing over the top of her half-glasses, silenced him. Back at the desk she began collecting her things.

"Noreen," he went on, "hold up just a moment." A cigarette was dangling from the corner of his mouth, unlit. "We're after having gotten off on the wrong hoof. But we're both adults here," he blundered on. "*Experts.*" This was said with difficulty, as though he had had to prise the admission (along with the hoof) from his mouth, and he did not care for its taste. His hand reached for the cigarette. "Can't we cooperate on this lot?"

But she was already at the door, the gas-blue satin of her suit crackling. "I've no time for beginners."

"But—I'd like to *learn.*" The last word was a kind of wail.

"Then listen to your wife," she advised, moving into the shadows of the antiques shop which was sweet with the odor of aging wood and lemon oil.

Near the door to the office, an old woman—doubtless the housemaid, Noreen thought—was leaning over the gleaming surface of an oval table, her elbow raised, her old, gnarled hand working a polishing cloth.

She did not look up.

6

By the time McGarr arrived at his Dublin Castle office it was well past noon, and Roche's appearance seemed to belie the suggestion in the preferred pronunciation of his name. Rock.

His skin appeared jaundiced and hot, his brow was beaded, and sweat had darkly patched the front of his shirt. Even his tie, a deep Prussian-blue like his suit, seemed damp.

His solicitor—one Glennon by name—rose to complain about the delay, but Roche, his eyes on McGarr, merely eased the man back into the seat. Under the definite ridges of his eyebrows, they seemed deep and recessed. Watchful. Pensive. And they moved not from McGarr.

Yellow shades, drawn like old parchment down tall dayroom windows, diffused the direct sunlight and radiated its heat. The amber glow was heavy and hot. Caught between panes, a fly had assumed the size of a bird, its shape blurring whenever the shade moved. Its blatting buzz was angry and loud. Its shadows darted across the dayroom table and the papers that were now set before McGarr.

O'Shaughnessy—erect, massive, and unruffled in the heat—sat to McGarr's right, a notebook before him. To Mc-Garr's left was Bernie McKeon, a small, round, and nervous man with quick, dark eyes and a thick shock of yellow hair. Slouched in a chair, he had a knee against the table. His tie was undone, his shirt sodden. For the most part an inside man, he was the desk sergeant; his specialty was interrogations, and he acted as McGarr's foil.

"Feckin' bastard," he had muttered when McGarr, who was very late, had entered the room. Now he changed his position yet again, jarring the table as he crossed his legs. "Christ, it's hot. Blazin'. Let's get the agony over wit'."

McGarr only continued to scan the pages before him, knowing that Roche was watching him closely.

Roche, Pierre Jacques Louis. His immigration papers said he was born in 1917 in Strasbourg of a German mother and a French father. He was educated both in Freiburg and at the Sorbonne, having specialized in modern languages and literature at the former university, and art history at the latter. There a doctorate was awarded in 1939, the same year that he joined the staff of the Musée du Jeu de Paume, a department of the Louvre.

With the occupation of Paris, he became involved in the Resistance. Early in 1943 he was arrested by the Gestapo, interrogated, brutally tortured, and left for dead; but because he had played such an important part in the movement, his comrades searched for him and he was saved.

For his bravery, Roche was made an officer of the Legion of Honor, a Commander of Arts and Letters, and he received the Resistance medal.

His recuperation, however, took years, most of it spent in a private clinic near Strasbourg. In 1948 he emigrated to Ireland, sponsored by William Craig. In a statement, Craig cited Roche's war record, their friendship, and his background as an art expert. Roche also brought just over forty thousand pounds into what was then a country in desperate need of even such relatively small amounts of cash. In his own statement, Roche said that he was tired of war and fighting and wanted to establish himself in a country the neutrality of which had been proven.

At that time he had been six feet three inches tall and one hundred ninety-six pounds. He had blue eyes, and his hair was then blond. Seven of eight fingers had been partially amputated, both final fingers down to the second knuckle. Four toes were missing. Roche had scarring over 90 percent of his back and his right shoulder and arm, both sides. The bones of his face, having been smashed, had had to be reconstructed, which explained the reddened and thin quality of his skin, but in no way—McGarr glanced up at the man—did any of what he had read explain the man's fleshiness.

Far from weighing fourteen stone, as he had in 1948, Roche was now more like eighteen, and the excess seemed to be concentrated in his chest and—as McGarr had noted in the studio the day before—other parts of his body, which made him appear almost feminine. In the heat he was the only man in the room besides O'Shaughnessy who was still wearing a jacket; no matter the conditions, the tall Gárda Superintendent did not appear in public without one.

Roche had placed his gloved hands, blue and stubby, on the table before him.

Roche's dossier also listed the several companies that Craig & Son, through a holding company—a tax shelter—on Grand Cayman Island, controlled: export-import, shipping, mining, and land development, most of it now abroad. As Henry Craig had said, the antiques shop, even packed as it was with valuables, had been only the tip of the financial iceberg, and his mother and Roche were now quite wealthy.

Roche had three known residences in addition to the Ballsbridge flat, and all on the water—Wexford, Roaringwater Bay, and Westport. He was a sailor, and his boat had competed in the disastrous 1979 Fastnet race which claimed boats and lives. There was a newspaper clipping of Roche standing next to its sleek expanse.

McGarr turned to the autopsy report on William Craig, noting that the coroner had found traces of an explosive bullet, which was a rarity. The time of death had been pegged at between half four and half five in the morning, still very much night by Irish standards at this time of year. At half four, the sky would just have been taking on color.

McGarr thought of the smoky fog and wondered if it had been heavy down by the quays that morning.

Witnesses? The woman, the wife.

With deliberation McGarr grouped the two reports and set them to his left, then squared the remaining one in front of him. He reached for the packet of Woodbines in the pocket of his sportshirt.

The fly had come to rest on the window once again, and its magnified image—the rounded disks of its eyes, the sweep of its wings—was imposed on the trapezium of amber light that had fallen across the table.

McGarr wondered if there had been a fly in whatever room or bunker or basement it had been in which Roche had been questioned by the Gestapo, and with what sort of instrument they had beaten and/or burned him so severely that the best that plastic surgery could do was the grotesque and shadowed visage—helmetlike with the sweep of white hair—of the man on the other side of the table.

McGarr removed a flake of tobacco from his tongue and then began speaking in low, measured tones. "Our apologies for the lateness of the hour, and the heat, about which we can do nothing. We're only civil servants, and this building is what you have given us." The click of the transcriber, placed as it was on an old oak desk in the corner, was sharp. It disturbed the fly, and Glennon—his specialty was criminal defense; McGarr had had dealings with him before—asked him to speak up, though McGarr continued as before.

In his seat, McKeon changed his position once again, pained, as though the languor of the interview, the heat of the room, the drone of McGarr's voice were an agony that he might not be able to endure.

Said McGarr, "I can appreciate your position, Mister Roche, having been William Craig's partner and friend. But I also hope you can understand ours. This interview is a matter of form. My staff has prepared some questions here which I must ask."

O'Shaughnessy reached between the lapels of his suitcoat and drew out a pen. McGarr waited until the cap had been unscrewed and placed on the end and the nib struck the pad.

McKeon sighed and with a finger began wiping sweat from an eyebrow.

"Question," said McGarr. "Had William Craig any enemies that you know of?"

"No, Mr. McGarr," said Roche. "He had only a small circle of friends and acquaintances. Intimates, none of whom would have had motive or cause to have murdered him."

McGarr glanced up, wondering if Roche knew of the missing painting. Certainly one hundred twenty-five thousand pounds sterling would be considered by some motive enough.

"In business, then—what was the state of that? Had any dealings been acrimonious of late? And, if so, could you give us the names of those parties?"

"Again, none that I know of. But, of course, I had little touch with the antiques and objets d'art. It was William's specialty."

McGarr glanced up from the papers in front of him. Roche with his doctorate in art history, his service at the Louvre?

"He had the eye, you see. I, the training. So much of that

sort of thing is feel—for innate value that will increase over time and for the market. Being a native of this country, William was better acquainted with tastes and preferences. And then we discovered, as our involvements grew, that my own strengths lay in other areas."

McGarr waited. The fly had started buzzing again.

"Investments," Roche said simply.

"Over the past, say, two weeks, what were William Craig's activities? Who would he have seen? Who would have visited him at the shop?"

"I'm sorry, but I couldn't tell you. Not only was that, as I have said, something which he and he alone controlled, but also I was out of the country. Argentina mostly."

"You left?"

"May ninth."

"And returned?"

"Yesterday. Which was the reason I came down to the shop."

Information volunteered. McGarr merely stared at the man.

"Usually we met in my—*our*—Ballsbridge offices. For business. Or my flat for"—another pause—"conviviality. Dinner. A drink or two."

"Your flight returned from—?"

"Buenos Aires."

"Via?"

"New York and Shannon. I changed planes there to Dublin."

The gold cap of O'Shaughnessy's fountain pen flashed as the nib moved across the page.

McKeon stuffed his hands under his arms.

"You're French," said McGarr.

"No longer. I'm now an Irish citizen."

"You were born?"

Said Glennon, "Come now, Superintendent—you have all that before you and don't tell me—"

But Roche's gloved hand came out, quieting him. "Strasbourg."

McGarr had abandoned the typed question on the sheet in front of him, but he continued to stare down at it, playing out what he and McKeon had arranged. "Your first language?"

"German. My mother, her name was Hochstäder. My father died in the First War. French was my second language, and then, of course, you know that I studied languages at university. Freiburg, Mister McGarr." A new and playful note now tinged Roche's voice.

Again McGarr thought of the Gestapo. Their technique had been to so humiliate and brutalize a suspect that the person who was experiencing the pain would reveal all about the person that he had been, perhaps even making things up about himself—anything to stop the pain. A Gestapo interrogation had begun with torture, and, from what McGarr had read about their methods, he wondered if torture itself had been their purpose.

The suspect, who was naked and had his thumbs tied behind his back, was first plunged into a tub of water and asphyxiated until he became unconscious, then revived, questioned, and even if information was forthcoming, nearly drowned again. With kicks and blows the process was repeated and then—by the thong that joined his thumbs—the subject was hoisted off the floor and left there dangling to reflect on the wisdom of telling all, his weight having been brought to bear on the sockets of his arms, which often became dislocated.

The next step, which McGarr assumed had caused the fore-shortening of Roche's fingers, was the driving of wooden match sticks under the nails of both hands and feet and then the lighting of them until they burned down into the quick. The pain was so excruciating that many of the tortured lapsed consciousness, whence the first technique—plunging their heads under water—was used in reverse to revive them. If the burns that resulted were not treated, gangrene set in.

Other forms of torture—ice-water enemas, beatings with bats, testicle crushing, to name only a few—were employed, but McGarr guessed that the match sticks were responsible for Roche's stubby fingers.

"When you got to the shop, what did you find?"

McKeon scraped back his chair and began pacing the shadowed wall of the room.

"The lights were on."

"Was it dim or bright, the day?"

"Dim, so to speak. There was fog off the river. Coal smoke. Early-morning pollution, I should think."

"Did you have to walk round?"

"Round?"

"The shop itself."

Roche's brow furrowed. "No."

"Then the shop door was open. The one on the street. The front door."

A pause. "Yes."

"Were you expected?"

"No, I don't think so. Unless William had called my office—the Ballsbridge office—to learn when I was to return. Then, of course, he would have been expecting me."

"Why, *of course?*"

"Well, we were very close, William and I. I had been in Argentina on a matter of some moment to him and me. More, it was my custom to come to the shop first thing upon returning, after I was away."

McGarr waited.

Under McKeon's step the flooring creaked.

"I don't fancy coming home to an empty flat."

Fancy and *flat*—an Irish touch. Was he *after* wanting to be believed? McGarr wondered.

McKeon had stopped. He now let out a small cry of disbelief.

"Can't we get him to sit down?" Glennon demanded, adjusting the fit of his modish glasses.

"Why?" asked McKeon. "Am I bothering you, Mr. Glennon? Or is it your client's answers?"

"What is *that* supposed to mean?"

"*Bernie,*" said McGarr. He pointed to the chair that McKeon had vacated.

"A pack of damn lies," McKeon complained.

Glennon himself was moved to stand, but again the gloved hand restrained him.

"And in this heat." McKeon sat. "The gobshite."

And did McGarr see Roche smile? He thought he did.

"You found—?"

"I beg your pardon?"

"At the shop. The door was open. The lights were on. The sign, the 'Ring Please' sign, was it hung out?"

"Now that you mention it, I remember distinctly that it was."

"As though Mr. Craig had been expecting somebody."

Roche nodded.

"Business?"

"I wouldn't know."

"Was it usual for Mr. Craig to conduct business at such an hour?"

"Again, I don't know. It wasn't my concern. I shouldn't think so, though it was the first time ever that I had arrived there at that time in the morning. Perhaps the lights were on and the door open from the evening of the day before?"

Not if the autopsy was correct and Craig had been murdered between half four and half five in the morning. And at that time, for whom would he have left the shop door open but a trusted customer, a friend, or, say, his partner?

"What did you do, once you were in the shop?"

"I went straight to the office, thinking that William, as he usually was, would be there. He wasn't. I then took the lift to the third floor. There too I found nobody about, so I left, going out the way I had come. I went to my flat, showered, changed my clothes, dropped into my office at nine, and then returned to the shop, arriving at around ten."

"Your initial visit there. How early was that?"

"Actually I checked the clock then, to ascertain the hour, my sense of time having been disrupted by my journey, and my wristwatch being set to New York time. Six, it was."

"You were?"

"In the kitchen."

McKeon had begun laughing. "Actually, I checked the clock then," he muttered. "Jaysus, that's gas. A great crack. Me sense of time having been disrupted, you see." He craned back his head and said to the darkness of the ceiling, "But *you* see, Monsieur—or is it Herr?—Roche, there *is* no feckin' working clock in the feckin' kitchen!"

"Wait. Wait!" Glennon was on his feet. "All of this—is it really necessary? If—"

"Nor in the hall."

"If it is, then I would like you to inform my client of his rights."

"Nor in the dining room, the sitting room, the parlor, if you could call it that—"

"And *formally.*"

"Only in the"—McKeon lowered his head and turned to Roche—"studio. A big clock there, so there is, Mr. Roche. Bought it yourself, last year. Christmas, it was. Expensive. Art Deco. The missus thought it brilliant, so she did."

And yet again the gloved hand controlled the moment, easing Glennon back into his seat. "We're here to help the police, or at least"—the reddened skin pulled back in what McGarr judged was an approximation of a smile—"some of them.

"To be honest, I don't rightly remember if I looked at a clock or added five hours to the time on my wristwatch, but I remember distinctly that the time was just going six." Irish phrasing again.

McGarr waited, trying to assess the tone. He did not know what to make of it: a manipulation and playful, by a man who was gifted in the use of several languages? Or just the attempt of a foreigner to appropriate the colloquial, the better to be understood?

McKeon and Glennon had locked eyeballs now. With a finger, the solicitor pushed the heavy frames of his eyeglasses back on the bridge of his nose. His ears were pulled back, his forehead an expanse of clear, angry skin. McKeon had folded his hands under his biceps, which bulged from his short-sleeved shirt.

Said McGarr, "Let's back up a moment, Mr. Roche, if you don't mind. The office. When you entered that room, what did you see?"

Roche paused, glancing down at his gloved hands. "I don't know what you mean. I saw nothing. I was looking for William. The light was on, on his desk. As I remember, I could"—he glanced up at McKeon—"hear the clock, the musical, floor clock behind the door, ringing the hour." He smiled. "There, Mr."—he glanced at McKeon—"is where I first learned the time. It plays twelve tunes. At six it plays the chorus of Bobby Burns's 'When Oft' Through the Glens.' "

"Did you step into the office?"

"I really don't see the point—" Glennon began saying.

But Roche spoke over him. "No. A half step, perhaps, just to look around."

"Then you didn't look behind the door?"

Roche shook his head.

"Or see the paint chips that had sprayed over the carpet?"

Roche's head came up and his eyes met McGarr's for a moment only, before moving off to the shaded window and the nagging buzz of the fly. "I'm afraid I missed that detail. Paint chips?" There was concern in his voice. Was it worry?

And why, even as a "silent" partner in the antiques shop, had he not inquired about any loss? Half of all contained there was his.

"Oil paint chips. From the painting."

Roche's eyes had now dropped to the gloves. He waited.

McKeon once again shifted nervously.

Finally, McGarr said, "The one behind the door, Mr. Roche. Did you not know that it had been stolen? The Sisley."

Roche said nothing, nor did he move, and McGarr judged that he had not known.

"I wonder—such a painting would have a provenance, would it not?"

Roche's head inclined, his brow furrowed, a gloved hand reached out. "I should imagine, but again, I—"

"—really wouldn't know," McKeon completed, mimicking the man's deep voice and neutral accent. Then, "Horse—"

"That's enough," Glennon fairly shouted.

"—feathers."

Said McGarr, "And when you got up to the second floor, did you not open the studio door and look in?"

Roche shook his head.

"Or any of the other doors? Craig's?"

Another head shake.

"Or perhaps his wife's?"

The reddened, thin skin of Roche's face fluttered in what approximated a half smile. "I should imagine that over time this sort of work causes one to select a limited set of motives that then can be applied to most situations. Labels. Tags.

"Then again"—a gloved hand flicked out—"perhaps my presumption in so assuming is no less ignorant than your own. Perhaps you have to ask such questions?"

"Not of you," McKeon said in a low, threatening tone, the pale skin of his moonish face having taken on color, his close-set, dark eyes narrowing down on Roche. "Not those questions. No need."

"Bernie!" McGarr again warned.

McKeon's head swung around, "Don't *Bernie* me, McGarr." Shoving himself away from the table, he stood. The chair, falling behind him, cracked on the floor. He pushed his blond hair off his forehead and stabbed at the shirt-sleeves that cuffed his biceps. "I've had it with him and you, arsing around with these feckin' gurriers . . ." He pushed his blond hair, which had the color and aspect of corn silk, out of his eyes and took a step toward the window, his skin beaded with sweat. "When what we want is something that makes sense."

He spun around. "You. *Roche.*" He pronounced it like the word for the insect. "Don't tell me that you—an art historian trained, a man who wrote his paper at the Sorbonne on Monet and the impressionists—and Craig, your dear, dead partner, were both so feckin' wealthy and feckin' uninterested in plain old cash that you didn't insure or bother with the provenance of an impressionist masterpiece worth hundreds of thousands of pounds, and hung the feckin' t'ing behind a door in the back of a shop in a building that a boy with a nail file and some balls could break into? Don't hand me that. *Don't.*"

The heel of his fist, resounding on the sill of the window, startled the fly, which began careening from pane to pane, smacking into the glass. McKeon's face, being round, full, and now red, resembled that of a cranky, spoiled baby. "And that shite about Craig not being able to tell the man he called a son for thirty-four years who he was and where he came from . . . What was so strange about Craig that he couldn't bring himself to face the man and say it? Let's hear it, Christ. Maybe they'll"—his thumb jerked back toward McGarr and O'Shaughnessy—"believe you, but not me." His hand then reached out and grasped the bottom of the yellow shade.

"And, starting at ten or whenever it was you surfaced the second time, how long were you in that studio with that woman? The missus. Henry Craig's missus. One hour? Two? Or wasn't it more like six, you feckin' liar, and don't tell me you or she didn't look out that feckin' window onc't."

His hand released the shade, which shot up the long window and smacked into its roll, the cord whipping around it.

A harsh, pinkish light now fell across the table and made the rough scarring of Roche's face seem like tabs of red and only partially healed flesh.

Yet he did not look up from his gloves.

Said McGarr to McKeon, "Get out. Wait for me in my office."

"This is *unprecedented*," Glennon roared. "Unheard of. It constitutes an assault. Defamation of character. I'll take this to Phoenix Park," he said, referring to the location of Gárda Síochána headquarters.

But even after McKeon had closed the door behind him, McGarr only waited.

Moments went by in which the fly buzzed nastily against

the panes. Only when it had stopped did Roche look up. His eyes met McGarr's and held his gaze while he spoke. "Taking Mr.—"

"McKeon," McGarr supplied.

A gloved hand gestured to Glennon, who made notes on his pad.

"Taking Mr. McKeon's queries in order. First, the painting. Did you say it was a Sisley?"

McGarr nodded.

"I believe I am acquainted with the painting. I saw it years ago. A lovely thing with Sisley's delicate manner. There's one like it in the Louvre, and it pains me that Louise and Henry have lost it. But it was William's, not mine.

"Insurance? The contents of the shop, that is, whatever was held by us jointly, *are* insured up to a maximum value of one hundred thousand pounds. The bill for the insurance premium, which is substantial, passes through my office. Whether this Sisley canvas is covered is a matter that Solicitor Glennon here and the underwriters will have to work out, but I can assure you I will endeavor to collect the limit. If the theft is covered by some other policy I could not tell you. It was his affair. Not everything"—a slight, wry smile tugged at the corner of his mouth—"was held in common.

"About the relations between William and Henry and my intervening in what constituted a family crisis: William Craig was a refined, reticent man. A gentleman. Far be it for him to discuss such matters. When I suggested to him that the boy really should be told whatever was known about his past, William actually blushed. He was embarrassed, it seemed. Why? I cannot say. That was his character, for which I shall make no excuses. William Craig was"—Roche paused, but his eyes did not stray from McGarr's—"perhaps the finest man that I could have the pleasure of knowing. An ally. A friend.

"And finally, the matter of how long I was in the studio with Louise and why I did not look out the window. My business in Argentina, which I shall divulge to you only if compelled by a writ to do so, was of much significance to Craig & Son, and I had to discuss the matter with Louise."

McGarr tried not to look surprised, but Roche understood that he was.

"Contrary to what others might think, Louise has been acting for Craig as the other half of the partnership for many years now, having left William to his antiques, paintings, and such. In spite of appearances, she is sagacious and"—one of his eyebrows, which had seemed to McGarr immobile and artificial, flicked up. He cocked his head, and McGarr thought he saw him smile—"shrewd."

McGarr thought for a moment. Somehow he could not imagine the dark woman, seated on the stool that seemed almost to have been composed in the center of the spare studio, taking an active part in the mundane affairs of Craig & Son, but he let the statement pass. It could—it would—be checked, Roche being nothing if not shrewd himself.

"Five weeks ago William Craig ordered his solicitor to write Henry Craig out of his will. Why?"

"William told me that Henry's anticipation of receiving his inheritance had effectively crippled him. He wasn't aggressive enough even in his chosen career. Rather than pursuing the large commissions—housing estates, office complexes, the like—he was content to build houses, many times pitching in with his own hands, something which William himself would never have done and looked down upon.

"We discussed it, William and I. He told me he should have done it earlier. I remember his words exactly: 'Sometimes manifest cruelty is the handmaiden of love.' His intent was, I believe, to goad Henry into making a mark in life. Having

86

failed to enlist the"—a pause—"no-longer-actually young man in our business, he chose this other tack.

"Admittedly it was harsh—suddenly, after thirty-odd years of having thoroughly spoiled the lad, to cut him off like that—but we all make mistakes. Henry's reaction was typical of him—wild, impulsive. He's always had everything he's wanted, including"—Roche paused again—"unlimited, enviable freedom, and the imposing of constraints perhaps came too late.

"But then, you see, it is not as if Henry Craig were entirely cut off. His mother's present will leaves all to him, as does mine."

McGarr waited.

"I myself have no family besides"—he inclined his head—"Henry and Louise and, well, William was like a brother to me. We as much as grew up together." A gloved hand came up. "By that I mean we were in Paris together during the War. In due time Henry will find himself quite wealthy. In *due* time." Again the flicker at the corner of the mouth.

"Your passport says you stopped in Paris on your way to Argentina. Why?"

"It was simply the quickest way to get to Buenos Aires, no flights leave directly from this country."

"Why did William Craig keep a handgun in the top drawer of his office desk?"

"I have no idea—that he did or why—though it would surprise me."

"What is the name of your insurer, the one for the shop?"

"Lloyds. Nobody else would assume the risk."

Roche waited for several moments. "Will that be all?"

"Not by a long shot," said Glennon, collecting his things. But Roche, standing, abjured. "Ah—Detective Sergeant McKeon was only off his form this morning, Edward. Not himself at all. On other occasions I should imagine he could grace boards less sorry"—with a foot, Roche tested for and found the creaking section of flooring—"than these. His talents here are wasted altogether."

At the door Roche added, "Would that he had chosen differently in his career."

His hand on the sill of the raised window, McGarr shoved it up slightly, and the fly escaped into the glare.

7

In spite of the rich sunlight outside, the north-facing windows of the laboratory of the National Gallery seemed to retain the chill of winter. They were drafty and rattled in the breeze. But Noreen, pushing through heavy double doors, soon found herself in the clinical atmosphere of the work area which was sectioned off by glass panels.

On a clean, white sheet of museum board, she spread the paint chips, varnish-side up, and it struck her how dim they looked. It could be, she knew, merely the effect of the varnish that had been painted over the surface of the painting to protect the color below. Over time it yellowed naturally and became impregnated with a surface layer of grime. But this varnish was smooth and had a high-gloss finish, like the mastic varnish that was preferred during the nineteenth century and was replaced in the first half of the twentieth by Damar. Mastic yellowed, bloomed (clouded), and cracked with age, whereas Damar proved less susceptible to such deterioration.

But *mastic* varnish? Again, as with the absence of a liner, Noreen had wondered why a painting of such worth had never been cleaned. It was the process of removing aged varnish by rubbing the surface with cotton wool and solvent and then applying a new coat of varnish.

Lifting the largest flake with a tweezers, she placed it under a table magnifying glass, through which she focused as she drew the head of a pin across it several times, flaking off the varnish. Here too, however, she was presented with another anomaly, for beneath the varnish the paint appeared to be the same color as it was when glimpsed through the surface layer. Why?

As paint oxidized and hardened it lost color. New paintings were bright and glossy but mellowed with the passage of time, sometimes not achieving stable tones for many years. The addition of reactive agents—hardeners and driers that were essential for certain difficult glazes—forced the absorption of oxygen and overcame other conditions that might inhibit drying. But such substances also accelerated the maturation of color. Paints into which hardeners had been mixed got darker faster than those that contained a more usual medium. Over the course of time driers made pictures much darker than when first painted.

Would Sisley, whose concern for slight variations in a delimited palette was seemingly paramount, have employed a drying agent? Drying agents were often unpredictable, and a painter who could not know what effect they might have over, say, fifty years, used those substances at his peril. Would the fastidious Sisley have taken chances with the subtle harmonies of his palette?

There were three methods of determining the composition of paint chips: chemical, which was surest but took a great deal of time; and spectroscopic and X-ray analysis. Noreen chose the last.

Using Hall's Box, a device developed by Dr. E. T. Hall at Oxford's Clarendon Laboratory, she bombarded a paint chip at a time with X rays that were reflected off the elements within at different but established angles. A collimator absorbed the irradiations, and a computer processed the information, estimating the type and quantity of elements present. Having first to adjust the "Box" to accommodate the diminutive chips and then seek help in selecting the proper program for the computer, Noreen worked through the remainder of the afternoon and learned several seemingly incongruous facts:

Yes, mastic varnish covered the surface of the stolen painting. Yes, glazing had been employed. And, finally, a siccative or drying agent *had* been employed—but not a linoleate (linseed oil–based) substance, which would have been available to Sisley in 1876. Rather, a naphthenate compound of cobalt—the best and quickest drier—had triggered the absorption of oxygen by the oil in the paint.

She considered the problem: cobalt linoleate, made by cooking cobalt salts in linseed oil, was first used in Belgium in 1852, but cobalt naphthenate was a more recent development, which had entered oil painting, after first having been used for industrial coatings, well into the twentieth century.

What, then did it mean? Perhaps only that the painting had once been damaged and "restored" by the use of techniques that were not usual and materials that had not been available to the painter. Or perhaps that Sisley himself had gotten hold of cobalt naphthenate, using it earlier than had previously been reported.

On her way through the laboratory toward the door, she placed the other half of the paint chips and the slides that contained the dust samples taken from the frame and stretcher on the desk of the chief chemist, who had promised to give her inquiry a few hours at the end of the day. He was an old flame, as it were, and would do just about anything for her.

Glancing up at the clock in that office, she saw that it had nearly gone four. She had her shop to close up, the receipts to go over, and she would return to the Craig & Son shop on the quays before going home. Because of McAnulty's presence, she had not completed her examination of the stretcher, which was all but obscured by the ornate frame. Given what she had discovered here, that was now essential.

Turning to the door out of the laboratory, she wondered what the chances might be of her husband's coming home at a reasonable hour. They had not had a night out together in . . . ? She could scarcely remember. He was always too busy, or they had some dreary Gárda social function to attend or an opening to pop into. She thought they might do something simple together, for a change—go out for a drink at Slattery's and listen to some music or even out to Tamango's in Baldoyle and dance. Then, there were all the after-hours clubs in Leeson Street.

Perhaps . . .

But more likely not, for earlier in the afternoon McGarr had returned to the shop on the quays and the scene of the murder. There in the kitchen the maid, Rose Marie Coyne, had said to him, "A ball of malt, Peter? Just a drop? Sure, I'll pop it into a teacup and your man"—she meant the cook who, as before, was working in the kitchen—"won't be a bit the wiser."

A conspiracy, no less. She and he, two Dublin Jackeens against the rest of the uncivilized world, when in fact under the patina of genteel poverty the Inchicore that McGarr had been raised in had been as brutal as any barracks room muster, filled with thugs, assorted gougers, and several generations of gunmen.

And it had been the necessity of averting the head, turning a blind eye to the inequities of life there—families of twenty-three, blessed by a bishop but cursed by the bravado of a barroom bowsie: T.B., rickets, the weak "little wans" with the gray-green skin and the saintly sick eyes; tired, tried cows' last half-dozen calves—that had led McGarr to police work. About the cruelty of the society in general he could do little, but in the particular, where details mattered, he had found his niche, although sometimes he thought of himself as just another hard man who had seized upon a different agenda.

"The shop now—who would have keys to the shop, Rose Marie?"

Her hand jumped to her mouth, saucer-wide with sincerity. "The son. The missus, somewhere, surely. But . . ."

She would have had no need for keys.

"Roche." Pronounced Rock. "Though he always rang."

Not by Roche's say-so. He said he had found the door open, having tried it in spite of the "Ring Please" sign with its imperative.

"Now, when you yourself arrived, you found—?"

"It locked, so. Amn't I after telling you that?" A tsk. Another. A shake of the head, her muddy eyes regarding him.

"You had to walk round?"

A nod.

McGarr waited; then, "Which side?"

The eyes cleared. They shied. Her old hand—the right one—jumped out, like the knobbed end of a thin stick. "The other."

"The *other*?"

She turned, orienting herself to the door of the building. "The one"—again she gestured with the hand—"facing. The one where the mister wasn't."

Old age? Senility? Perhaps. A lie? Could she have known all through the day that he was there and not have let on, hoping that somebody else would discover the corpse? Why? Fear?

Once again he thought of the IRA. The old lads who drank out at the Silver Tassie.

"When you called Henry Craig to tell him what had happened to the mister, did you mention that a painting had been stolen?"

Her brow knitted. "Where was I now, when I phoned?" She thought for a moment, a finger to her wrinkled upper lip. Her forehead then cleared. "I don't think so. No. In fact, no, I didn't, because, you see, I used the one in the office, and it was only in turning around, after having rung off, that I noticed it. The stuff"—pronounced shtoof—"the chips was all over the carpet, which is mine to care for."

"And the clock? Was that yours?"

She shook her head. "No, a complicated oul t'ing. The mister wound it."

"You're sure?"

"As I live and breathe, please God."

And then the cook, Jean-Jacques Dupuis by name, a native of Rochefort in Charente-Maritime and not far from Segonzac. A double coincidence, in Roche's name and that of the city and the origin of the bottle of cognac? McGarr could not know.

And as in his formal statement, the cook—a chef, McGarr noted in a pyramidal *meringue croquembouche* that topped a pastry on a counter—said that the lights had indeed been on when he had arrived, but at the back, which, "as domestic staff," he always used and was locked. "I too had to ring." All in French.

"Qui est allé à la porte?"

"You speak their lingo, Peter?" interrupted the maid. "Good man." She tapped his shoulder.

"Madame," said the cook. He was a man of medium height with a burly build that was running to fat. The pouch of flesh beneath his chin was blue-green in the now-failing spring light. His forearms, exposed in a short-sleeved, uniform shirt, were powerful and covered with tufts of fine, black hair. His nose was long, thinly bridged, and so straight that his nostrils

94

appeared flared and diaphanous. The tiny capillaries revealed there were maroon, as though filled with dried or sludgy blood.

"How was the madame dressed?"

"As she later appeared. In a"—the nostrils flared—"dress."

"Later appeared?"

"When Monsieur Roche arrived at ten. I heard the bell ringing over and over again until, finally, I thought I should answer it." His eyes, which were dark and clear, lighted briefly upon the maid.

She said, "And where did you pick it up, Peter—their talk?"

"Synge Street," said McGarr, meaning the Christian Brothers College there, which so many highly placed business, professional, and government leaders had attended that they were now known to the press as the "Synge Street Mafia." An old-boy network, but whose members were from decidedly different backgrounds from the English model.

"Synge Street—now wouldn't it be just like your mither."

To put on airs and send her youngest to a Christian Brothers school, to want her son to better himself and break out of Inchicore, McGarr completed, although he was trying to concentrate on what the cook had to say. And he was after wondering why she thought she could or should break in on him, like this, and now he thought he knew why.

He turned to her. "Where were you at ten yesterday morning that you didn't hear the bell ringing when Mister Roche arrived?"

The skin of her forehead wrinkled as her eyebrows went up, and her head turned to the windows. "Ten? Ten, now? Where was I? Doing something or other."

She blinked. Her eyes cleared. She raised the bony cudgel of her fist, which she shook. "The garden, I was. The clouds had parted for a moment, mind, and I used the excuse of looking in on the gardener, poor oul soul, to sit meself down in the sun."

"But the shop—?"

"Ach—like I said. We have little custom in off the street, and wasn't I after camped there hours already and not so much as a rattle at the door?"

"And how was the gardener?"

"I didn't bother the misfortunate man. The reek off the place was enough. Story told." She cupped a hand to her mouth. "Bee, double oh, zed, eee. Straits, he was, from the night before. I just plunked me"—she smiled, an eyelid dipping slightly in an approximation of a wink—"*self* down on a garden bench.

"But, sure, there's nothing in it anymore. The sun. With all them satellites and volcanoes and pollution, you know. Five minutes, maybe ten. I got a chill, so, and"—she turned to direct the thought to the cook—"I was back at it, hard, until as before, like I said yesterday, I saw the mister and went out to him and then up to the missus."

"The gardener," said McGarr, turning from the cook and taking her by the elbow. He directed her to the kitchen window, from which they could look down at the roses, the ragged boxwood maze, and the corrugated metal hut painted green that reclined against the back wall. "Curtin, isn't it?"

She nodded. Under his hand the old muscle of her forearm was taut.

"Why would he of all people have use of the mister's Mercedes?"

Her head jerked up to him. "Sure and he wouldn't."

"I have it that he would. Last night, for instance. A long drive, all about the town. Out to Collins Avenue. Through Phoenix Park."

Reaching out behind her she grasped the back of a chair, seemingly for support.

"Out to the Silver Tassie on the road to Enniskerry. Know the place I mean?"

She shook her head.

"How would he have gotten the keys?"

Another head shake. "Nicked them, no doubt. He's here long enough to know where things is." Her old eyes suddenly glazed over and her facial expression hardened. "Always nosing about, looking for whatever he could scrounge in the way of a drink."

"When was the last time the car was used?"

"That I wouldn't know. Weeks ago. Maybe months. The mister was one for taxis, you see. And public transportation. 'I'm a democrat,' he would say to me. 'It's necessary to retain the common touch.' "

Yet he kept a handgun in the top drawer of his desk, thought McGarr, in case that touch should become too complete.

"The desk in the office, Rose Marie. Had you ever occasion to go into that?"

"Never." Too fast. "It was locked, always." McGarr's staff had found it open and not forced.

"The key?" he asked. It had not been found on the body.

She shook her head. "And I'm after needing a wee rest. You'll have to ask the missus. She's in the studio waiting for you."

8

Although suddenly, precipitously, in a way peculiar to Irish weather, it had become a season for open windows, McGarr was surprised to find the one in the studio that looked out on the death scene wide to the breeze.

Like a drunken sailor, the wind blustered across the gleaming parquet, rolled through the open hall door, and plummeted down the stairs into the shop. There the brine musk, sour from its tussle with the Liffey, coupled with the sweet propriety of old wood, silk, and lace, then lurched out the door, requited.

That too was open, a Guard standing in the deep shop shadows, as though to make sure the wind took nothing away. By his side was the P.M., resting out of the sun.

"Have ya got a fella?" McGarr now heard through the open studio window."

"Yah."

"What's his name?"

"Dermot."

"Does he love yuh?" A catechistic inversion with several voices questioning, but only one—thin and reedy—replying.

"He says he does."

"Does he kiss yuh?"

"He tries."

"Where?"

Giggles. A shriek. Uniformed schoolgirls with pleated skirts strolling along the granite blocks of the quays, the breeze baring pink, knobby knees.

Among them was the inevitable redhead, her hair flowing in the breeze. Red himself, McGarr followed the thin-legged twist of her hips as she stepped over the mated blocks of the quay wall. Her skin was as pale as chalk against the jade of the tide-swollen river, and she was squinting and seemed out of sorts, as though she knew without having to be told that her season—the subtle hues of winter; the amber glow of firelight in the gloss of her hair; skies that muted like a troubled mood—had passed and the umber, fecund tones of summer had arrived.

There was something engagingly precious and unpredictable about redheaded women—McGarr, after all, had married one—but when the earth took on heat, dark-haired, dark-skinned, dark-eyed, deep women, like Louise Craig, were required. She was sitting on a stool in the middle of the floor, dressed not in the black of mourning but rather in a natural linen suit which contrasted with the tones of her skin.

Today, far from crossing her legs, which were shapely, away from him, she had twined them primly but also in the way of a woman who well understands, and has decided to employ, her attractiveness. And she had followed him with her body, turning herself to him as he had entered the room.

Auras of the personality, animal magnetism—call it what you will—McGarr was far too experienced in dealing with people not to believe in such power, and in contrast, say, to Henry Craig's woman in Glencree whose presence was hot, throbbing, like a full sun, Louise Craig's was a silent presence, a warmth—McGarr could feel it—that was mellow and radiant.

A motherly presence? Yes, but not in the usual way, for in the waves of her age-streaked hair, set off by gold barrettes and the lightly powdered, scalloped shadows of her wide upper chest, McGarr read the promise of the affection of that other mother, the one tasted only fleetingly in those dreams that are most secret and sweet and wake one with a guilty start, making further sleep impossible.

And in her eyes there was now a kind of mature and purposeful acquiescence, as though to say that she had prepared herself for him and was now inquiring of his pleasure. Dark and darkly ringed, her eyes were set in a strong, sensual face—the upper lip heavy, slightly protrusive, with a chiseled edge—and the promise in them was undeniable. He wondered of what, and, if she had thought that necessary, why.

Or could she be one of those unfortunate persons (and McGarr had met some) whose auras are so strong and compelling that they cannot themselves conceal an attractiveness, which tyrannizes everybody concerned with them, including themselves.

How little of what we do or cause others to do, he wondered, and certainly not for the first time, can be explained reasonably. As a policeman, it was the Greater Task that society had set him: to make sense of the untoward, to couch the senseless in terms that would allow expiation, to define the culture's Higher Faith in the reasoned approach to life. And the attractiveness of Louise Craig and her effect upon others could not be proved.

If the Honorable Justice will indulge me, McGarr imagined himself saying in Central Criminal Court before what he sometimes thought was the hardest and most jaded man in the universe. *The key to this case is this woman's magnetism.*

She attracts . . . fumbling for words here . . . *men . . . such that somebody—her son or her husband's partner or a thief or just a lonely stranger passing in the night—felt compelled to open the unlocked* (said Roche) *door of the lighted shop* (had the killer been expected?) *and had then dragged her husband out through two doors into the lot below her window and, while she looked on, had shot him in the groin.*

It was absurd, of course, and he could hear the justice interposing lightly, Correction—she attracts *McGarr,* much to the diversion of all present.

Yet it was undeniable. Everybody from the victim, to the son, to Roche had been drawn to this woman, had concentrated his thoughts, words, and actions upon her, and McGarr felt it himself, now that she had turned her attention to him.

Perceptions. How much were they like the tap of a blind man's cane on the pavement, but more deceiving—here the feel of something real but indefinite and there the void below a curb. Or was it a precipice?

McGarr shifted uneasily under her gaze. The missus. She who had either witnessed or had been party to the murder, he was now convinced. Could he prove it? Perhaps, if he could get her to admit to having been up and in the studio between half four and half five yesterday morning.

Time. He thought of Roche, who admitted to having arrived at the shop early in the morning, though he said he neither entered the studio nor opened any other doors. Roche, who then returned later. When had his plane arrived? McGarr would have to check.

And the son, who denied having been on the premises for weeks but whose car might have been seen there. By the maid.

As McGarr began speaking he nodded to a Ban Gárda, a uniformed policewoman who was seated at one of the several drawing tables, a transcriber in front of her. A necessary intrusion. For the record, no lies.

He prefaced his questions by thanking her for the interview here, as requested, in the studio.

She smiled slightly, timidly, her eyes glinting, yet she retained her reticence in a way that was fetching. No billows of sex, no gusts, but rather a quiet promise, silent, like warm, moist air on a summer night. She would be seen best then, he imagined, her dark features in shadow. She was a woman of full curves, of size, and just deliciously overripe.

Roche at six? The son perhaps earlier or later? Impossible? Maybe not.

"I'd like to go through the day, yesterday, from the beginning. What time did you arise?"

Holding her cigarette like a pointer, she glanced down at the lighted end, which was being made to glow in the strong breeze, the smoke fanning back over her bare arm. Gauloises or Gitanes, some dark, strong tobacco.

The cigarette swirled once, and she glanced up at the clock near the open window. Metallic ribs, Art Deco. A present, much appreciated, from Roche, but she had allowed it to stop. It said 4:47, though McGarr, checking his watch, noted that it had just gone 4:00. "I'm not a clock-watcher, Mr. McGarr." A deep voice, husky, heavily accented and entirely appropriate. *She appeals to McGarr?* He judged that her appeal would be lost only on the insensible.

"I retire at night, I arise in the morning."

"First light?" which was half four at this time of year.

She shrugged.

"The birds were singing?" It would place the time about a half hour earlier.

"We have no birds here. No song birds." Her eyes met his briefly and moved off toward the twilight in the window. "Pigeons. Crows. Sea gulls."

"You heard them?"

Another kind of shrug, a flick of a wide shoulder. She drew deeply on the cigarette.

"Then can we say half four?"

"Yes. Half four."

"And you did what? Upon arising."

Her head turned, and she looked at the prim figure of the navy-blue-skirted Ban Gárda with the sky-blue blouse and epaulets at the machine. "The usual. I completed my toilet, dressed. I took coffee in the kitchen, a second cup here."

"You remained here?"

Without looking at him, she nodded.

"How long?"

"Most of the day."

"Were the windows open or closed?"

"Closed."

"Early visitors—did you have any?"

She paused, drew on the cigarette, and looked off to the other side, away from the transcriber. She shook her head.

"Not Monsieur Roche?" He waited.

No reply.

"Or your son, Henry Craig?"

She shook her head.

"I can't hear you."

"No."

"No—Pierre Roche?"

"No, not him." There was an edge to her pronunciation of the pronoun.

"No—not your son?"

"Neither."

"Both of them were here. They told me so."

Again she raised the cigarette.

"Roche said he opened the door and looked in," a lie, but one he believed necessary. "You weren't here."

"He must not have seen me."

"Were you smoking then?"

She shrugged once more. "Of course."

"Did you hear anything unusual between half four and half five?"

She tilted her head slightly. Her eyes were now back down on the sheen of the floor, as they had been a day ago when McGarr first saw her. *"Oui."*

McGarr waited.

In French she said, "Downstairs. William was up. I could hear him. The lights were on everywhere."

The Ban Gárda looked up at McGarr, who motioned that it was all right and continued the questioning in French. "Was that unusual?

"Yes, but then not so when he was preparing for an auction."

"Was he?"

"I wouldn't know."

"You took no active interest in his business?"

She shook her head.

"In the larger business, in, say, the purpose of Mr. Roche's trip to Argentina?"

Her brow furrowed. The hand with the cigarette flicked out. "He tells me things, asks my opinion, but . . ." Her voice trailed off.

"And you give your opinion."

"When he demands it."

"Why does he *demand* it?"

"Because he is an egoist, because he thinks that everything that interests him should interest everybody else, because . . . he began his initial investments with my money, or so he says."

"Says?"

"When he came to this country he brought with him some of my family's money."

"And you allowed him to use it?"

She only looked away.

"Is he used to making demands of you?"

Her eyes moved up to his. "He would, were he capable."

"I don't understand."

Once more her eyes fell to the floor, then to the ashtray by her feet. As she bent to snub out the cigarette, the lapels of her linen suit opened, and McGarr caught a glimpse of full breasts, a delicate olive in color. "His injuries. Perhaps you'd best ask him."

"Then yesterday morning you heard sounds different from most other mornings."

A nod. "Moving around. The shop door."

"Ringing? The bell?"

She shook her head.

"Were you not interested or concerned with those sounds?"

Another head shake.

"Then what are your interests, may I ask?"

"You may, of course." But she offered no more, and McGarr listened to the rumble and thump of a lorry in the street, the ringing of a winch cog over the teeth of its wheel, the groan of a ship's horn out in Dublin Bay, all coming to him clearly down the granite, canalized banks of the Liffey here at quayside. Out in the hall beyond the closed door he heard a footstep.

"*I'm* interested in what you did from half four until ten, when Monsieur Roche says he finally managed to locate you here."

"Rose Marie came in with my breakfast. We—*she*—chatted. She said she had some things that she wanted to discard—bedding, blankets, things from Henry's room, now that he's"—a pause—"departed. She wanted my permission. They were in the press. After breakfast we went through them."

"Until Monsieur Roche got here?"

She nodded. "I was just returning to the studio when he arrived, and he"—she drew on the cigarette—"importuned me with talk of Argentina. Business." She waved the cigarette dismissively. "World affairs. *Jusqu' à la gauche.*" An Irish touch that, but in French.

"And Roche left?"

"He kept speaking until half two, when Rose Marie knocked to tell you about your husband's corpse?"

"For . . . hours, yes. Interminably, it seemed. But then he removed some papers from his folder and began to go through them."

"For how long?"

A shrug. "Some time."

"And he sat where?"

"There—at the drawing table." It looked out not on the rubble-strewn lot in which Craig had been slain, but rather upon the back garden.

"And what did *you* do?"

"The usual. I either painted or drew. Or . . ." She glanced down at the cigarette which was now nearly burning her fingers. She snubbed it out.

"Where did you do all of that?"

"Painting—the easel."

To catch the north light, it had been placed off on an angle to the window and the lot. If while standing there she had looked out, she could have seen him.

"The drawing. Here. I"—her hands came down on her thighs—"work here on the stool. In my lap."

"Which was it, then. Painting, drawing, or—?"

Again, only a shrug.

"You don't remember?"

"No."

"Why not?"

"One day is like another."

Self-pitying? McGarr did not think so. "Did you look out this window?" Again McGarr rapped the sill, as he had the window the day before.

Her eyes met his. "Perhaps."

"Then did you notice"—that he almost had to pull the words from his mouth, without knowing why exasperated McGarr—"notice your husband there? Murdered? In that ditch?"

She said nothing, though her eyes—shadowed in the near darkness—held his gaze.

McGarr waited. When at length she had added nothing, he asked. "Earlier. Early in the morning. Between half four and half five, when, as you have just told me, you were probably in this room, did you not hear the report of a pistol or something like a pop? Short and sharp. Something unusual."

"As now, I hear many things."

Somewhere off in the distance a pneumatic drill was pounding stone.

"All day long you did not once look out this window?"

No answer. Only the eyes.

"You did not see your slain husband out there in that ditch?"

Nothing.

McGarr thought for a moment, then said, "Can it be that you fear for your own life, that you did see him murdered and you are afraid to tell me what you saw?"

Nor did she answer that. She only changed her position with McGarr, who moved away from the window into the now nearly dark room.

After a while, McGarr asked, "Your husband's murder—what does it mean to you?"

Her nostrils flared. She reached for yet another cigarette. "That he is no longer here."

"No more?"

"No less."

"Will you miss him?"

"Perhaps."

"And the way in which he was murdered? Out there in the ditch. Do you know it was an explosive bullet that was used on him? It blew away his whole lower, middle anatomy."

"Death is never pretty."

"What were you thinking about when I looked up and saw you in this window, staring down at your husband?"

Once more she shrugged. "That at least it was quick. Or so I assume."

McGarr looked away. "Your marriage—was it a loving one?"

No reply. She merely struck a match and held it to the end of the cigarette, the flame making her face seem suddenly haggard and old.

"You loved him?"

"At one time I needed him."

"Why?"

"Because I was young, alone, and very pregnant."

"And now?"

"That is a question without a point. I shall have to see, shan't I?"

"Could it have been your son that your husband had been expecting?"

A nod.

"Why?"

In her eyes McGarr read the ennui that he had noticed the day before, except that she now seemed to suggest that he was its cause. He wondered if it was by her moods that she controlled the men in her life. McGarr had met women like that. And if she had no—or at least a different kind of—concern for her husband, he wondered what she had felt for her son.

"Did your son take an active part in your husband's business?"

"You should ask him."

"When was the last time you saw your son?"

"Monday week."

"Six weeks ago he came to you wanting to know about his parentage—who his father was. Why?"

"Because he is the sort of fool to whom such things matter."

"What did you tell him?"

"That I did not know."

"It seems strange to me that you would not know."

She only let that pass.

"Why did he then fly to Paris?"

"I understand he received a bequest. From my uncle. A painting. Henry has a collection." There was a touch of pride in that.

"The argument he had with your husband—was it before he left for or after he returned from Paris?"

"I know of no argument."

"Then when did he come to you with the question?"

Another shrug. "Some time ago."

"What was his mood?"

"He wanted to know. I told him I didn't know. He asked me what kind of woman was I. I told him I was no *kind* of woman but merely a woman. I had known men. I became pregnant. He was the issue of that pregnancy. He had been well looked after since his birth. He had never lacked for anything. He had health, strength, and talent and would one day become a wealthy man because of the nature of his birth, which was now distressing him. Of that he should be thankful."

"And—?"

"He wanted to know who were the men that I have known. How many, their names. I told him too many to have remembered and some"—she drew on the cigarette—"I never asked their names."

"Frenchmen?"

She shook her head. "Mostly Germans. It was war. Paris was occupied."

"Against your will?"

Her eyebrow flicked up. "What is will?"

"And he?"

She raised her wide shoulders and let them fall. "I should have told him long ago. Perhaps it would have helped him mature."

"And by that you mean?"

"To have settled this very question long ago. He has a woman now, I've met her. He has talent." Pride, definite and distinct. "Even if it is, like my own, restricted to"—a long pause—"smaller forms. Houses and such. And he should—get on with life."

"Do you mean he should have a family?"

"Whatever pleases them."

McGarr was now at the row of light switches. With the flat of his hand he snapped them all on.

Her head rose to the eccentric circles of colored light in the oval recess of the ceiling—a yellowish but deep pink, a greenish-blue, and a light reddish-yellow.

Again he heard a footstep in the hall. The maid, the cook, one of McGarr's own staff seeking him out but not wanting to disturb the interview?

"The painting. The Sisley that was stolen. *L'Inondation à Port-Marly.* Are you acquainted with it?"

She nodded.

"Its provenance—where would your husband have kept that?"

She shook her head.

"Why was it hanging in the office and not in the shop or here in your apartment?"

Her eyes drifted up into the colors again. "It was not for sale. It was William's own, to do with as he pleased. He spent much of his life there in that room."

There were several framed paintings hanging on the wall—a still life of a vase with roses; a market scene that McGarr recognized from his years in Paris as the old Les Halles market-place; racing at the Hippodrome de Longchamp with the Tribunes in the background—which he found attractive and worthy of further study. It was as though he had seen them before, but then, on closer scrutiny, he realized he had not and was moved to linger over details. "Yours?" he asked, when he had satisfied his curiosity.

She only inclined her head and looked away.

McGarr turned to the window that looked out on the garden. "Your roses. Tend them yourself?"

"I saw them last spring. I might again soon."

"Who hired the gardener?"

"William. Or Rose Marie."

"When?"

"Years ago. Five. Ten."

"Why is Pierre Roche so"—he searched for a term—"solicitous of you? Is it because, as your son told me, you have been diagnosed schizophrenic?"

She did not reply.

McGarr only asked, "May I look around?" and did not wait for a reply. He opened the door.

Out in the kitchen the telephone was ringing, and as he walked down the hall, he thought he heard the sound of heels on the stairs down into the shop. A woman's and careful. The maid?

In the kitchen the cook was placidly squeezing potato rosettes from a force bag while the phone jangled. McGarr wondered how he could possibly get on—order supplies, haggle, even give directions to a cabbie—in Dublin without speaking English. McGarr knew his own people, and they would take his sullen, even forbidding, presence and silence as an affront. Eventually he would be ignored, perhaps even abused. Certainly he had to know at least a few words.

"We finally ran down the 'Curtin' alias, and get this," said McKeon on the phone. "His name is Coyne."

McGarr heard a door closing somewhere off in the quiet of the old building. Tugging the cord of the receiver to its maximum length, he looked out the kitchen window, down into the back garden.

There on the path, in the shadowed light from the shop, he saw the old woman, Rose Marie Coyne, advance out into the garden toward the hut at the end of the wall and then stop suddenly, as though having seen or heard something.

"The old woman's last child," McKeon went on, "Edward. Ned, he was known as in the nick. A weapons offense. Then a succession of U.O. charges," by which McKeon meant membership in an unlawful organization, which was proscribed under the Offences Against the State Act.

Over the shoulder of her coat the old woman carried a large bag, black like the bonnet on her head.

"But for the last—let's see—four years, we've got nothing for him. Not even a registration address, so we can lift him, if that's what you want."

Suddenly the old woman turned and in moving off toward the wall and the door through which two days before Craig had either tried to flee or had been led, cast her eyes up to the kitchen windows and McGarr.

Horror, was it? Yes. And fear.

"Then there's a writ outstanding on a—"

McGarr pivoted and in two long strides toward the kitchen door slammed the receiver into its yoke.

He took the steps down three at a time, one hand on the wall, the other before him for whatever he might meet in the dark.

Down in the shop he groped, like a blind man, down the corridor that led to the door into the half-light of the garden.

But the maid was gone, along with the key for the low, arched door into the lot, which she had locked behind her.

Back within the building, McGarr rushed out the way he had come until he reached a lighted showroom, where he broke into a sprint, the P.M. and the guard at the door rising when they saw him.

"Quick—the old woman, the maid. Out in the lot." McGarr tugged open the door, the bell jangling on its brace, and stepped into the street.

It was almost night, with only a stripe of indigo paling the horizon to the west, and through the sifting haze of fog, coal smoke, and fumes, McGarr could just pick out the figure of the old woman, her legs like two thin sticks, stumbling near the far margin of the lot, the bag which she now clutched in her hand dragging through the rubble.

The P.M. McGarr reached down and grabbed up a fistful of the nearly deaf dog's crest and shot his other hand forward toward the woman. "Watch!" he shouted, and the dog was off on its hobbling gait, picking its way, like an errant mote through the scarred surface of the lot.

But she gained the sidewalk of the street beyond and moved toward a car that had pulled out of an alley into the cadmium cone of a streetlamp. A door opened and she was pulled roughly into its dark interior. A hand reached out and snatched up her bag, which had fallen into the street. And the car was off; lightless; the dog following it a short way up the street.

McGarr turned to the Rover, tugged open the door, and began to reach for the microphone on the dash.

He stopped. Curtin/Coyne in the kip. Why had she not given him the warning, the old cow to her last and sorry calf, who had broken his cover on the night before? McGarr himself had told her so.

The car. It had been waiting for her, having pulled out of the alley behind the shop. He thought of the expression on her face, as in the shaft of light out the showroom window she had glanced up at him—the sagging, spent features drawn in a kind of terror, hopeless. What had she seen?

Reaching under the seat, McGarr felt for and found the cold butt of his P.P.K. He checked the clip and slid the weapon under his belt.

The dog had returned to the car.

From a web beneath the dashboard McGarr drew a shotgun and a brace of shells. "Can you use this?" he asked the uniformed Guard.

"I"—a slight hesitation—"can, sure." Heavy hands fumbled for the barrel, the brace. A tall, dark young man.

"Go round the building and cover the alley. Stop anybody who comes out the back way. If they're armed, use it and that's an order."

In the shop the dog followed McGarr's heel—back down through the lighted showrooms to the dark corridor and then out into the garden.

The hut door was nearly closed, but the gate leading into the alley was swinging open. A shaft of yellow light fell onto the pathway. McGarr could hear a radio playing from inside the hut, and the sweet stink of cognac was still present in the entry.

McGarr paused where Rose Marie Coyne had. What had she seen that had thrown her into a panic? Through the hut window: a section of wall, the paint peeling; a triangle of greasy porcelain that was the corner sink; a hand that had partially released its grip on a bedpost. Through the window in the door he could see the bottom of the bed, a leg, and a battered boot.

But the P.M., now advancing without him, had begun a low, steady growl, its right shoulder rocking down with its careful steps. In the entry, it stopped suddenly. The growling ceased. It turned and looked back at McGarr, and then raised its snout to the gap between the door and its jamb, scenting. Farther up was the dirt-ringed knob of a bony chest and a head thrown back on the pillow. The eyes were open, staring at the ceiling.

The dog whined once, turned back to McGarr, and then whined again, reaching out with its left and able paw as though wanting but not daring to push open the door of the kip.

McGarr rushed forward and grasped the dog by the tail, tugging it once, and then turned and rushed back into the darkness of the garden, only to have—in a flash that he saw repeated in the sixteen shop windows—his feet swept out from under him and his body blown in a jarring tumble into a clump of rhododendron bushes. And suddenly it was raining—glass, metal, rubble, and brick—all in a searing fireball that scorched his face and made him turn his head into his arms.

He tried to pick himself up, to stand and run away from the searing flames, but he was disoriented or in shock, his legs numb, his balance gone, and he blundered, stumbling, through the rough bushes that tore at his flesh until he felt himself falling, this time in a psychic tumble through the large and ever-deeper hole that was his waning consciousness.

9

Through the pavement three blocks distant, Noreen first felt the tremor in her knees. It jarred the cobblestones of the street beneath her feet. Next she saw the fireball blossom up over the roofs of nearby buildings in a puff of vivid orange. Only when it burst, as though igniting the mauve and gaseous flux of the early evening air, did she hear the report, which staggered her.

Clutching her bag under an arm, she began to run, her steps resounding off the brick of the businesses there. Office blinds were parted. Navvies, their faces soot-blackened from a day of work, appeared in coal-yard gates, staring up at the conflagration on the quays.

Approaching the shop from the rear, she saw first the fire at the back of the garden, the Gárda Rover—like her husband's—parked in the street out front, and a figure lying on the stone of the alley near the crackling flames.

It struck her how strangely recumbent he appeared with the hat still on his head, the cinch tight about his chin and his hands crossed on his chest. His mouth was closed, the dark sweep of his mustache untouched. Even his eyes, in which the flames danced, were open. And it was not the shard of searing metal that still hissed in his blood and had nearly cut his torso in half that made him seem sculptural, like an un-finished sarcophagal carving, but rather the chunk, the size of a baby's fist, that was missing from his forehead. Curiously, it was not bleeding.

Turning, she lost her footing and stumbled and then blundered through the rubble by the side of the building to reach the front and the door that was open there. In the distance she could now hear Klaxons and saw in the street others running toward her.

She passed quickly through the lighted showrooms, hating in a vagrant thought the immobility of the inanimate antiques, and groped along the passage that led to the back of the shop, where the shattered glass crunched under her feet. There in a paneless window she saw what she had hoped she would not see:

In the dancing shadows of a withered bush, the dog, the P.M.—its coat smoking, its mouth open, whining, turning its head back toward the building imploringly but either unable or unwilling to leave the other figure upon or beside which it crouched. Her husband.

Mindless of the glass and the wreckage below the window, she jumped down into the garden, the dog rising to meet her then returning to McGarr. She had to swing her back to the scorching flames to reach the shelter of the bush, only to discover that she could neither pull nor tug McGarr from the branches, and it was in glancing back to the building for help that she saw the woman standing full in the frame of the brilliantly lit, blown-out, upstairs window, looking down at them.

Noreen thought of yelling, of beseeching her help, but first one soot-blackened face and then another and a third appeared in the window she had jumped from, and soon the navvies from the coal yard she had run past were by her side.

"Easy with him now, lads. Just out of the heat now, back

117

there in the corner," where a team from the St. John ambulance brigade soon appeared.

McGarr's eyes were glassy and unfocusing, opening briefly and then closing, as if the lids were weighted. But when they tried to place him in a litter, he would have none of it, and he struggled to his feet.

Stepping through the door into the building, he rocked against the wall. His face was drawn, haggard. His shirt, left side, was in tatters, and his arm hung limp by his side. There was a burn the size of a ten-penny piece on his cheek, and he was sweating, although his skin was ashen.

"Peter," Noreen shouted, "do as they tell you. Get into that litter. You're not yourself, so. They'll take us to the Richmond," which was a hospital.

With that McGarr lurched down the darkened hallway, reeling, staggering, using the wall for support, his head lowered, the hand that was uninjured groping at his belt.

Noreen reached out and stopped him, turning him around into the light from one of the blown-out windows and the fire beyond. "What's that? Jesus, Mary, and Joseph—a gun, is it? And just where do you think you're going in your condition? Look at your flippin' shoulder. Your cheek. Your arm, sure— you've broken it, and you know that yourself. Out here arsing around—"

He pulled himself away and set off again.

"Wait. Stop!"

McGarr had turned a corner and now was staggering dumbly through one of the lighted showrooms, walking on his heels, his feet falling like planks on the old floorboards.

"With bombers and gunmen, like you were some rookie inspector with a death urge. Do you know that the Guard, the one out in the alley, is dead?"

McGarr stopped, his hand reaching out to the back of a

piano to gather himself. Dead. He remembered the young man's hesitation before accepting the shotgun. "I can—sure." Can die.

She stepped in front of him, the P.M. standing off a few paces, regarding them. "Yes—a death urge, definite and undeniable, and it's hardly fair, is it? To me.

"It would be one thing if you were—" There were tears in the green eyes that now searched his face.

Twenty years younger, McGarr completed in his head, at first having thought her an apparition and only now realizing why she was here. He tried to step past her, but she remained in front of him. "But—listen to me—you're—"

An old buck, he thought, who still had something to do before he could consider how badly he was hurt, and at the moment—trying to ease her away—he believed that his greatest mistake in life was to have married a woman who *was* twenty years younger than he or in fact to have married at all.

"—Chief Superintendent now, and you should realize that you're—"

"Beyond—" he prompted, lurching by her again toward the front of the shop and the Gárda Rover that was parked there. What he had to do could only be done by him and him alone. Nobody else in his squad had the rank or authority, and he had to get to them fast before Special Branch, which dealt with all crimes committed by unlawful organizations, was called in. And while they were still at their ease, those who had planted the bomb. What were the chances of anybody having made the connection? of Curtin/Coyne having been followed? they were now asking themselves. Doubtless over a pint.

"Yes, *beyond* all these"—her copper-colored curls shook in anger, as she tried to spin him around—"histrionics. Get those other lummoxes to take the chances."

Other? McGarr asked himself, following her thought in an attempt to distance himself from the pain.

Some uniformed Gárdai on the sidewalk began to salute, but, seeing his face and shirt, they could not quite bring their hands to their caps.

"And your head. Mother of God, you could have been kilt. A bleedin' firebomb and you with that shooter under your belt. Didn't we agree that you wouldn't jeopardize yourself unnecessarily, that you'd just do your job at the desk and that would be it?"

Easing himself into the Rover, McGarr glanced at the other men, who were now looking everywhere but at him, trying to absent themselves from the wrangle without the possibility of leaving. He had to lift the injured leg and pull the arm into the car.

"What if you were home alone waiting up for my return and not knowing who or what or what kind of bust-up I was in or if I'd ever get back? Or those times you just popped off here or there for days without so much as a by-your-leave? Your work, it is. Always your work. No time. The *situation*. All that tripe about arrest percentages declining so many hours after a crime. You don't even believe in that yourself."

McGarr eased the door to and stared out the windscreen at the twirling beacons of the fire-brigade pumpers at the end of the street.

It was the theatrical touch in Dubliners, he decided— hadn't she even mentioned the possibility?—and no chance of playing a time-honored role could be ignored. Here she was Juno out of O'Casey's *Paycock*.

"Just look at your puss and your scalp. Go on—look. Janie, you should be in hospital. I won't have you looking like a grotesquerie for some foolish act of forensic bravado. Where do you think you're going?"

120

McGarr glanced in the rearview mirror. His face was blood-stained and blackened. Scorched. He would have to stop and clean himself up. There was a jacket in the back seat and a cap.

In the console between the seats, McGarr's fingers fumbled for the flask that he kept there, while two Guards cleared the bystanders from in front of the car.

Marriage—the search for brief moments of wholeness that seduced joy from what had formerly been perceived as the complete pleasures of life. There was only a nagging sense of loss when it could not be sustained. Reaching out with his good hand, he grasped hers on the door.

"You go on home now, and I'll be there by-and-by."

"You're an eedjit, so. I don't think you understood a word I just said."

McGarr started the car. He was tempted to say, I did, but I can't help you. I can only be me. But he forbore.

Noreen was not conscious of how much time—minutes, an hour—transpired before she found herself back in the shop office, where she sat at the desk and asked herself what it meant and where it all would lead: the arguments, though he never actually argued; the risks he took; the way he abused himself, smoking and drinking. He had not seen the corpse of the young Guard, as had she, but even if he had, would it have made a difference?

And the fact that it was chance, mere luck, that the concussion, fireball, and debris of the corrugated metal hut, the bomb that had decimated the garden and blown out the windows of the building, the shrapnel that had killed the Guard not once but twice, had not struck her husband, had not injured him any worse than he was, more than simply frightened her. It was a gift—something like Divine Providence, in which, now, she was tempted to believe—that he was living at all. And then to have him go off like this, as though her concern for his injuries and complaints about the chances he took were merely bothersome, now made her about as angry as she had ever been. He wasn't just his own person to do with or destroy as he pleased, he was hers, too. It was what made a completeness.

She now felt something wet—the dog, which pushed its nose into her lap, raising her hands, wanting to be petted, soothed, comforted. She ran her hands over its coat, rank with the sour singe of burnt hair, calming the animal, feeling for a cut or a burn in its skin, and finding none. And there in the darkness they waited until, at length, a figure appeared in the door.

"Noreen?" It was McAnulty, the Technical Bureau Chief. His men had been passing along the hall for what, she judged, was over an hour now, though the clock behind the door was stopped at 4:47.

What was he doing here now at this hour? she asked herself, only to remember that he was another one who could not keep himself away from the job.

"Are you after having seen Peter? Commissioner Farrell is wanting to speak to him, but then I heard he got all banged up in the blast. Lucky though. Not so the Guard."

She reached out and switched on the desk lamp with the turquoise-colored bezel, then stepped over the P.M., which was asleep on the floor by her feet. At the front of the desk she opened her purse and began removing her magnifying half-glasses, several twist clamps, a small hammer, a pair of pliers, a screwdriver, a scalpel, and a nail puller.

"Aren't you going to say something?" he asked, his small, dark eyes narrowing down on her gear.

"Any suggestions?" she asked, stepping past him to the wall

and the empty frame, which she lifted off its hook and carried back to the desk.

"I just thought you might know where he was." The gluey stub of an unlit cigarette was stuck to his lower lip. "His being your husband and all."

"Him? He's not accountable to me in any way." She pushed back her hair to fit the bows of the half-glasses over her eyes. "And I wouldn't have it otherwise. Sure, and what's a husband? Here one moment, blown away the next."

McAnulty looked off, then scratched at his head. "I reckon . . ." He peeled the butt off his lip and—ever careful of any "sweep" his men had made of an area—tried to place it in his jacket pocket. It stuck to his middle finger. He tried again. "I reckon you wouldn't be talking so, had he been 'blown away,' as you put it."

"Really?" Drawing the light to her, she now tilted the frame. "A penny a bushel, husbands. They walk the streets by the hundreds every day of the week, going to and from their work. Easy to recognize—trousers, coats, newspapers under one arm.

"Their jobs? Story told in the pay packet. Some good, some adequate, others less so, but they get on. A contented lot, mostly. Life expectancy—seventy or so. Set your watch by some of them. Regular hours. The odd ulcer. Case of toper's elbow. Gout.

"But then there's the other sort. No accounting for ambition, a death urge or other manias. Easy to recognize those rotters. Usually little fellas . . ."

McAnulty, who had lit a fresh cigarette, exhaled a cloud of smoke and stared down at it, as though disappointed with the taste.

"Never at home. Round the bloody clock. Seven days a week when the curse is on them. In spite—what am I saying?—*because* of the risk." She now played the light over the frame.

"That's the sort to get. Always the chance of trading them in for a widow's pension. Sure, and it's better than having them under foot a morning a week and them a bit 'banged-up'— consoling phrase that—a broken arm or leg, and a burn"—she had seen it herself—"the size of a donkey's cack on the cheek and a head lacerated from ear to ear.

"Sure, it'll give the little gurrier character, something to talk about until his number comes up.

"Any more questions, *Chief?*" She bent back the canvas and, lowering her head, stared down at its outer edge.

Said McAnulty, as though highly insulted for McGarr, "I'm after never onct hearing Peter tell a 'story.' Yet."

Men, she thought—especially Irishmen—were so child-ishly ignorant and simplistic in their pursuits. They were spoiled certainly and mostly by their mothers, but it was as though they had received some extra gene at conception that negated any need to explain themselves to the world. They were what they were—bakers, bankers, barmen—and that was that.

Life for the women unfortunate enough to become involved with them thus became a Menippean dialectic: was your man a good bookie or a bad bookie, a proficient bomber or a dead bomber? Did he make a living from his farm or did he and his family starve?

On a social level, the reactionary implications of that as-sumption rather frightened her. Could it be accurate? Might all the ostensible perfections of society be mere froth on the waves of a history that was ultimately immutable? Redirecting her attention to the edge of the canvas, she addressed herself to whatever hard facts might be presented there.

If, say, the canvas had been cut down from some suitably

antiquated but valueless painting and scraped clean (a Sisley "mock-up" having been applied to that surface), then whoever had completed the work would not have been able to remove the paint from the cut edge of the material, try as he might. Even when soaked in solvent, some pigment would have remained.

"And I hope you're not meaning to say that he *wanted* to get blown up. Not that, please. It's tripe, so it is. All bugger and rot."

And then removing the curious frame, which wrapped the stretcher on three sides, would give her a better idea of the antiquity of its construction, the stretcher probably having been made by the artist, who was impoverished at the time.

She clamped one side of the frame and stretcher to the top of the desk and reached for the hammer.

McAnulty pushed himself away from the wall. "What do you propose to do with that?"

She straightened up and turned to him, her anger having only subsided not decreased. "I propose to attempt to learn why this painting was stolen." Her voice was restrained, even dulcet, and suggested an infinite patience. "Or is that not important?"

" 'Tis, surely, but with a hammer?" McAnulty's small, dark eyes narrowed down on her. They blinked, as he tried to assess her change in tone. "And we know the reason already, don't we?"

It was Noreen's turn to let the silence carry her question.

"Because of its value."

"To which you are willing to swear?"

"Well . . ." Into his mouth moved the cigarette, like a pacifier, she observed. Too bad mammy wasn't here to beat off the threat to his ego, and another woman at that. "It really isn't my pitch, is it?" She found the reference to a game apt, but still she said nothing. "It says right here, 'Alfred Sisley,' doesn't it? And Craig's reputation was spotless, you said so yourself."

His head turned to the door and the musical, long clock between which the painting had been hanging. "But then, what was it doing in here and without any—"

"Provenance."

"Just so." Now the cigarette was in the very center of his mouth. The right hand moved to the greasy knot of his tie and then to the source of the grease—his head, which he scratched.

"Another possibility is"—with a pop the cigarette exited from his lips—"that the murderer and the thief were not one in the same, the thief knowing that Craig had been murdered and taking the opportunity . . ." McAnulty's features glowered. His nose, which was rough and porous, twitched. The nostrils pulsed, as at something that had gone bad. He plunged a hand into the pocket of his shiny, rumpled suit.

"No. No, no—I've never known an art thief to steal something valueless. It's a—"

"Contradiction," she prompted.

"That's just what it is, a contradiction in"—before Noreen could supply the missing word, McAnulty blurted out—"terms," and brightened, having consummated the phrase.

Noreen paused to consider how her husband, who, if nothing else, possessed a clear, insightful intelligence, managed to function on a daily basis with colleagues such as the man in front of her. She suspicioned that having to bring all of a limited intelligence to bear on his task was the cause of McAnulty's near-total dedication to his job. No wonder he had been relegated to managing the Technical Bureau, which required thoroughness and little else.

Amazingly, however, he now followed the thought to its

conclusion. "And what with all that's here and the thief having *chosen* to steal only the painting . . ."

Noreen now raised the hammer. "Shall we?"

"Shall we what?"

Why investigate, you fool, she was tempted to say. "A tap or two, just to get it apart."

"But why?" His features crumpled in a way that caused her to wonder if he had been drinking, only to realize that for him this was the highest form of fun. They had regressed, she and he, and they were playing a game in which the stakes—life and death—were higher than any.

"To examine the ends. The junctures. The cuts."

His face, registering a pleasure/pain that was yet more exquisite, turned to her, imploring her not to make him have to ask the questions that were on his mind.

"The ends, silly. A forger always tries too hard. Not satisfied with buying some daub of about the same antiquity and size that Sisley had worked in, he would have researched this Port-Marly piece and cut down both the canvas and the stretcher to match the dimensions of one of the famous *L'Inondation* paintings exactly. In that way both the canvas and wood would be genuinely old, but there would be two things that he could never hide."

McAnulty's brow was now twitching. In the center of his mouth the cigarette glowed like a poker.

"The paint in the very edge of the canvas, the weave itself, which no amount of solvent could ever get out, and the corners of the stretcher"—the heavy frame of which she tapped with the hammer—"where he made the fresh cuts to conform to an exact size.

"Now, Sisley's most famous *L'Inondation à Port-Marly* painting, which is hanging in the Louvre, is 24 inches by 19⅝ inches. This canvas was exactly that, not a quarter inch this way or that. There is a blush of color in the weave all around the very edge of this canvas."

McAnulty's eyebrows jumped.

Noreen reached for the bow of her half-glasses. "Look for yourself, so." She prised up an edge toward which McAnulty lowered his face.

"I see it—yes. Blue, some red. There's a touch of yellow. Gray."

"Then, shall we?"

"Shall we what?"

She handed him the hammer. "You to play."

"But"—peering over the half-glasses, he accepted it weakly —"it's *evidence*."

"About which we do not as yet know all. Go ahead, give it a go."

"Ah"—he took a step back—"no."

"You can do it; I know you can."

"I can't. Janie, no. Not me. You."

"Why me? Aren't you the chief here? I'm"—she hunched her shoulders—"only the consultant. A blow-in. A woman and somebody's wife. You couldn't have it said . . ."

McAnulty stepped, as though lunging, toward the desk. Far from tapping it, he uttered a little cry of distress and took a swipe at the stretcher and frame, shivering it on one side.

He dropped the hammer. "Jesus. It's ruint. Destroyed."

Noreen picked up the pieces and held them under the lamp.

"And they're black, the ends," said McAnulty. "Ancient. The t'ing's the real McCoy. I'm in the damper, sure."

But Noreen had not yet examined the ends. Of more interest to her were the inventory markings which were burned into the stretcher and had been concealed by the odd frame: "Camondo 201, L. 2021." The latter was a Louvre designation and—she reached into her bag for her notebook—exactly the same as that of the *L'Inondation* canvas hanging there.

"Up before the Commissioner they'll have me," he lamented. "And after all these years of . . ." He could not find a word.

"Scrupulosity," she supplied, picking up the scalpel and nicking off a bit of the blackened end. She held it to him. He opened his palm and she dropped it in.

She turned, collected her things, and began to leave.

"What am I to do with this?"

She hunched her shoulders. "It's all one to me. You can put it under a microscope, or—since you're the chief here and will have to write the report—hand it to a chemist. He'll tell you the blackness was caused not by age and dehydration but rather by paint or carbon or perhaps plain, ordinary, bootblacking.

"Better still"—with her hand she gestured to the P.M., which was lying in the shadows at the farther end of the desk—"you can put it in your pipe and smoke it."

McAnulty's eyes rose from the chip.

Noreen stepped into the hall.

"But—your glasses."

"Keep them. You need them more than I."

In the blown-out frame of a window she stopped and looked down on the steaming crater of the bomb site, a part of which members of the fire brigade were still hosing down. In the center a group of men had brought achromatic lights to bear on what looked like a boot with a leg in it. By a tiny corner sink, which still stood upright on its drainpipe, other lights had been trained on a charred and blackened skull. The gardener, she assumed.

Growls came to her from the office, and McAnulty said, "Clear out, ya brute. I don't care who you are, you don't get cheeky with me," and the P.M. appeared in the hall.

She reached down for his ear—almost useless now because of a bomb—and decided that she was still very much what she was and could pursue that about as well as anybody. And would.

10

With the brim of the cap pulled down over his eyes and the collar of the jacket raised, McGarr kept his eyes on the clutch gathered at the corner of the bar to which Briscoe, the publican, referred periodically, fetching their drinks on the nod of a head or a slightly longer blink of the eye. Regulars. The lads. The "in the Army" (IRA) crowd, but years ago.

McGarr now wished he could be sitting among them, hearing what was being said, but his time would come. Driving to the Silver Tassie, he had thought back on the device that had been used to destroy the gardener's kip. It had been dirty and cheap, dating from the days when IRA funds had been scarce—just enough explosive to vaporize the petrol and spew it everywhere, making the interior of the hut both an inferno and a kind of larger, more lethal bomb.

And there they sat in their dour, winter clothes—overcoats even now in spring; dun suits with shiny elbows and even a cardigan below; shirts with yellowing collars; ties with darkened knots; on their feet heavy, heeled brogues with clips—sharing a quiet jar. Their lives were a ritual of pub and job. They had little to say, and that in a kind of formal chant, wide-eyed and unblinking, as though struggling, but knowing that their variations on those tired themes would not be believed.

And yet they spoke endlessly, incessantly, their voices sounding to McGarr like the lower register of a bagpipe, a drone that resembled music only in that it was at once form and content. To McGarr's ears their patter warped most vowels into some approximation of the ancient lament, *oi* (moi for my, point for pint, loife for life), and their gait to the Gents to compose themselves was Dublin's special, masculine stride. With their upper bodies erect, they moved only their heads forward—never side to side—with each step, their pace, carried by the click of heavy heels, steady, even quick, as though life were a death march set to double time. Species: *Homo cauponorum Dublinensis*. There were hundreds of thousands of their type in pubs the city over, but with a difference that perhaps only McGarr could appreciate.

Having found a cramped seat at a table between a perfumed and fleshy housewife, who was extracting a week's hilarity from two drinks of a Saturday night, and a sullen youth, all sharp shoulders and elbows, McGarr pulled over an empty pint glass. He filled the bottom three inches with the fluid from his flask, nursing his pain—but carefully—in the only way that he knew.

Until what he saw at the bar made him forget it: Craig, the son, tall and blond; the angular, blonder woman with him. They were served as quickly as the men in the corner, but by a young barman who, McGarr guessed, was Briscoe's son.

Chat. Five minutes. Ten. Then Briscoe, the elder, approached, and Craig nodded to him. Briscoe then shook the woman's hand. Smiles. A laugh.

Briscoe motioned to the son that they should have a drink on him, then returned to the men in the corner, and Craig and the woman went into the lounge. Her hips, which flared from a narrow waist, collected many stares. Her careful athletic step. Her sparkle and tan and the glint of the gold bracelet on her wrist. In parallelograms.

Time. It weighed heavily on McGarr, and the ritual of the stampede to the bar for last call, the flashing of lights, Briscoe's gracious, greedy extension of ten minutes overtime, and then the sing-song litany of "Gentlemen, pleece. Pleece, gentlemen. Time. Time now" seemed interminable. He sipped slowly at his drink, measuring its effect, planning his move. Beneath his forearm and under the left side of his jacket, he could feel the reassuring bulk of the P.P.K., which he almost hoped they would make him use.

The bomb. It complicated matters. Special Branch, which dealt exclusively with unlawful organizations, would be called in and the case taken from McGarr's hands if he could not make the link tonight. And he was angry. Hot. Three deaths, wanton and at will, and he had nearly been killed himself.

Why? What connection had those five old men, who now remained on their stools as the other patrons filed out, to Craig & Son, the antiques shop on the quays? And how had they been able to place the Coynes in Craig's employ?

McGarr now thought of Roche, the surviving partner, who eschewed all responsibility for the shop. He knew more, far more, than he had told.

The son perhaps? McGarr did not yet know, but he would.

"Gentlemen," a barman beseeched. "You're destroying us. Pleece! Time. Time now. Have yuh no homes to go to?"

Most lights had been extinguished and only the door into the parking lot was unlocked, through which the remaining patrons were being asked to exit. McGarr checked his watch—11:52—and hoped he had parked the Rover far enough back in the shadows that it would not be noticed and checked. Official blue. The radio.

How many employees? Four that he could see. A fifth at the door. In the back? Doubtless others.

McGarr, alone now in the corner of the long, padded wall seat, began singing, low at first, rocking slowly from side to

133

side. "The Rising of the Moon." A Republican tune. An inch of amber fluid remained in the glass.

Briscoe, seeing him, cleared his throat, and his son looked up from his work of filling washracks with dirty glasses. He swore.

"Seamus," the son called, and a few moments later, a square and heavy young man looked into the bar.

The men there kept drinking, pints stacked before them. A celebration? McGarr hoped so. Briscoe, in holding his own short glass under a whiskey dispenser, glanced in McGarr's direction, his eyes glassy and uncaring.

McGarr raised his voice.

"Jasus," said the young man. "You're locked. And what've yuh been into? What's that in yer glass?" And he reached for it and sniffed. "Malt. Who gave you that?" He glanced at the bar, as though expecting help from Briscoe's son, then turned back to McGarr.

"How's it going to be, friend—easy or hard? Come along, now. It's finished here, now, and you've had yours." He placed the glass on a nearby table and reached for the arm that McGarr offered him, the good one. The injured arm he kept at his side, securely over the butt of the Walther. In the fist of that hand he held a scrunched-up five-pound note.

On his feet, McGarr teetered into a table, which screeched back into some others.

"Paddy," the young man shouted, "for feck's sake, give us a hand." And he shoved McGarr roughly out onto the floor, which was filled with tables and low stools, three of which McGarr knocked over before the man took his arm once more.

Paddy Briscoe, the son, had a round face and a small mouth, the chin a knob that could be grasped, cheekbones so prominent that they were like ridges that had to be peered over. In the father they were points, from which the sagging skin of the lower face now hung; in the son two pink patches, as though made with rouge.

"Got the bag on, does he?"

"And he didn't get it here."

When Briscoe, the younger, grabbed his injured arm, McGarr opened his fingers and let the note fall. "Me foiver," he muttered, shambling back on his heels, looking down.

It lay balled at his feet, and, when he moved to pick it up, the bouncer pulled his arm back.

"For what he owes us." His eyes met Paddy Briscoe's, who glanced toward his father and the bar.

"Take it, lads. Take it, fellas," McGarr mumbled, staggering. "I meant you to have it, I did. So. I did."

There was a moment of indecision. A second or two, no more. And then he felt the hands release their hold on his arm.

When the bouncer, the more powerful of the two, began bending at the waist, McGarr raised an arm, as though he would fall backwards, but then suddenly, whipping his body with all his force, slammed his forearm down into the lowered neck, snapping the face into his rising knee. His hand, following through the motion, came to rest on the butt of the Walther.

The bouncer, limp, fell heavily to one side, blood spurting from his nose, a piece of tooth stuck on his lower lip.

Briscoe, the younger, had not moved.

McGarr ran the stubby barrel up under his right ear. "Pick it up," he meant the bank note, "and walk toward the bar."

There all conversation had ceased. McGarr could hear only water running and a radio playing in the kitchen beyond an open door.

Briscoe, the elder, had turned his back to them, his hand in a drawer behind the bar, his eyes—the pouches ruffled on his cheekbones like the gills on an oyster—meeting McGarr's in the mirror.

"Whatever you have, keep it in that hand and draw it out slowly. Lay it on the bar."

Briscoe's eyes flashed across the register, angling off in the mirror toward the other men. In them was caution, concern.

One nodded slightly.

From the drawer a gun emerged, a large-bore, nickel-plated revolver. Briscoe slid it across the bar.

Taking long strides, McGarr rushed the boy forward and shoved him into the bar. "Kneel," he ordered. "Hands on top."

"Easy, now," the father said, and the men behind him echoed the warning.

"That your weapon?" McGarr asked. When the father did not answer, McGarr snugged the muzzle up under the son's ear, tightening his face down on the bar. The boy's eyes were bulging, his mouth open. He gasped.

"Is that your weapon?"

"If it is, I'm telling you under duress."

"*Duress*," McGarr roared, thinking of the bomb blast and the dead Guard. And Curtin/Coyne.

With his own good hand, he snatched up the son's hand and slammed it down on the revolver, picking up the weapon with both their hands. Thumbing down the hammer, he aimed it at the father, jerked the barrel up slightly, and squeezed the son's finger over the trigger.

The blast was deafening and shattered the large mirror behind Briscoe, cascading jagged shards, fragments, and slivers of glass into the bottles stacked there, which fell and broke on the floor behind the bar.

Again.

And again.

Yet Briscoe, it seemed, had hardly moved. His bald head and shoulders were spangled with fragments of glass, his eyes still on his son's face.

McGarr lowered the gun and shook it from the son's hand onto the floor by their feet. He then tugged back the slide of the P.P.K. that was jammed under the son's ear, cocking it. "Now—is that your weapon or is it his?"

"Tobin won't fancy this," said Briscoe, the threat in his voice obvious.

It was the one thing that McGarr wanted—his connection in Special Branch and right at the top. A few names, a tip here and there. Over the years it mounted up, McGarr well knew, especially if you kept out of things, as these old men would have.

Then why toss the bomb now? he wondered. Where was the edge, the percentage? And the proper sort of tout being hard come by, Tobin, who was no less than S.B. Chief, would not want to know.

"And you are?"

Very quietly, McGarr said, "The man who has been sent to end your son's life."

Briscoe looked down at the son, as though condemning his bulging eyes, his gasps, his fear. But he nodded.

"I didn't hear you."

"It's mine."

"Louder—I want these men to hear you."

"It's my revolver," said Briscoe.

"Will you help the police in the investigation of three murders in Dublin?" "Helping the police" was the phrase used when a subject agreed to interrogation without being placed under arrest.

Briscoe shook his head.

"Then I charge you with possession of an illegal weapon and

membership in an unlawful organization. And that"—McGarr glanced at the men on the stools—"goes all around."

The bouncer on the floor behind him had begun to revive.

McGarr reached into his shirt pocket and pulled out a card. He tossed it on the bar toward Briscoe. "Call that number. Ask for McKeon. Then hand me the receiver." Easing up on the boy, McGarr grabbed up a fistful of shirt in the middle of his back and shoved him toward the old men. Reaching for the revolver on the floor below him, he tucked it under his belt. "Use that phone." He pointed to a slim device on the sideboard of the bar. Turning to the men at the bar, he leaned his weight into the padded rail. "Now, gentlemen. Please."

After a while, a hand reached out for a pint, another followed, and yet another. It was in front of them, and they would drink while they still could.

"McGarr," said Briscoe, looking down at the card. "We'll soon see who Chief Superintendent McGarr is."

Bravado? McGarr rather doubted it. Confidence? He wondered how many and what class of favors Briscoe and his mates could have provided.

11

It was brisk and springlike by the time Noreen reached Paris. The sky was tempestuous. Billows of pewter-gray clouds were sweeping up the Seine. Now and again sheets of rain forced walkers into the doorways of buildings, but as quickly the water was carried away on the breeze. The chill edge of winter had left the city, and Noreen, who had studied here, judged that spring had come to stay.

She had the cabbie pull up at the Place de la Concorde on the far side of the Jeu de Paume. In newspapers she had read that the river had been rising, threatening to pour over the quays. Reports from the country told of vast inundations, villages stranded, and commerce by boat. She wanted to stroll toward the river and look downstream to where water met sky. Troubled and turbulent, they made one medium today, and she considered the flux closely.

And yet in the Jeu de Paume, the former tennis court of French kings that now housed the Louvre's collection of impressionist paintings, she was disappointed. *L'Inondation à Port-Marly*—perhaps Sisley's rarest atmosphere—seemed dim and lusterless. Glancing down at a brown patent-leather shoe, she wondered why the picture had not been conserved and if perchance it was merely the light.

It was still early, and the museum had as yet attracted only school groups and pensioners who seemed merely to be getting in out of the elements. And she was tired. Having abandoned her husband in what some would see as his extremity, she felt disloyal and had begun to doubt herself. She looked from the shoe to find a museum guard staring at her leg.

He was large and fat, with a shaggy crescent of mustache and bleary eyes. He smiled. He winked.

She drew in her leg, stepped to a bench, and sat.

The light? She glanced up through a window at the troubled gray sky and then back at the painting, which again disappointed her. What had always struck her about Sisley was his fastidiousness. When he was at his best—and by all accounts nowhere more than here—he kept the elements of his talent under strict control. To her the special strength of the Port-Marly canvases had always been the tension that obtained between the tempestuous scene depicted and the mellow brush that he had brought to this work.

But the brush strokes in the water of the foreground seemed nearly reminiscent of Pissarro, and the whole painting had a tone that was wild and un-Sisley-like. Then again, who was she to say? There were those—Hector Langlois for one, whom she was about to see—who had praised it for just those reasons, considering Sisley's work otherwise timid.

Which was the way of it, she concluded, standing again: once you could question one piece, you could question all, the activity of a forger being insidious, an infection.

She turned and tightened the lapels of her otter jacket.

Moving past the guard, she thought she heard him mumble "Hollandaise" or perhaps "Irlandaise," and glancing at her wristwatch she noted that it was nearly noon.

Hector Langlois was a study in brown. Small and plump but

muscular for his age, he wore a brown suit with a matching tie and a tan shirt. His face was smooth, round, and slightly tanned from—Noreen guessed—a winter holiday. His nose was curved. It supported gold glasses, the rims of which flared like sea gulls' wings. In the rich light that flooded through tall Louvre windows, the lenses had darkened to another brown shade.

Having finished scanning her documents, he rearranged the papers and slid them across the desk toward her. "Yes—you are all that and how delightfully so much more?" He allowed his eyes to dwindle down into the brown areas of the eyeglass lenses, and Noreen was reminded that Frenchmen had foibles no less tiresome than, if different from, those of her own countrymen.

"And I envy you your shop, Madame McGarr. As a civil servant, I have been told I must retire soon." In addition to his scholarly activities and after a long career at the museum, Langlois was now Directeur of the Jeu de Paume. "Yet I still feel and act"—rising from his desk with exaggerated effort, he placed a palm against his back, as though in pain—"so very young."

Noreen smiled.

"Ireland. Is it lovely in the spring?" He moved across the carpet toward the several windows and the tumbling patchwork of differing grays that was presented there. "I have been told that it is."

He opened his jacket and placed his hands on his hips, as he stared up at the sky. "Spring. With its transitions, its turbulent, often tempestuous skies. How hard they are to capture with, say, Sisley's immaculate modesty. I'm thinking of the Port-Marly pieces, as doubtless you are yourself.

"And, you know, it was that"—Langlois now wagged a finger at the window—"the transmission of the Sisley personality into her first—how shall I term it?—'reproduction'? which confounded our poor, dear Louisine. That and the Sisley palette, although at the time the resources of the museum and the conservation department had yet to be placed at her disposal." Langlois turned only his head to her. "Would you care for coffee?"

Noreen said no.

"Please stop me whenever you think I'm running on." Langlois turned and began walking toward the windows on the other side of the office, his eyes in front of him as though careful of the steps he was taking.

"It all seems so long ago now. Like an eternity. And I suppose it is in a way. Forty years. Some people and so many of the principals in this tale, didn't—don't live that long. Anyhow, in the later canvases she kept to the slate-blues, the rose-salmons, and delicate tones of mauve-lilac that marked what I shall call Sisley's spring palette. But in that first canvas, she was just learning." He had stopped in front of a window. "Where to begin?" He turned.

"Louisine came to the Louvre in 1938." He went on to say that two entry-level jobs had opened up then, one in the curatorial, the other in the conservation department. Pierre Roche filled the first, and Louisine Faure the second. She was a grandniece of Jean-Baptiste Faure, who had been a baritone with the Paris Opera and an early friend, collector, and patron of the impressionist painters.

"And I think Roche fell in love with Louisine from the moment he first saw her. She was like a tall, dark, voluptuous child—a girl/woman—but sensitive, intelligent, and not without certain talent and charm. And she was very frank in the way that she carried herself. Above all the wiles that other so-called liberated women even now still employ."

Noreen crossed her legs and leaned back into the chair.

"One day, after he'd taken her out a few times, he told me—later, of course, much later when we were reminiscing—that he saw her in a vault where they were both doing some work and, as though an afterthought, she said she had grown fond of him. And that was that. Roche said he hadn't been about to try to resist her. But none of this is of interest to you, and"—Langlois pivoted and began walking in the other direction—"does not address the problem with which you've been presented.

"The point is that the Germans had attacked and pillaged Czechoslovakia and Poland, and some of us realized that France was next on the list. I too, you see, was working here at the time and, as you know, we began our preparations for evacuating most of the collection long before the actual fighting began."

The story was legend in the art world: how the Louvre staff had padded, crated, and then shipped the most valuable items in the vast collection to the unoccupied zone, constantly moving the caches ahead of the advancing Germans.

"We worked so long and hard that it seems now the whole period of preparation and shipment took only a few days and then the Germans were upon us.

"Louisine and Roche were among those who were chosen to stay with the museum, and quite soon after the Germans arrived they became involved in setting up exhibitions of 'decadent' and 'Jewish' art in the Orangerie and the Jeu de Paume. To be laughed at, of course.

"So they hung an impressionist show, and the German officers poured in, some of them merely lifting canvases that pleased them right off the walls. Until Rosenberg, acting for Göring and Hitler, put a stop to that. They wanted everything for themselves. They fabricated pet projects and museums that they were planning to build—but it was pure sham. They never made a move to begin construction. They just wanted everything for themselves. It was rapine, plain and simple."

Langlois now removed his glasses and placed them in the center of the blotter on his desk. Without them his eyes seemed small and dim. "The temptation, to which I'm succumbing now, is to cast all Germans as villains." He shook his head. "It wasn't the case. Are you acquainted with this period?"

Before Noreen could answer, Langlois went on. "No. Of course, you couldn't be. It was not a proud moment in our history, and we French, perhaps more than others, prefer to mythify the past.

"In a nutshell, then. There were three German confiscatory agencies: the *Kunstschutz*, or Art Protection Service, under Count Franz Wolff Metternich, who was a man of dignity and honor. He tried to prevent art thefts from whatever source. Because of his fairness he was awarded the French Legion of Honor at the end of the War. Wilhelm Krugger, who plays a role in your little drama, I believe, was employed by him.

"The second was the Germany Embassy itself, where Ambassador Otto Abetz, a former art student, declared the confiscation and tried to direct the seizure of all art objects in France.

"And the third, which concerns us for the moment, was Hitler's *Einsatzstab Reichleiter* Rosenberg, which here in Paris a certain Baron Kurt von Behr—as unscrupulous and dissolute a man as the Nazi movement possessed—controlled, with the Gestapo providing the muscle.

"It's interesting how opposites attract. Von Behr was corrupt, decadent, even then an old man. He was a savage, albeit an aristocratic savage, but it was to the Sisley paintings and to our lovely Louisine that he was particularly attracted, and he chose her to take him through the collection here at the Louvre.

"And a good thing too, for Louisine would note where she had taken him and what he had seemed to like and then that night some of our workers would transfer those pieces to some other part of the museum. The Louvre, you see, was being used as the repository of their plunder, and even vaunted German efficiency could not keep up with the mountain of material—paintings, sculpture, furniture, tapestries, rugs, silver and plate—that was pouring in here. Cataloging became sporadic. Their avarice bred a kind of confusion that permitted us a certain degree of deception. And in chaos there is opportunity.

"Some degree of civility still obtained, however, and Louisine could refuse von Behr's advances toward her but not those to the Sisleys. He kept returning to see them, along with, say, a dozen or so other impressionist pieces, and we began to speak of the situation resignedly—that there was nothing we could do. Eventually von Behr would take them."

Langlois raised his palms. "Well, Louisine sealed her fate, it turned out, in a sentence. She said that it didn't matter much anyhow, that Sisley had a facile talent. I was there at the time myself, in the commissary where we were all having coffee. Villanbrecque, who was head of the conservation department at the time, challenged her. 'If they're so easy,' he said, 'you bring us one.' A fortnight later she showed up with a Sisley Port-Marly flood scene.

"It was good. For a first effort it was masterful. Eventually she got the tone down pat and without, mind you, having to resort to glazing and studio work. Villanbrecque was astounded and not a little bit envious. Still, there was nothing he could do but show it to the Directeur, who insisted that Louisine begin copying the Sisleys before the real canvases were taken away. This time, however, she was offered the assistance of other trusted members of the staff." Langlois reached for his glasses and fitted them back on the bridge of

145

his nose. "After all, we were being attacked, raped, and pillaged, and it was perhaps our only means of fighting back. At least it was perceived so at the time."

Noreen crossed her legs the other way and considered the wisdom of a museum's conspiring to create "reproductions," as Langlois had termed them, under any circumstances, but she had read of other work that had been labeled *entartete Kunst*, or degenerate art, and had not survived the War. In 1943 a panel of German art "judges," led by a certain Dr. Borchers, who was second in command to the infamous von Behr, condemned some five hundred or six hundred paintings as "degenerate art," drew out long knives, hacked the canvases to shreds, and then had them burned in a pyre behind the Jeu de Paume. Included in the destruction were canvases by Miró, Picabia, Valadon, Klee, Ernst, Masson, Leger, Picasso, Kisling, La Fresnaye, Mané-Katz, and other artists of vision and talent.

And she considered the difficulty of producing a copy of another artist's work under the best of conditions—the mannerisms that would have to be learned, the singularities—but she imagined that with three rival German agencies vying for the spoils, doubts of authenticity had been less likely to arise, their greed causing them to look closest at signatures.

"It was remarkable, really," Langlois continued, "her completing seven 'Sisley' canvases in slightly over three months. And difficult. She had to obtain old canvases, cut and scrape them down. Then frames and stretchers. She had to mix and use driers to mute the palette and make the paints look old. She had to study brush-stroke patterns, mimic craquelure, and since she couldn't work here in the Louvre, she had to do all from memory, working at night in the apartment that she was sharing with Pierre Roche.

"Von Behr and certain of the other Germans would have

missed her here, you see, and it was that, the work that made her unavailable for"—Langlois paused—"a dinner engagement and such, which eventually led to her discovery, or so I believe. As I said, Louisine was a young woman with rather advanced ideas in regard to men, even though she was living with Roche.

"For instance, Wilhelm Krugger from the *Kunstschutz* felt himself snubbed and went round to her flat. He walked in without knocking, which was the manner of the conqueror then, and discovered what she was doing. At the time he said he thought it a great joke on von Behr, whom he despised, and he aided in the effort, passing on to Louisine some of the materials that had become unavailable here in France.

"But"—Langlois's hands rose and fell onto the back of the desk chair—"it was too good to last. It was wartime, food was scarce, and loyalties could be bought, sold, and by the S.S. extorted. More to the point—*I* believe—was Louisine's particular"—he spun away from the chair and again walked to the window—"attractiveness. Certain men found her irresistible, and too many people had become involved. Eventually somebody—it was never clear who—told von Behr what a fool she had made of him. By that time he had taken away all seven Sisleys and had them hanging in the townhouse that he had requisitioned.

"The affront to his person was compounded by the suspicion—which, I've found, lingers in certain German minds—of cultural inferiority. Like Paris and France, she could be captured but never possessed. It was Mars, if you will, falling for Venus, who played him false and before a gallery of spectators." Langlois's smile was wry.

"Von Behr?" he went on. "Outrage both moral and ethnic. The world as he knew it had been turned on its ear for a moment, and he would not have that. In personal command of a squad of Gestapo, he stormed their apartment—Louisine and Pierre's—and took them away. What happened to Pierre is well known. They tortured and brutalized him, battered him beyond recognition, and left him for dead. Fortunately, he had friends who searched him out. We found him barely alive and put him in hospital, and, I'm sorry to admit, I lost track of him until I learned only a few weeks ago that he has been living in Dublin these many years.

"Louisine? Well . . ." Langlois, who was now again looking out a window, seemed to sigh. "Her story is not as easy to tell. Von Behr kept her incommunicado at his residence, where no excess of 'degenerate' French civilization was too much for him and his cronies. Since his arrival he had been throwing lavish parties, at which the very best champagnes and cognacs were consumed by the case. Artwork dripped from the walls. Convoys of provisions rolled in and out of there, as to the Ritz.

"Like Göring, von Behr had a drug habit and he passed drugs around freely. Like Himmler, von Behr also enjoyed young men from time to time, and if their tastes sometimes ran to women, he provided for them"—Langlois raised his hands—"Louisine. I'll go no further, the point being that he was trying to debase and break her.

"At least until Krugger discovered her whereabouts and with the personal intervention of General von Choltitz, who, as you remember, had distinguished himself by *not* burning Paris, managed to free her. I'm afraid, though, that her experience had been too untoward and something in her had snapped—her joy, her will to go on. And then she was by that time both addicted to drugs, which Krugger at great personal expense weaned her from, and pregnant. She was living with him when she gave birth to the child."

"Henry Craig."

Langlois turned to face her. "So he told me he called himself when he sat where you are—let me see—six or seven weeks ago."

"And Wilhelm Krugger—what happened to him?"

Langlois looked away. He shook his head. "I don't know. A kind man, a gentleman. He continued to perform his function until the end of the Occupation, and"—he paused—"I heard no more of him. Nor of Louisine. The chaos, you see, as the Germans were pulling out and trying to take anything they could with them, required our, my presence. . . . Perhaps you can understand. The collection—not people, not friends—came first. Always the collection. For me, I suppose, even now."

"You have no family?" Noreen asked.

"Me?" With a certain delicacy of movement Langlois's fingertips touched his chest. "Please, Madame. Really." Again the glasses came off, this time to be cleaned on the lining of his jacket. "As you can imagine, Henry Craig's arrival here and his questions, his statements . . . Well, the information I have just told you took me some time to recollect, I assure you." He smiled. His teeth were short and widely spaced and appeared stubby.

"And you told Henry Craig what you've just told me?"

"It pained me, but I thought I'd save him the trouble of weeks of research. And then I, having been an insider, know rather more than the archives contain."

"How did he react?"

"He remained in command of himself, certainly, but I could see that he was disturbed, as well we can imagine. His mother had been a heroine of the Republic, though to some she might have seemed otherwise, living with von Behr and Krugger as she did, bearing the child. That she suffered, that her life was changed irrevocably—and diminished—is incontestable."

"William Craig—were you acquainted with him?"

"No. Should I have been?"

Noreen canted her head and noticed how Langlois's eyes followed the line of her neck, then rose to her eyes, her hair. "I thought perhaps you might. He was an arts liaison officer with the British Army at the close of the War. I thought that perhaps you, having been in charge of returns . . ."

Again Langlois's hands came up. "I wasn't aware that my life was such an open book." In art circles Langlois was, of course, quite well known. The smile, tugging at the corners of his mouth, seemed more one of approval—of what he was seeing, of her—than of mirth. Or of how the interview was progressing. They had dealt with so much, so quickly.

Taking up her purse, Noreen stood. "I'm curious to know why you assumed I came here about a Louisine Faure 'Sisley.' I told nobody of my purpose."

Langlois eased back in the desk chair, the better, it seemed, to view her body. "Madame McGarr, for over forty years I have had visitors, researchers, scholars, men and women of letters from the four corners of the world stopping in to discuss their projects with me, but until six weeks ago none from Ireland. You with your art background were the second and fairly soon after the visit of Henry Craig. He had asked me about a Port-Marly Sisley which was, I believe, hanging in some obscure corner of an antiques shop that his father controls. I merely put two and two together."

Langlois made a point of glancing at his watch. "Now, I hope I've answered your questions. I'm afraid I already have a luncheon appointment. Otherwise . . ."

Stepping to the door, Noreen thanked Langlois, adding, "Unfortunately, mine is a forensic investigation in which"—she dismissed the term hearsay—"information from secondary sources is not quite as valuable as hard evidence, and the inventory of your Port-Marly Sisley would be invaluable to my search." By that she meant the scientific inventory which would detail the Louvre analysis of the painting, listing brush-stroke patterns, a chemical analysis of pigments, varnishes, and grounds, the weave of the canvas, its size, and blemishes, cuts, nicks, or other disfigurations, and so on. She knew for fact that the Louvre had a long-standing policy of fully documenting all of its major works and most of its collection. It had begun well before the Second World War.

Langlois's chair had come down slightly, and his pause was hardly discernible. "But, of course. Certainly." His brow furrowed. "Forensic?"

"Yes. William Craig, the young man's father, was murdered."

The chair fell yet more. "When?"

"Two days ago. Thanks again for your time. I'll ask your secretary to direct me to the archives."

"*No.* I mean—allow me, Madame McGarr. Please." Langlois was now on his feet.

"But your schedule. I don't want to put you out."

"*You* put *me* out? Please." Now Langlois's smile was saccharine. He was doubtless a man used to visitors and interruptions, and she wondered how he managed to write his books. "It'll give the old women in the archives something to gossip about. Langlois seen with a gorgeous Celt." He took her arm.

12

It was well past noon by the time McGarr stepped into the long carpeted hallway that led to the Commissioner's office at Gárda Síochána headquarters in Phoenix Park. Because of Briscoe and the others, whom he and his staff had interrogated through the night and much of the morning, McGarr had had little sleep and no chance to change. His trousers were ripped, his shoes scuffed, and the skin that was not bruised or scorched on the left side of his face had developed a cratered scab that was yellowing at the edges. The burn. McKeon had told him it resembled the map of Ireland. "The twenty-six counties. Far be it from me to wish the scourge of Unification on a mug like that." But McGarr now believed that his appearance would here prove useful.

The scrubbed faces of properly attired bureaucrats turned to him as he passed the open doors: all the gray and drab-green files, the in- and out-baskets heaped with paper, the *clack* of typewriters, the phones ringing, the whispers into receivers. All of it was merely another—but more pernicious, because organized—form of gossip; and even though he had to employ it from time to time, McGarr's aversion to the static memory of state was personal, involuntary, and total. The bureaucratic stab in the back, which the ordinary citizen would scarcely feel until the blade had touched the quick. The impersonal offense, but permanent. Amend or destroy *The Record?* Hardly, for in that and that alone lay the bureaucrat's power.

Too much? Passing by other, barer, quieter rooms, the fingers on the keys of computer terminals sounding like hands passing through heaps of old bones, McGarr hardly thought so. It was the new language of social institutions that he was hearing, and its inaccessibility rather frightened him: secret records in cryptic codes to be interpreted with Yahwistic arbitrariness by the high priests of the printout. It was a bureaucrat's Greater Dream, the one of Omnipotence.

McGarr himself, however, had not come hat in hand to the temple. Nodding to the two men who were huddled at the end of a long table in the dining room that adjoined the Commissioner's office, he placed his own sheaf of papers before him and sat. He was late, and all dishes except teacups had been removed.

Thick lenses made Fergus Farrell's watery eyes fill the frames of his eyeglasses. They were a moiling stream of color and never seemed the same, one glance to the next, as though the vicissitudes of his consciousness were being constantly exposed to view, but the revelation remained unavailing and a challenge. Look into my soul, he seemed to be saying, and what do you see? A perpetual chaos which I have conquered, have you? In spite of the amount of alcohol Farrell put by daily, McGarr had never known a shrewder bureaucrat. Farrell's was a political appointment, yet he had weathered every change in government and was now himself an institution.

Tobin, who was sitting to his right, was his protégé.

"Morning, Peter," said Farrell.

It was half one.

"In bits again, I see. Made the papers, so." Without looking up from his notepad, Farrell shoved folded copies of the front pages of the day's newspapers across the table.

McGarr ignored them.

"Ray, here, is after piecing out your exploits. Unexpurgated. The facts, says he. I'd like you to tell me where they're not."

Tobin's eyes had not met McGarr's, and for a reason. A man of medium height with a round, fleshy build, he was trained in the law. In his mid-thirties, he was a rising star in the Gárda Síochána. Hoping that he would fail, officers more senior even than McGarr had insisted that he be given the Chief Superintendency of Special Branch, which dealt with Ireland's peculiar and most delicate problem. But Tobin had learned quickly and soon proved himself to have a sure political touch. He was now spoken of as an inevitability.

He had a red, pixyish beard that exaggerated rather than concealed the slight smile that McGarr had not once seen him abandon. It was a disarming smile, like that of a penitent acolyte, and remained no matter the situation, while his eyes, which were quick, black buttons, revealed every passing mood.

"We'll start with this Coyne person, alias Curtin. Ray here says that as early as two days ago, hours after the Craig murder, you knew of his connection to an unlawful organization, yet you did not inform him of it."

McGarr wondered who had told him that—certainly nobody on his own staff. Rose Marie? If so, McGarr wanted her and badly. And nowhere was it *written* that he had to inform Tobin of anything. Certainly one of the reasons he and the young man on the other side of the table had never locked horns was that neither had ever told the other anything beyond the reports or requests that had been sent out to all agencies.

"This Coyne fella—deceased now, I gather—"

The last word grated on McGarr, but he kept himself from glancing up. He had his own cards, and he would play them his way.

"—then 'borrowed' the Craig Mercedes and drove to the Silver Tassie—"

"*Straight* to the Silver Tassie?" McGarr asked.

Farrell scanned what appeared to be notes. "So it says here. Ray?"

The smile still complete, Tobin only allowed his eyes to flicker toward McGarr's. He would give nothing away, but it was enough. He could have gotten that only from the old woman.

"Why?" Farrell asked.

McGarr said nothing. Tobin knew he knew.

"The Silver Tassie, as you should have known," Farrell went on, "is a Code Six site, and as such under 'Article Three' of the 'Interdepartmental Memorandum' dated twelfth January"— Farrell's wet eyes flickered over to Tobin, doubtless the source of his documentation—"of this year, you were requested to submit a report of same.

"Twenty-seven hours elapsed from that time until the bombing incident at the Craig & Son premises. No report.

"After that incident nobody from your office bothered to inform Phoenix Park or Special Branch of the particulars involving this case. Ray here learned of it only when he saw it on the telly.

"Had you bothered to inform yourself of Code Six—"

McGarr now allowed his eyes to meet Farrell's.

"—requests . . ."

He was pleased to note that Farrell was at least being accurate; by no means had he been required to make notification of Curtin/Coyne's visit to the Silver Tassie, and, in fact, had the site been of current interest to Tobin he should have staked it out himself.

"Perhaps . . ." Farrell's wet eyes left McGarr's. It was too much to assume that Tobin or McGarr or any combination of Gárdai could keep somebody from planting a bomb. "Well, perhaps Ray could have been some help to you.

"As it was, you went out to the Silver Tassie on your own without even informing your own desk sergeant."

McGarr wondered where Tobin had gotten that, certainly not from McKeon.

"No support. No search order. You didn't even identify yourself. You"—Farrell paused to reach for the teacup; he sipped—"relieved a certain Mr. Burke of his front teeth, upper and lower. You fractured his jaw. His nose is shattered. You then drew a weapon, threatened the life and limb of one Padraic Briscoe. You threatened his father, firing another weapon at him three times and causing property damage and bodily injury, namely, a laceration of the scalp. The property damage has been placed at over a thousand pounds.

"Still not having identified yourself, still threatening the life and limb of both Briscoes and some eight other individuals gathered there, you coerced the elder Briscoe into making a statement, which you then used as the basis for the arrest of seven persons and the imposition of"—Farrell glanced once at McGarr—"a Closing Order upon said premises.

"Ray here tells me that it will be just about all he can do to get the Briscoes to withdraw counter-charges against you and the Gárda Síochána, providing restitution is made for damages and compensation for false arrest and bodily harm. But there are eight other men involved, seven of whom are known to Ray and Special Branch and who have in the past proved themselves helpful. Well, it's all here." Farrell closed the document he had been reading from and moved the thick stack toward McGarr, as though it were a heavy bet made at a poker table.

All? McGarr rather doubted it, and his anger was intense. He wondered if Farrell could possibly value the heap of paper between them more than, say, the life of the Guard who had been killed. Or Curtin/Coyne's.

"It seems," Farrell went on, "all sorts of people, even your wife, were and perhaps still are involved in the investigation at your end, but the proper channels and contacts, well . . ." Again his hand flicked out at the paper, then reached for the teacup.

A cheap shot. The cheapest. Noreen was an acknowledged art expert, one of the most highly regarded in the country, and had been called on by Farrell himself in the past.

"That's Ray's version, Peter. Am I being unfair, asking you in here on short notice and taking you away from . . ."

Your investigation, which in a matter of minutes will be passed on to Tobin, along with an apology to seven bloody bastards who blew the life from a colleague? Even the sorry Curtin/Coyne—if their concern for areas of organizational responsibility had brought them so low as to be weighing the relative value of human life—had been worth more than whatever small change of tips Briscoe and the Silver Tassie had yielded over the years, all factions of the Republican movement sharing a profound intolerance of touts.

"Would you care for a cup of tea?" Farrell asked, meaning, Will you still drink with me? A test within a test. There were two teapots on the table, one of which poured another familiar amber liquid.

Tobin—still smiling, eternally smiling—now glanced up at McGarr, who nodded to Farrell and began speaking in low, rhythmic tones, incantatory, like prayer, but one that he judged proper to this cathedral of bureaucratic virtue. Having attacked certain, supposedly helpful elements of the IRA—which, although now an unlawful organization, had freed the country from the British and was still for many something of a sacred cow—having ignored Farrell's significations from the altar, McGarr, the apostate, would have to prove his canonicity.

He said, "Where an officer of the Gárda Síochána not below the rank of Chief Superintendent, in giving evidence in proceedings relating to an offense under said Section Twenty-one, states that he believes that the accused was at a material time a member of an unlawful organization, the statement shall be evidence that he has been such a member."

McGarr opened his own sheaf of paper and began sliding copies of each formal charge that he had made against Briscoe and the others across the gleaming surface of the table, as he spoke out the laws. Unlike Farrell or Tobin, whose staff was much larger, he had had to enforce the dictates of the Oireachtas on a daily basis, but not merely because of that had he committed the laws to memory. McGarr's command of the details that affected his life was comprehensive and exact, a facility which, he well knew, any bureaucrat would envy, and, more, he hoped they could appreciate the irony. The laws he had charged Briscoe and the others with breaking had been written with Special Branch specifically in mind, the Gárda having many superintendents, but few chief superintendents, who might enforce them.

"The meaning of such an organization is defined in the original Offences Against the State Act of 1939, Number Thirteen, Part Three, 'an unlawful organization is any organization which, (d) engages in, promotes, encourages or advocates the commission of any criminal offence or the obstruction of or interference with the administration of justice or the enforcement of law.

"Or, '(e) engages in, promotes, encourages, or advocates the attainment—' "

"Yes, yes," said Farrell, "we know all that."

"Do you?" McGarr asked, sliding that specific charge across the table toward them. "Do you indeed?"

Yet he kept reciting verbatim the laws that the men at the Silver Tassie had broken, all the boring legal detail which was their commission to enforce but which in this instance both of the other men wished to ignore. McGarr wanted to know why. What had Craig and the Coynes, what did Briscoe and the Silver Tassie mean to the state that its laws could be suspended for them?

"Under the Offences Against the State (Amendment) Act of nineteen seventy-two . . .

"Under Section Twenty-Nine of the Criminal Law Act of nineteen seventy-six . . .

"Under Sections Nine and Eleven of the Dangerous Substances Act . . ."

Until each time he was stopped by Farrell, who, looking down into his teacup, finally said, "I must tell you, Peter, that I find this unavailing and not a little bit tedious. We know. We've read the list of charges that you're laying against these men. And"—he paused to sip from the cup—"we know the law.

"Haven't you any reply to the counter-charges? We're not dealing simply with citizens here, these men are . . ."

McGarr glanced up from his open sheaf of documents and waited for Farrell's definition of the men whom he had arrested at the Silver Tassie.

"I believe we've been through that," Farrell said.

Not completely, McGarr said to himself. Not by half, and

pushing aside the copies of the remaining charges, he began his own definition of Briscoe *et al.*, but now in silence.

First he slid across to them six 8-inch by 10-inch forensic photos of what little had been found of Curtin/Coyne in the smoldering ruin of the garden hut—half of his head beside half of the corner sink; a boot with a leg in it to the knee; his pelvic area. Then the bomb-site itself, the garden a smoking, cindery cavity with the blown-out windows in the shop and the flat beyond.

McGarr then added the pathologist's preliminary report on both the Guard's and Curtin/Coyne's deaths, opening the letter to a paragraph that he had underlined. It said that Coyne had died before the blast, much of his head having been carried away by an explosive bullet. It was what his mother, Rose Marie, had seen before she turned and fled.

A Technical Bureau report came next, noting that tests performed on the clothes, shoes, facial area, hair, and hands of the men whom McGarr had arrested at the Silver Tassie revealed that Enda Briscoe, publican, and two others bore traces of the very same type of gelignite that had been found in the crater of the bomb-site. Within the past twenty-four hours, Briscoe had fired a ballistic weapon.

Following that, McGarr slid the dossiers of Briscoe and the others, which documented their former service in the Official IRA.

Last, he showed Farrell and Tobin the forensic photos taken of the corpse of the Guard, their colleague, his head seemingly untouched except for the bloodless chunk that was missing from his forehead, his hands clutching to his body the jagged piece of metal that had nearly cut him in half.

Farrell frowned. He passed Tobin the final photograph and removed his eyeglasses, placing them on the table. Without them he looked like another man. Reaching for the teapot, he poured McGarr nearly a full cup, adding a splash to his own. The livid color of his face had darkened, and he turned to look out the window, as though considering something important.

Facts, incontrovertible. What did they mean? More to the point, McGarr wondered what Tobin could make of them. Tobin's smile remained, though his eyes were darting around the documents, which were now spread on the table before him.

To be swept under the carpet?

Not now. McGarr and his staff had done their work too well. The evidence was circumstantial but overwhelming—Curtin/Coyne's visit to the Silver Tassie coming directly after Craig's murder; the gelignite test; the ballistics test—and the justices in Special Criminal Court who would deal with such charges would be quick to affirm the correlation. They had little sympathy for bombers.

"Ray?" Farrell asked.

Tobin's hand had reached out for the sets of formal charges that McGarr had shown them first. Tobin fanned them on the table, noting that there were four copies of each. "You haven't filed these charges yet?"

McGarr said nothing, only continued to stare at Tobin.

"You're not going to file these charges. You never intended it." His smile grew fuller as he turned to Farrell, as much as to say, I told you so, it's a ploy.

Farrell, who knew McGarr better, looked dubious and reached for the final photograph, the one that pictured the young Guard. He fitted on his eyeglasses.

And then, McGarr had credibility. Perhaps with suspects he might bluff, but within the organization of the Gárda Síochána never. "Peter?" Farrell asked.

"Bank holiday," said McGarr. The courts were not in session.

Tobin's smile faded only slightly, but his eyes darted around the mass of paper that was spread before them. "Well, what . . ." His tone was too strident. He looked away, out through the long drapes onto a green field in which horse-mounted Gárdai were parading. He then renewed his smile. "I'm after wondering what Peter wants?"

Everything, of course. Rose Marie Coyne, an explanation of Briscoe and the Silver Tassie's importance to Special Branch. More, McGarr wanted to know what relationship the Silver Tassie had borne to the shop on the quays and why the Coynes had been placed in Craig's employ. In return he would be willing to withdraw certain of the charges from certain of the men, but not until Tobin covered the bet that McGarr had laid down.

And pointless was Tobin's appeal to Farrell, who had not remained Commissioner by siding with bombers of any stamp.

Reaching across the table with his one good arm, McGarr reassembled the documents of his file, placing them in the manila folder. He then lifted the teacup and, in three swallows that scorched, drank off its contents.

He stood. "Fergus." He turned to Tobin. "Ray." He began leaving the room.

"What the Christ is he after wanting?" he heard Tobin demand.

Said Farrell, "You'll have to ask him yourself. And I'm to be left out of this now. He's very particular when it comes to anything that has to do with one of"—a pause—"us. As am I."

"Commissioner, please—isn't it enough that we've got two people dead by explosive bullets? We haven't seen that class of thing since the postwar era. And then the gelignite, the gun. Briscoe. The Army." Again Tobin had to collect himself. "This thing's got Special Branch written all over it, and I'll see whoever's responsible for the murders in the dock myself.

And that's a promise. But we can't have that ballocks thrashing all over the place. Consider the infrastructure. It's taken years to build, and in one night alone he's as much as—"

"That's enough now. I'm out of it. It's you and him. Perhaps you can work something out."

13

"**A** Camondo acquisition, I believe," Langlois had said, while leading Noreen down narrow aisles stacked to the ceiling with files. "Number two-oh-one, if I'm not mistaken." His step was rangy and quick for a small, older man, and his sponge-rubber soles squeaked on the metal floor of the stacks.

"Your memory is remarkable."

"Yes." He turned to her. "But it's not everything. Facts are one thing, correlations quite another." He smiled, again baring his small, widely spaced teeth.

"Ah—here it is." Craning back his head, Langlois had adjusted the fit of his glasses and squinted up at the labels with their ornate, French lettering, faded and dim. He had passed his hand over the oak tag and stepped back, dust spangling the harsh, pinkish light from bare bulbs that were activated by timers.

"As you can see, poor Sisley has not been of much interest of late." Again careful of the dust, Langlois had slid the file from the shelf, and then, having to squeeze past Noreen—his eyes fixing hers, his stomach rubbing up against her—had taken her back into the reading room of the archival collection by a route that seemed to her circuitous. Even Langlois himself had gotten lost, having to use a key on doors, one of which set off an alarm someplace deep within the building. "*Merde*—I always do that. I get so turned around in here. I'm afraid I just don't possess the researcher's instinct."

And in the reading room itself, when he had placed the file on a table and begun to leave, again mentioning a luncheon engagement, they had been approached by an older woman, who demanded to know if the material had been signed for.

Langlois had tried to make apologies, saying that it was a matter of forensic concern. All that was required was a certain number of photocopies and then Noreen would be off, but the old woman, with what Noreen then interpreted as Gallic excessiveness, had said, "I'm shocked and, may I say, not a little disgusted with you, Monsieur Langlois." Her head was shaking, and her eyes were glassy and hard. "This isn't the first time I've had to speak to you about this. It doesn't matter who you are, you must sign for the records you removed from the stacks. That is the rule.

"And this woman must sign the register." Her arms could barely place the thick log book in front of Noreen. "Name, date, and legal address. If foreign, passport number and country of issue."

After the old woman had left, Langlois had said, "The officious old wretch. You'd think somebody was trying to steal from her." And he then asked if Noreen could manage by herself.

She could, of course, and from the first. Not only would she have signed the register, but she would have entered through the usual door and introduced herself to the archivist, whose acquaintance with and proprietary regard for the collection it was always best, she had found, to acknowledge.

Now she was glad that Langlois had left, but after photocopying the inventory of the Sisley flood-scenes, which she had noted was complete and exhaustive, she glanced up at the clock and discovered that she had four hours until the next scheduled flight to Dublin.

Langlois: it struck her how different he seemed from his writing, which was clear, reasoned, insightful, and always poised. Instead he seemed nervous and quirky, what was most probably an ill humor only thinly disguised. But that was the way of the printed page—a skilled craftsman could there conceal so much of the personality or adopt one entirely different from his own.

What he had told her about the events during the Occupation had been helpful in explaining the painting itself and why the inventory numbers had been burned into the stretcher. But she still knew no more about why William Craig's murderer or somebody else had chosen to steal it. Also, it was strictly hearsay, and the chance of inaccuracies and omissions was probable after forty years, even from a mind as acute as Langlois's.

At the catalog she found that the archives contained biographical entries for artists, collectors, and persons important to the world of French art. Not only were Louisine Faure, Pierre Roche, and Wilhelm Krugger listed, but those entries were shelved in stacks directly off the reading room, not the circuitous passage with several locked doors that Langlois had taken her on.

Louisine Faure: the file was thin but contained photographs taken of her when she first joined the Louvre staff, as Langlois had said, in 1938, and Noreen recognized her but vaguely as the woman who had been standing in the blown-out window after the bomb blast at the shop on the quays. A handsome, striking woman here in the picture, with dark eyes of the sort that Noreen thought of as quiet—deep and containing reserves of calm which nothing could disrupt. And how deceiving that impression, Noreen speculated, turning to the record of her employment. Again, as Langlois had said, she had left the Louvre in 1943, 11 January to be exact, "after service which none has rendered more valorous than she." It was the only allusion to her activities during the War and the entry was annotated H.V.L. Hector Valéry Langlois? It was likely, but she could not be sure.

Also contained in the file were photographs of what Noreen guessed were some of Louisine Faure's original work, dated just shortly before the Occupation: vibrant and inviting cityscapes, all of Paris. At first Noreen was reminded of Derain, but Faure's brush had been quicker, more mannered and modern, more like the Parisian street artists whose work, still wet from the palette, could be bought for a few hundred francs along the Seine in the summer. But far better.

Noreen passed over a fall scene, the sort of late afternoon in autumn when one realized how short the days were growing and how night had begun to creep into the high tones of the early evening sky. It was still blue, but the buildings and streets below were deep in shadows that seemed cold. The streetlamps were on, the restaurants and shops well lighted, but steps had quickened as people hurried home to a warm kitchen or a deep chair and a good book. Winter had announced its intentions and people were reacquainting themselves with their homes.

There were scenes of snow dumps melting on the banks of the Seine; sidewalk cafés thronged on the first balmy day of spring; a leafstorm in the Bois and nobody, not the people on the benches or the passersby, seeming to notice.

A major talent, one that could have been important to its period? Certainly not. Perhaps not even one that would have garnered a modicum of critical praise. Everything was too quick and energized, and the scenes were lamentably hackneyed now, but how many painters had Noreen viewed who had attempted trifles of the sort without carrying them off? There was a freshness and ease in her treatment, and it was not as if she had been attempting to break new ground. Noreen imagined that Faure had simply been having fun, and from her experiences in her own picture gallery she knew that there was a good market for such things.

And then, what more might the woman have done, if . . .

Roche, Pierre Jacques Louis: the file was thicker because it contained the record of his recovery, an expense that the Louvre had assumed. Remembering Langlois's saying that Krugger had had to wean Louisine Faure from a drug habit at great personal expense, Noreen wondered why the same consideration had not been extended to Faure, though she believed she knew without having to be told. A woman, especially a beautiful woman, did not unwillingly take drugs or cohabit with the enemy or become pregnant, no matter the situation. And how to renounce such suppositions, given what had been her immediate concerns?

But her pathos for Faure and her plight paled somewhat before the information in the text which her eyes had passed over and to which she now returned. In addition to the other depravities wreaked upon him during his interrogation and torture by the Gestapo, Roche had had his testicles crushed. By the time he could be treated, a massive infection had set in and a radical amputative procedure had had to be performed on the entire area. She found it difficult both to read further and understand without resorting to a medical dictionary, but she understood that some type of catheter had been fitted to the man, and the supervising physician recommended a regimen of hormone injections to prevent the gradual "effeminization" of his body.

Noreen looked away toward the archivist's glass-enclosed

cubicle and the window above it. It was getting dark, and the old woman and her assistant, who had already donned a raincoat, were staring out at her. At the door the guard had folded his arms and was tapping his foot. He had begun a low whistle.

,She checked her watch—3:45—and guessed that she still had a few minutes until the archives closed, most probably at 4:00.

She slid the medical report back into the folder, but in the *K*s she could find no entry for Krugger, though she was certain the name had appeared in the catalog.

Quickly she returned to the large bound volumes. "Krugger, Wilhelm Friederich Norbert, b. 1905, Strasbourg. d. 1944. Oberst. Kunstschutz."

Was the file being used? But where? As in most Continental libraries, no material would be allowed to leave the archives. And if it did, its whereabouts would be so noted in the catalog.

Steeling herself, Noreen picked up the heavy volume and approached the Gorgon glares of the two women in the office.

"Yes?" the archivist asked before she had reached the cubicle door.

But Noreen continued in. "Krugger, Wilhelm Friederich Norbert—why is there no file on that subject when there is an entry here?" She shook the catalog once.

Said the assistant, "Perhaps she should ask her countryman."

"Quiet, Françoise," the old woman replied. "We won't become involved."

"Involved in what?" Noreen asked. "And what do you mean by my countryman?"

The assistant only turned away.

Said the archivist, "Try *Kunstschutz*. Most all of our information concerning Krugger was duplicated in that file. We close at four." Her eyes were the color of milky-turquoise and as hard.

But on Krugger the *Kunstschutz* file was not complete, and it appeared that several pages had been removed from the text, those that dealt with that agency's operations at the end of the War and might have explained the man's death, in which she was now most interested.

Said the assistant, her back still turned, "Try Langlois, Hector Valéry. He's too vain to have removed that little bit from his own file."

Reading against the clock and distracted by the jangle of the door guard's keys, Noreen discovered newspaper articles, personal reports, even the text of a French Legion of Honor commendation given him for the recovery of Louvre artworks at the close of the German occupation of Paris.

It seemed that the German yen for plunder only increased as the conflict wore on and defeat became apparent, all knowing that something tangible would help them through whatever dislocation would follow surrender. Resistance observers thus kept a close watch on all roads and train stations, and a few days before the liberation of Paris it was noticed that a certain train was being loaded at night under tight security and given a priority clearance. Lightless, it left in the early hours of the morning.

Before it departed, however, certain Nazi bigwigs and other German officials had boarded with all they could carry. Included among them was the *Kunstschutz* officer, William Krugger, accompanied by a dark young woman and a child. She was tentatively identified as Louisine Faure.

Just outside Strasbourg, the train was stopped and fighting broke out, after which it was found to contain, among other French treasures, thirty-eight impressionist paintings from the Louvre that had fallen under the protection of the *Kunst-*

schutz. Krugger was found among the dead, his throat having been slashed. His papers and clothes were discovered on the corpse, but positive identification was made by one Hector V. Langlois, then an assistant curator at the Louvre. The body was buried in a mass grave. The woman and child had vanished, and it was assumed they had escaped.

Included were clippings from newspapers showing the return of the paintings to the Louvre. Accepting them for the museum was again a young Hector Langlois. He was pictured in the middle of a group of people shaking the hand of the man who led the Resistance party that had stopped the train. It had been Langlois who had identified Krugger and Faure at the train station and had alerted the Resistance about part of the contents of the train.

Noreen glanced at her watch. Five minutes.

She carried the file out of the stacks and, again under the scrutiny of the archive employees, copied the several sheets, then strode toward the cubicle and the two women. "Pardon me, please—I know you're anxious to leave, but this is a matter of utmost importance. You mentioned that my countryman might have removed the Krugger entry from your archives. Was he Henry Craig?"

"No. We won't get involved," said the archivist.

"Yes," said the assistant, who, Noreen judged, was only slightly younger than the archivist. "As far as we know. Professor Langlois—"

"That's enough. I won't have you saying that, at least not in my hearing." The old woman rose from her desk and moved toward the door. "And it's time to leave, Madame."

"Langlois," the other woman continued, "brought him here, as he has you." To the archivist, she added, "I won't have him steal from us, Hélène. Not without a word.

"And later—a day or two—we found a gap on the shelves.

Three weeks ago we noticed another reader at the file. A tall man with a scarred, red face, though he took nothing away. He presented documents that said his name was Briscoe, again from Dublin. Now you tell us the *Kunstschutz* files are no longer complete."

Said the archivist from the door, "I'm leaving, Françoise, and I advise you to leave with me. If not, whatever comes down will be on your head, and you're a fool."

"What does that mean?" Noreen asked, but the assistant rose from her chair and, as though weary and contemptuous of the archivist's timidity, moved past her, out into the reading room and toward the stacks.

"Do you have a list of the paintings?"

Noreen held out the clipping that named the recovered works.

"We'll take the Sisley. It's closest," she said, reaching out for a light switch as they entered another area of the stacks. "Whoever certified one, certified all. Things were very hectic then." She was a small woman with a narrow, bony face, wrinkled skin, and sloped shoulders. Her rubber boots barely left the floor as she shuffled deeper into the stacks.

Asked Noreen, "The archivist—she seems afraid of Monsieur Langlois. Why?"

The woman, who was wearing a babushka that only emphasized the thrust of her nose and her lack of a chin, inclined her head. "Natural caution. She was born with it. That's why she's archivist, and I? I am a fool, she said it herself."

"But what can Langlois—?"

"He's a man, is he not? He's got position, and he's getting old, feeling threatened. With you—well, he was probably courtly. Am I right? But with us he is usually something else.

"Here we are."

The area, which contained provenances and certifications,

was under lock and key. The 27 August 1944 certification of A. Sisley's *L'Inondation à Port-Marly* was signed H.V.L.

"Would this painting have been recertified since then?"

"What would be the need? And, if so, that certification would be here."

Even before they had returned to the reading room, they could hear Langlois's voice. "*When* did she leave?"

"I don't know."

"Was she using the file from which this was taken?" From the darkness of the stacks they could see him standing by the copy machine, the flap of which was open.

"I don't know. I have my work, I was busy," said the archivist.

Langlois raised a slip of yellowed newspaper which Noreen in her haste had evidently left in the machine, then turned suddenly and moved to the register by the guard at the door. "She didn't sign out. *Why?*" he demanded, his voice echoing through the vaulted room.

Her old eyes only moved toward him, as she observed, "Nor did you." She looked away.

"*Did* she leave?" he asked the guard.

He only blinked.

"I've never seen him like this," the assistant said in a whisper. "What's it all about?"

"Three murders," said Noreen, though she now knew it was something more as well.

"Where's Françoise?" Langlois demanded.

"Come—we'll leave through the gallery," the diminutive assistant said.

There Noreen discovered that the Sisley flood scene had been removed. In its place was Morisot's *The Cradle*.

But Langlois was standing just inside the entrance, out of the rain, waiting for them.

14

The tall, maroon crane in a construction site two blocks from Belgrave Square was mercifully quiet, the sun having driven the workers off and established a silent hegemony over the neighborhood, saturating its old brick and new-green lawns and gardens. A shopping arcade it would be, the urbanization of what had once been Dublin's Pale seemingly inexorable with the availability of cheap road transportation and cars.

McGarr thought of all the claptrap they had been fed in school, how Dublin had in times past been one of the great cities of Europe, meaning one of the largest. An elaboration, of course, but the assumption of quantitative grandiosity remained fixed in the minds of politicians, developers, bureaucrats, and other boomers of that stripe, and McGarr guessed that only an all-out depression would deflate their aspirations. Then perhaps Dublin would return to the reasoned growth of the past, though he wished poverty on nobody.

Nor would the fair weather last, he imagined, shielding his eyes with the forearm that was not in a sling, as he reclined in a lounger on the patio in the center of his garden, the P.M. and a cold bottle of lager by his side. Clouds, like smoke from a distant war, had established a line of ruffled billows to the west. They would be afforded the rest of the day but no more before Ireland's guaranteed 320 days of dirty weather began again.

McGarr glanced at the dog and picked up Noreen's pair of sun blinds, closing his eyes. The slap of plates on the sideboard in the kitchen came to him now along with a voice—high, wavering—raised in song: Maisie Edgerton-Jones, who must have been watching the house, waiting for his return.

"Ah, there you are, Inspector. The lad has been waiting up for you all night. Pacing he was." She meant the dog, which had nudged open the back door and come to McGarr's side. "And Noreen is after handing me this for you. Last night as well." She had paused, while McGarr had opened the letter and read its contents, before adding, "Left, she did. With a case and all."

McGarr had glanced at her long, thin face with its narrow bridged nose and her neatly coiffured gray hair. Her light-brown eyes were still acute for all her years. He took in the old cardigan rolled up past the elbows, the tennis dress with a tea stain or two on the front, and runners on her feet. During Horse Show week it would be jodhpurs, boots, and an old houndstooth riding jacket from Callaghans with even a crop in her hand.

"She asked me to look after you while she was gone, and I see you're in need of it." She meant the sling that contained McGarr's left arm. The patch on his cheek.

"Nothing wrong, I hope?" Gossip, but not in that alone was she more Irish than McGarr himself. "You'd better put that away or tuck it farther under your belt." She pointed to the butt of the Walther. "People might misunderstand, the neighborhood—like the world—being a small place, and you and the lad having made the papers, so."

There had been pride in that, and while McGarr had gone

into the den to lock the weapon in the gun drawer, she had again mentioned her girlhood, when her father and brothers, though British genealogically and Protestant, had fought for the Cause, their having put up in the house next door no lesser figures than Roger Casement and the Countess Markievicz. One brother had been killed by the Black-and-Tans, another in a British barracks in Strabane.

Hanging the key on the rack behind the pantry door, McGarr had returned to the kitchen to find her at the stove. "You're knackered sure, the both of you. There's a time for everything, and yours now for rest. Tea, is it? Or coffee?"

"Tea, please," McGarr had said, "but I've got the staff coming. I thought I'd—"

"Tea and sandwiches," she had said. "For how many? There's the big fella, O'Shaughnessy, and the little one, Ward. Then McKeon with the sharp eyes and tongue. And the smile—"

"Delaney, Greaves, and Sinclaire," McGarr had prompted, cocking his head, regarding her thin but sprightly figure and realizing for the first time how much she lived through Noreen—the gallery openings, Noreen's stories of her buying trips to Rome and Vienna—and him. Although their names sometimes appeared in the newspapers, she had met McGarr's staff only a few times and in passing.

"Six, is it? Or seven including yourself and . . ." Stooping, with one hand on the open refrigerator door, she had reached out with the other hand to pat the dog's head wildly, ecstatically, her tongue clenched between her teeth, her old eyes closing. "Welly, who'd like a little bite himself, sure he would. And why not? Life being short and sometimes brutal.

"Then eight it is. And tea, though they're drinking men. But"—she had straightened up—"it's not proper for them to be drinking with the Chief and during hours.

"Here's a bottle for yourself, now. Go on out to your garden and leave the lot to me."

Chief. It was the first time she had ever referred to his proper title, and if making them tea gave her pleasure . . .

McGarr now fitted the plastic sun blinds over his eyes. They looked like the half shells of a white egg. Tugging the cap down on his brow, he eased his sore back into the lounger, and with the sun warming, it seemed, his very soul, he fell into a deep and dreamless sleep.

For how long he could not tell, but gradually through the layers of his sleep he became aware of the presence of others at the table nearby. Opening his eyes, he saw through the sun blinds only a flame-red burst, like the blast of the evening before, and he closed them once more, realizing that he had not heard the P.M. bark.

The staff. They had brought their own drink with them, and he now heard bottles being opened, all praising his garden in low tones. "He'll not miss one," he heard McKeon say, and then from the kitchen Maisie shouted, "Hold on, Sergeant. The grub is coming now, and you'll not be needing that."

They ate and drank, while McGarr continued dozing, moving in and out of sleep seemingly with the sun and its warmth, which from time to time was diminished by thickening clouds.

At length O'Shaughnessy said, "I was hoping Peter'd be coming round, but we'd better thrash this out while we can. It seems he stopped in to see Farrell and Tobin in Phoenix Park this after'. And now Tobin, through 'sources'—"

Somebody swore.

"—has gotten back to us. A neat little package. They've put the whole thing together for us, they have. No more for us to do but, they say, turn what we've got over to the proper channels and get on with our sorry pursuits.

"Unofficially, mind. Subject to"—McGarr heard a notebook

open and the sounds of glasses or bottles being placed back on the table—"change, I'm sure.

"They say that the Coynes came on the place about fourteen years ago when the son, Henry Craig, was in university here with young Briscoe. The son had joined the Sinn Fein and him and young Briscoe worked constituencies for candidates, passing out fliers, shaking hands, door-to-door—that truck. Little else was asked of them, Briscoe, the father, not wanting his son to become a gunman. That is, until it was found that the Liberation Army in breaking away took not only most of the loonies and louts but much of the fund-raising and money-laundering apparatus as well. Men like Briscoe still had the name and the tradition, but needed cover.

"I'm told," O'Shaughnessy went on, "they then read Henry Craig right. He'd been spoiled by the father, allowed to get and do anything. In his enthusiasm for the Cause he'd even made a kind of bomb himself that blew up and left him with a bit of paralysis in the face. Anyhow, they convinced him to impose on the father to use the antiques operation as a front for cash. The father went along with it, thinking that at least this way the son would have to keep a low profile and not jeopardize himself or the setup.

"The technique was to get sympathizers here and abroad to purchase antiques and such from Craig and pay double or triple cost, the excess being raked off by the Army. From time to time they also used the place to store weapons, records, et-cetera, and the kip out back for temporary cover in Dublin city center. Coyne and his failing—drinking buddies and so forth. It all dovetailed, a great crack, until Craig's death.

"They have it that the son killed the father."

"Why?" asked McKeon.

"The son's affairs were in a shambles."

McGarr again heard the ruffle of a page turning.

"Eighteen months ago he completed a house out on Spinnan's Hill in Baltinglass. It carries a price tag of over three hundred thousand pounds and remains unsold. Underwritten, incidentally, by Mammy, but that's not the half of it. They also have information—dead cert, I've checked—from one of our 'godfather's' that young Craig gambles and heavily and he's owing more than twenty thousand just to that fella alone and who knows to who else?

"Then there's the matter of the painting, which wasn't insured, but in looking into that we found that Lloyds, which covered all else in the shop, also covered the father's life. Sum? Given paid-in values and interest, one hundred and eighty-three thousand pounds. The beneficiary?" O'Shaughnessy paused. "Himself, Henry Craig. The son.

"With the painting worth, say, one hundred and fifty thousand minimum by Mrs. McGarr's report, and his being able to flog it for, say, half that, Henry Craig would just about break even. And then there's the matter of him and the father recently being at odds about the shop and his—" Here O'Shaughnessy began searching for a word.

"Parentage," Ward supplied.

O'Shaughnessy grunted. "Then we've got the professional way the painting was removed from the frame and the bottle. Henry Craig is an architect. He studied painting. The bottle—we've been over that before. The trip to Paris about his—"

"Parentage," several of the others supplied.

"Everything seems to have begun with that. And then the way the father was shot. I mean, where he was shot—low and in front of the mother."

O'Shaughnessy flipped another page. "It goes on and on, most of it touted information that meshes pretty well with what we dug up ourselves, like the explosive bullets. The one that killed the father, the other that blew off the back of Coyne's head before the bomb blast." There was a pause, in which McGarr could almost feel their eyes turning to him. "In the kip out back of the shop. The word on that is Craig collected guns, exotic stuff. He'd have that, and we should look into the collection.

"And like the report of the BMW having been at the shop soon after the murder. Like the argument between father and son. That from the old woman."

"But why would the son have wanted to get rid of the gardener?" Greaves asked.

"I asked that, of course. They say he's just trying to lay it on them. Coyne, they say, being a toper was trusted with nothing. He knew no more about the Tassie than Special Branch knew themselves, and there was no reason for them to put him down." O'Shaughnessy sighed, and McGarr heard the flap of his notebook close.

A silence ensued, in which he knew all were asking themselves if it was enough—for Special Branch to charge the son, to quash the case, to preserve whatever hard-come-by link Tobin had forged to Briscoe and the IRA. It was based on the dictum that the devil known is better than the devil not, and certainly a tout's tout—somebody who would be willing to take a partial fall for a price—would be found among the men McGarr had arrested at the pub. Briscoe himself, McGarr was willing to bet.

And why? What else was at stake? Could the concern be political alone and in particular what?

Delaney, whose few words always fell emphatically upon their proceedings, said, "Yes. But it's both enough and too much."

They waited, doubtless while the small man with the mild, benignant face and large, clear eyes searched the garden or the house or the sky. He was an uncharacteristic policeman with a humorous, philosophical manner. McGarr had not heard him speak in a fortnight.

"Right from the first, nobody has wanted this to happen, and they've been trying to preserve the status quo. It's like a house of cards, one tumbled and they're afraid the whole thing'll fall in. And so we've got details—the bottle on the kip doorstep, the Orly Airport sticker, which the son, whose trip to Paris was an event, would have removed. The BMW. The gun collection and so forth.

"And Craig's murder? It's as much an unknown to most of the figures in this case as it remains to us. It's whatever Rose Marie Coyne and perhaps Roche and the missus were doing those hours between the death and the report of it. They scrambled, sure. They tried to move mountains to preserve whatever it is that's vital to them.

"The fund raising, the money-laundering fiddle? Well . . . yes, I'm inclined to believe that. But there's more to it than that, and more than Tobin—here playing the chancer—knows himself. *If*"—there was a pause—"he wants to know at all. At all."

Said Hughie Ward, "And then Rose Marie Coyne went to work for Craig in 1947, and not fourteen years ago. I've checked the books. Curiously, Craig kept precise records. He was compulsive about it—names and addresses of clients, types of purchases, differences between assessed values and prices realized at auctions and from out of the shop—and about three dozen names of known IRA sympathizers or organizations recur, year in and year out."

"From '45?" somebody asked.

"From day one of the shop. In some years over fifty thousand quid was passed them in this way. Then there are the William Craigs who served in the British Army during the

War, some seventy-six of them. Not one was mustered out with the scarring, the root canals, the porcelain-covered gold caps that were found in the dead man's mouth."

"Anything else?" O'Shaughnessy asked.

The silence that followed was near total, and McGarr listened to the wind soughing through the bowers of his mimosa tree. In the house Maisie Edgerton-Jones was speaking to the P.M., endearments undoubtedly dispensed with the touch of a hand or a tidbit.

Options? Had they any? They could lift the son and check his story against what had just been offered them. Over time and carefully, repetitively. Then there was the mother, who had given them little enough as it was, and who, McGarr did not doubt, would offer no more. And . . .

"I'm tired," said McKeon somewhat drunkenly, "sick unto the very death of gobshites—"

"Ah, Bernie, that kind of talk—"

"—and louts, and you—all of yous—mincing around with Tobin and his pack of Phoenix Park arse kissers."

"—it won't help and you know it."

"And him." He meant McGarr himself. "With his parry and thrust and them blinders on—look at them, they're fittin'—like he's hidin' out behind a pygmy's brassy-ear."

"A what?" one man asked.

"Two, tiny tits, like your wife supports—when we all know who's been propping up the whole bloody business from the first."

"How much of that has he drunk?"

"Not half enough." McGarr heard a bottle ring on the lip of a glass.

Said Greaves, "Well you can scrounge the other half out of your own pocket. We bought that for Peter, and it won't be long before he'll be needing a drop."

Well said, thought McGarr.

"Anyhow, it's Roche we want."

Somebody started laughing.

"You think it's not?" McKeon asked. "Then you're an igno-ramus, a fool, and a cretin, and I'm vastly overrating you. What's worse, you're an innocent man. Let me ask you this? Who is Roche? You spoke to him, but then you wouldn't have been able to tell. He's canny, he's shrewd, and he's got what the good Lord had sense enough not to waste on you—brains. He controls things, and it's a mini-feckin'-empire, which he built himself. Do you think he wouldn't have known that the Army had a piece of the shop? If you do, then you're naïve in addition to your other faults, and your mother should never have let you out of the house.

"And what do you know about the Army itself? Not much, even after all these years, but you've got to know at least this—that if the Army had enough on Craig and him to have a piece of the shop, they have enough to have a piece of the rest, and that's at least a part of whatever else they're willing to sacrifice a few lives to protect.

"All this malarkey—"

"Will ya leave the bottle alone?"

"—about the son convincing the father to run guns and channel funds is bloody shite. *Shite,* I tell you . . ."

There was a small pause, in which somebody cursed, and again the bottle thumped on the table.

"With Dick"—McKeon went on, his voice suddenly gone high from the drink—"I hang."

Laughter began again.

Said Delaney, to whom he had referred, "Pity—I was hop-ing they'd chop him up first, starting with his tongue, his sec-ond longest appendage."

"Craig was murdered, and then the others, for who every-

183

thing had been so sweet, had to scramble. Who could they pin it on—the mother? No, she knows too much. She has to, though we haven't found out what. One of themselves? Not unless absolutely necessary, as it became with Curtin/Coyne. Roche? Definitely, most assuredly, not.

"Go on and laugh, ya low-minded muckers, but think—if you're capable of an elevated thought—of the sacrifices that are being made. Rose Marie Coyne's, for instance. And now maybe Briscoe himself. And for what? For stakes that the son can supply? Or the mother sitting in her studio come day go day, puffin' on fags and paintin' pretty pictures? Who's left?

"Roche. Sacrifice him? Not on your life, since he's the Molly who's made everything so cushy. The son then? A natural, and when we didn't fall for it, and it looked like we had a line on them, they brought in the bomb, which would put it in Tobin's pitch, where they hoped it'd die.

"Why—*why* was Craig murdered? When we know that, we'll know all."

The men at the picnic table had quieted. Nothing was said while—McGarr imagined—McKeon reached for the bottle yet again.

"The most I can say is that it's for something personal and . . . unusual, or at least different from the possibilities that we've dug up so far.

"Let's remember that Roche himself went to France only a week or so after Henry Craig returned from Paris, and they had their confab there at the airport."

"But what can we make of that?" somebody asked. "He had subsidiaries there, business. He comes and goes. A dual national."

"I don't know, but . . ." Now on uncertain ground, McKeon paused. "Roche has got it for that woman, and she's—let me tell ya—she's just the bitch who—"

"Ah, give us a bloody break, Bernie, and if you kill that thing, you've got to replace it."

The garden was suddenly cold, and McGarr removed the sun blinds from his eyes.

Above him the sky was freighted with whisping armadas of buff-and-gray thunderheads, which on updrafts tumbled into and through each other, only to offer at incredible heights shafts of yellow-gold sun flooding tranquil plateaus that remained for a few moments and then were gone. Lower toward the horizon and the west, the sky was locked in immemorial gloom.

Ireland in spring. Its glory was evanescent and emphatic, and where in that movement of masses, the transit of the sun, the sowing of seed did McGarr—one of more than four billion of a single species—fit in? And how important could be his endeavors?

Ultimately, not very, though he realized in turning to McKeon, whose face was set in a drunkenly defensive scowl, there was at least one who would debate him.

Black wet rocks patterned the deep umber of the Wicklow hills at sundown, and a stiff breeze that swept rain in sheets was racking the slope of the Craig house in Glencree. Through the French windows beyond the pool in the patio, McGarr could see a bright wood fire burning, but he went around to what he still judged was the front door, though he had his doubts.

The woman's smile was sparkling and festive, until she saw who it was. But she resumed it, after a slight pause. "Chief Superintendent McGarr. It's cold out there. Won't you come in?" She stepped back, one hand still on the door, and in the precise and graceful positioning of her feet McGarr again made note of her poise.

The colors of her garb were reversed from the day before—a white sheer top with a low-cut bodice and brown pleated slacks—but the suggestion of both strength and femininity was still very much apparent.

McGarr removed his hat and smiled into the golden highlights of her dark eyes, again noting the jewelry, which was, like the house, parallelogram in shape, the stylish tufts of light-yellow hair that resembled heath grass in the sun. "I wonder if your man is about. I'd like to have a word with him."

The smile fell. The head moved to one side, and she clasped her palms histrionically. "I'm sorry, he's not. But I'm expecting him and . . ." She turned toward the fire. "Would you like to wait? Perhaps I can get you a drink."

"Smashing," said McGarr, not being able to keep his eyes from the ridges of her upper chest and its tan, her narrow waist, and her muscular stride as he followed her into the room toward the fire. She was exotic, and the tan again told McGarr that she had not spent all of the winter in Ireland alone.

"You're Danish," he said.

"Yes, but of course you could tell that from my name."

"And a dancer."

At a small bar, she tilted back her head and smiled, allowing the glitter of her eyes to move down his face to his lips. "Past tense. I was. How did you know?"

Still regarding him, she smirked in a way that broke the mask of youth. Wrinkles appeared around her eyes. And then her teeth were white in a way that was unnatural and had required great care. Her hand reached out to pass McGarr a large tot of malt. On the wrist was a thick chain of gold in what McGarr concluded was the requisite shape.

"You must be joking," she said, eliding the J. "I was a showgirl."

"In Copenhagen?"

Her head moved back yet more, as though appraising him, though she continued to face him squarely. "You're playing with me."

Not as McGarr would have wished.

"You know as well as I, sir, that Copenhagen nightclubs are no place for a proper girl to work."

"London? Paris?"

"No, Las Vegas, silly." The V was pronounced fetchingly, like a W, and she reached out to touch McGarr's sleeve. Even the nails—long and arcing out like cashews—were umber.

McGarr thought of Henry Craig and his ungainly frame, his long, curious face and the drooping eyelid, and now this woman who was so attractive and seemed so much of a piece with the stylish, exotic estate that was, mind, not in any proprietorial way, Henry Craig's.

And again McGarr wondered about her age. Could she be, say, forty? It was difficult to tell, given her tanned, leathery skin—a condition that the Irish sun alone would not have yielded—but he was willing to bet that she was older than Craig. And an expensive woman, that much was plain.

"Gambling, was he?"

"Yes, if you must know, I was." The voice came from behind McGarr and quite close, though in no way did it seem angry or put out.

McGarr turned, and Henry Craig stepped around him to the bar, where he had to bend to kiss the Danish woman's cheek. Fleetingly. A buss. "Sorry, I'm late. But all the details"—he turned to McGarr—"about William." His large features darkened. "The autopsy. The funeral."

"You gamble still," said McGarr, tasting the drink.

It was as though Craig, through an act of will, now composed himself. After removing his wet raincoat and pouring himself a drink, he turned to McGarr a face that seemed placid, unflappable, the mocking eye fully in command. "Yes, I gamble."

"And lose."

The woman looked away.

Smiling slightly, he considered his glass. "Like everybody else—sometimes."

"But you lose big."

The smile became definite now. "It's all relative, isn't it? Depending on how much one has to lose."

The woman drank from her glass.

"And your resources?"

"In a way you might conclude that I lose big."

"But in another?"

"There's always the chance . . ." He broke off and turned away from McGarr, lowering his large frame into an armchair of modern design. "And then I fully understand that for me there are three situations that I find impossible to endure in a reasonable manner: betting and winning, betting and losing, and not being able to bet at all. I've been struggling to maintain this last condition for—how long have you been with me, Lykke?"

"Seven months."

"But you have debts and not just from gambling."

Craig nodded.

"How do you propose to satisfy your creditors?"

The half-closed eye seemed nearly to wink at McGarr. "It seems all of that is being taken care of for me."

McGarr drank the remainder of the malt. "A gun collection. You have one, I'm told."

Craig nodded.

The woman came around the bar to take McGarr's glass.

"Explosive bullets. Would that be something you'd have?"

"You know it is, because you've checked. You'll find a dozen in a box in the top-right drawer beneath the gun case." He pointed to an open door to another room. "Purchased from Martin Brothers in town. Illegally, of course. The keys to the gun rack are there as well."

But it was on a shelf of the bookcase near the gun rack that McGarr found what he was after. A photograph of Henry Craig and Paddy Briscoe, arms around each other's shoulders, rifles clutched in their free hands. How old could they have been at the time? Fourteen or fifteen, too young to have been political, though Enda Briscoe, the father, could be seen standing in the background. In the photo Craig's drooping eyelid seemed to belie the idea, evident in the younger Briscoe's ecstatic smile, that they were having fun.

Out near the hearth and fire, McGarr asked, "Are you political?"

"Not anymore."

"Sinn Fein, wasn't it?"

Craig nodded. "That too is a matter of record."

"Last night around half eleven, where were you?"

The eye moved away from McGarr's. "Seeing some old friends."

"The bomb in the back garden of your father's shop on the quays. Who's responsible for that?"

"I understand you have some idea of that yourself."

"It doesn't disturb you that I've arrested your"—he paused—"old friends?"

This time the eye did wink, though without a doubt unconsciously. "Nothing that you could do would disturb me."

15

Noreen followed the archival assistant down the stairs of the Jeu de Paume, out into the darkness and the rain, which in sheets was now raking the rue de Rivoli. The assistant glanced back over her shoulder, buff crescents of sclera showing. As she did so, Langlois emerged from the museum entrance.

"Where are you staying?" the assistant asked Noreen.

"I'm not, I'm returning to Ireland tonight."

"Out of Orly?"

Noreen nodded.

"Good, if this is really about what you say it is."

Noreen wanted to ask the small woman with the tottering gait why she feared Langlois so much, but she had seized Noreen's hand and pulled her out into the traffic between a gap in the double wall of lights. Behind them, Noreen saw Langlois on the curb. "You won't find a taxi at this hour," she explained, "at least none that would take you as as far as Orly. And there's safety in numbers."

Nor did the older woman's pace slacken when they reached the farther sidewalk, rushing to make the traffic light at the rue de Castiglione and then hurrying toward the crowd that had formed in front of the Tuileries metro station on the corner of the rue du Marché-St.-Honoré.

Only then did she release Noreen's hand. "This has to do with the paintings, the ones in the article, the ones Langlois recovered?" She began digging in a purse for some coins.

Noreen thought for a moment. "Yes—I believe it does."

The babushka made the woman's head seem small and the features of her bony face even larger. She had not withdrawn her hand from the purse, and her eyes rose to Noreen's, round with concern. "Then you'd best listen to me. It makes much of what has been going on in the Jeu de Paume understandable—the choice of what's to be hung, the whole debate about how much conservation should be applied to the collection, Langlois's anger and . . . desperation when he's questioned.

"Here—take these." Into Noreen's hand she placed two tokens. "And remember what I tell you, in case we become separated." Once again she glanced over a shoulder. "We take the metro as far as the Place d'Italie, where you'll get off and walk—stay with the crowds, don't rush, I learned that during the War—to the Gare d'Austerlitz. There you can get a train straight to the airport. Stay on it, don't get off, and for heaven's sake, do something about your hair. Here." She tugged at the knot of the babushka, which she handed Noreen. "Put that on. There aren't three women in all of Paris with your hair."

But the line in front of the metro station had not moved. Casting another nervous glance over her shoulder, the woman again grasped Noreen's hand. "Come. In here. We'll wait for the queue to break up." And using her diminutive size and narrow shoulders to advantage, the little woman pushed and shoved her way into gaps in the crowd, pulling Noreen after her with an urgency Noreen did not quite understand, until they had gained the door of a small café. In trying to close the door, Noreen felt the knob being grasped roughly by a man. Langlois.

The café too was packed with people, and the desperation, of which she had spoken, seemed now all in the older woman's eyes. "You'll never get away with it—too many of us know. Hélène . . ." She pushed her way toward the bar and ordered two coffees, Langlois following them.

"Know what?" he demanded through his short, widely spaced teeth. "I'm not trying to get away with anything. I'm just trying to save my position and yours and the reputation"—he looked around at the other patrons and lowered his voice—"of the museum. Scandal is no good for anybody or for . . . art."

"How—by hanging forgeries?" she demanded, and the man behind the coffee machine looked up from his work of filling cups. "It puts all that you've done since you've become Directeur in perspective. And before that even, when you were Curator."

"Lower your voice, you fool."

People were now turning to them. Langlois's brown-tone glasses were steamy, his close-cropped hair wet.

"Listen to me, both of you. And try to understand my position. I made no mistake in '44 when I certified those paintings. I knew what they were, but had I any choice? What were my options?"

"None. You're an expert. Your word is—"

Langlois's hand now moved into the pocket of his raincoat. "Shut up and listen, you who've never had any more responsibility than saying yes to whatever Hélène or somebody else has told you, and why? *Just because* you can't be trusted."

He turned to Noreen. "When those paintings came back from the train, there was ostensibly nothing to distinguish them from the originals except a general evenness of tone. As copies"—he swung his head to the woman—"listen to me, Françoise, as copies they were perfect, except when viewed together, like that, fresh out of the packing cases and lined up against one wall. Only then, as I said, was Louisine's tone—

which one would have had to have viewed in her own work to know—perceptible.

"I waited until night when Villanbrecque and the others were gone, and I took three of the canvases into the lab, only to have confirmed what Krugger—it was he, it wasn't any part of Louisine except her talent, I'm sure—had done."

A large man, in trying to reach the top of the zinc bar for his drink, pushed Noreen into Langlois, and she felt something long and hard in the pocket of his raincoat.

"For that period of nearly two years between his 'rescuing' Louisine from von Behr and the German evacuation of Paris, Krugger forced her to continue doing what she had done for us, but to *his* purpose, all the time befriending us at the museum, ingratiating himself and making the *Kunstschutz* seem like an altruistic avatar of"—he flourished his hands—"*art.*

"I should have known, and in retrospect it seems almost as though she had tried to tell me. I met her—Louisine—once on the street. We had coffee together. I asked her if she was happy living with a German. 'German, French,' she said, 'is there a difference what name they go under?' When I asked her what she meant by *they*, she mentioned something about oppressors. When I asked her what she was doing, she said, 'Much of the same.' Her manner was distant, and at the time I thought perhaps it was drugs, but how could I have known then?

"And what was I faced with? Thirty-eight of our best paintings were gone. The very best of our collection and all series work, not merely Sisley's *L'Inondation* but—"

"The *Nymphéas*," the older woman said, looking away, meaning Monet's many paintings of the water lilies in his garden at Giverny. The Orangerie had devoted an entire room to their exhibition.

"Of course, it had been easier for her like that, the compositions being somewhat repetitious, and I was faced—as few others have been—with a dilemma."

The older woman shifted uncomfortably and opened her purse to pay for the coffees, even though Langlois had placed a ten-franc note on the bar.

"I'm not trying to make my actions seem heroic or even correct or anything but what they were, but consider the possibilities. Remember, I knew Krugger and well. A brilliant if a devious and deceitful man with what I could then see were unknowable reserves of quiet cunning. Up until then, everything he had planned had gone his way—his theft of the paintings right out from under the nose of Metternich, the *Kunstschutz* chief, doubtless one by one. His and Louisine's and the child's evacuation from Paris and their disappearance. Whatever logistics had had to have been in place to have gotten the genuine paintings out of Paris and without a doubt out of France—all of that was overwhelming, to say the least.

"Now, it had taken seventeen days to get the paintings back to Paris, three to get them into the Louvre, a day to uncrate them. I had no idea what Krugger's resources were and with whom—if anybody—he was in league, but I did know this: raising the cry would have made the dispersion of what then comprised his collection that much more likely and quicker, and already the tales reaching us from the Eastern Front were of the quick deals that could be consummated with the advancing Soviet forces. They were buying every type of thing, no questions asked, and paying in gold.

"Then, Krugger had evidently murdered once on the train to facilitate his escape. Of what else he was capable, I did not and could not know. Would my sounding the alarm cause him to sell them off quickly—Asia? South America? the U.S.?— their being well-known parts of a series making dealers or collectors, who would normally be chary of such things, more interested in acquiring them? Would he even resort to destroying them in order to keep himself from being caught?"

Noreen's eyes met those of the archival assistant, who looked out the window toward the entrance of the metro station.

"So instead I chose to do nothing, hoping . . ."

Noreen glanced down at a shoe.

"Hoping that some lead as to their whereabouts—"

The older woman's nostrils had flared. She tugged at the sleeve of Noreen's jacket that was away from Langlois.

"—would arise, *Françoise*." Langlois's tone had become icy once again. "We are not speaking of apples and oranges here."

"Nor of archives," she said, her eyes again darting toward the window.

Noreen, looking down, watched Langlois's hand come out of the pocket of the overcoat and take her arm. "Think, please—Madame McGarr—of Krugger's position. He now had millions of francs' worth of genuine impressionist masterpieces that would stand up to any, every sort of scrutiny. He would only have had to change the frames and stretchers, which he had probably already accomplished, given all the paintings of that vintage that had been destroyed during the Occupation, and one at a time he might let them go.

"You're a dealer. You understand these things—a quiet sale to settle an estate, a 'discovery,' even an attribution which the purchaser would discover on his own was, in fact, the real thing and keep quiet about to keep the price somewhat low. With thirty-eight of them, Krugger could afford that.

"Better still, why sell any at all? Why not wait decades before releasing them, since their value could only appreciate and all the memories of the Occupation and what happened then would have grown dim.

"And it was what I was hoping for, what has now finally occurred, that in reading everything that was written, spoken, even rumored about impressionism, by becoming the Expert of my generation, I'd learn of Krugger and the paintings, that someday something or somebody would come to me about one of them, and I'd be able to track them down. In the meantime, the public would not be denied the enjoyment of those works, either."

Yet again the older woman's hand moved to Noreen's sleeve.

"They'd be here to be seen, and, more, Krugger, wherever he was, would not be on guard, would begin to grow complacent, careless. He'd give himself away eventually, which is what we've seen.

"And, listen to me." Langlois paused as the large man reached past him to set his empty glass on the bar and ask for another, and the assistant whispered to Noreen, "Just follow me, when the time comes."

"There's precedent for this. The Louvre is no sacred cow, as you well know. The Campana Collection of majolica, acquired by Napoleon III, was a potpourri of doubtful objects and out-and-out forgeries. The Benivieni bust was another. The *vierge ouvrante* even had faulty iconography with a secular figure of knights and kings. And sentimental? It fairly reeked of the nineteenth century, and yet the great, all-knowing Louvre bought it."

When the man again reached for the fresh drink, the assistant tugged at Noreen's sleeve and stepped quickly away from the bar, Langlois's hand slipping off the slick fur of Noreen's jacket. The large man, jarred by Langlois, spilled the drink on his jacket and shoved Langlois back into the bar.

The assistant swung around, pointing at him. "He's pestering us, and we don't care for his attentions."

The café had quieted, and eyes swung from her to Noreen, who nodded.

"And who's going to pay for this?" the man asked, trying to flick the Chartreuse from his lapels.

Without responding, the assistant tugged open the door, and they rushed out into the night.

But they had only reached the landing that led to either track of the metro when Langlois caught up with them, his face flushed with anger. "Françoise," he shouted, spinning her around. "Why are you doing this to me?"

"You. It's always been you, Hector, who has been done to, and here it is no different, is it? You don't care that much"— she held up two fingers and a thumb and shook them at him, her eyes bulging, the veins in her forehead distended— "about the museum and you never have.

"And all your talk about precedents. It's *merde* and nothing more and you know it. Who was really behind the majolica and acquiring it for the Louvre? Pinelli, that wretch, and"— she flourished her hands—"*experts, such as you.* And the Benivieni bust? Was it Bastiani, from whom it was bought, who claimed it was by Verrocchio or Donatello? No. It was your ilk who talked it up and made the extravagant claims and drove the price to fourteen thousand francs. Why? You know yourself. For your own ends—so you could line your pockets or derive some other advantage.

"Monsieur le Directeur," she went on, taking a step toward him. He had one hand on the rail of the flight of steps that led down to one side of the metro, the other in the pocket of his raincoat. The station was still thronged with other metro riders. "We might grant you some knowledge of art, but you are ignorant of the ethics of your own profession, or you think us fools enough to agree that when you first learned of the forgery and chose to do 'nothing,' as you put it, you in any way exculpated yourself.

"No. On the contrary. And it wasn't just from that moment

that you began to conspire with Krugger and that woman, was it? No again. Then you only dropped the other shoe of the theft by notifying the world that those thirty-eight paintings were safe and sound in the Louvre and that any other paintings like it and genuine were just further examples of the series work of the impressionist painters. Then you only legitimized the entire conspiracy, along with demoting me, who dared to question your"—she waved a hand—"'expert eye,' routing me into the archives where you knew I'd languish. Remember that? I do well." Her laughter was mirthless. "Well enough to have watched you closely since then.

"And shall we tell her the real reason you've been waiting all these years for your precious evidence of their existence and why, once it arrived, you, an old man who could do nothing on your own, didn't contact any others?" She moved even closer to Langlois, who was perched on the final step of the staircase, craning her head up to him, her neck thrust out. "Or the board? The police? The government?

"From the day the memo came down from the Directeur effectively destroying my career, alluding to malfeasance, poor preparation, even laziness, I knew you had something to cover up. I put in all the time I soon had on my hands, all my negative attitude and insubordination into keeping tabs on you. Suspecting what I did, it was easy to understand why you became enraged anytime anybody tried to meddle in your little 'field of specialization'; why, after those two came, you decided it was time to remove the Krugger material from the files.

"They were the Magi you'd been waiting for all these years, weren't they? Arriving under a dark star, as it were—first the young one, and then the other whose name was Irish but whose French was as good as my own."

Langlois's head went back, his eyes behind the rain-streaked, yellow lenses narrowing.

"Shadow enough, you thought, to begin poring over the Irish subscription lists to *Impressionnisme*, cross-checking the address in Inchicore with inquiries to the magazines and the letters that have appeared from time to time from that address."

A sound now came from Langlois, guttural and involuntary, a kind of moan or growl. A muscle beside his temple had begun to twitch.

"Not tell her?" the assistant went on. "Why not? She knows everything else. You, the great researcher who's dedicated his life to impressionism, wouldn't want her returning to Ireland with any great gap in her knowledge of our collection, would you?

"No. Then shall we tell her why, long after November 1941 and von Behr's discovery of the Faure woman's deception, you kept on requisitioning supplies from the conservation department for, as you put it then, 'artist friends' whose work otherwise would have languished without supplies? Furtherance of the cause of art? Most certainly, especially all the documents which proved so difficult to destroy or alter, all of those that had to do with what you took, a little bit at a time, until it totaled nearly a liter and a half, all the little fibs and reasons and projects you had to dig up to justify the use of certain naphthenic acids of—"

Noreen scarcely saw Langlois's hand move. It was quick, deft, a swipe with a large, canvas-cutting mat knife, and then there was blood everywhere, it seemed.

The assistant, caught in mid-sentence, merely turned her widened eyes to Noreen, trying to say something like "Run," which only formed a bright bubble of blood on her lips before she began a soft tumble, raglike, down the long flight of stairs.

"What happened?" somebody asked Langlois, whose hand was back in his pocket.

"I don't know. A hemorrhage. She simply . . ." His eyes

scanned the crowd, which was quick to form, but Noreen had left—away with the part of the crowd who had not seen the woman fall, across the landing and down to the track on the other side of the metro and a train that pulled away just after she boarded. She kept the babushka wrapped tightly around her head.

There was another airport in Paris, and her first concern now was safety and a phone.

16

It was dark by the time Mc-Garr returned to the quays. A mist, stealing up over the banks of the Liffey, mixed with the vapors of a day's labor, the smoke from the still-smoking rubble in the garden, and the many fires that had been set against the coming cold.

"Yes?" she asked, one hand clutching at the lapels of the housecoat, the other brushing back a wisp of hair that had fallen over an eye. At first frightened but then relieved to see it was he. The woman whose choice of solitude had become complete with the death of her husband and the gardener and the abductor of the maid, the woman who now had to answer the door that led up to the flat.

She closed and locked it behind them, though Gárdai teams were still combing the new rubble, and a security squad had sealed off the quay. The silk of her housecoat crackled, sparking in the shadows, and, as he followed her up the stairs, the words of the day before came to him and then all his own:

"When did you notice your husband there? Murdered? In that ditch?"

No answer, only her eyes, dark and darkly ringed, holding his gaze.

And later, "All day long you did not once look out this window?"

Again no answer. Only the eyes.

"You did not see your slain husband out there in that ditch?"

Yet again nothing.

"Can it be that you fear for your own life, that you did see him murdered and you are afraid to tell me what you saw?"

Fear? Perhaps McGarr had mistaken her reticence and the matter was more complex than that.

Complexities. Tired of them he was, and now, snapping on the light in the kitchen, he brushed away the shattered glass and debris that had been blown onto the newspapers, magazines, and knitting basket of the maid at the corner table. And he began rummaging through stacks of bills and receipts, all, he noted, initialed L. F.C. Looking for what? He didn't know, but it was, he was convinced, there in the house. Something specific from the little world, the microcosm, that was her life in that flat. The missus's world.

The connection—Rose Marie Coyne and her son to the men at the Silver Tassie? It was real, but why would they have chosen to end that? It had only obscured things, Coyne's murder, as it was supposed to—the smoke and the fire. McGarr thought of Tobin, his "colleague," who seemed to know where the old woman was.

The son? It had been Henry Craig's desire to understand his own connection with the larger world that had seemed to initiate the chain of lethal events. McGarr, pawing through a stack of bills submitted by provisioners, butchers, specialty shops on Grafton Street, a parking ticket, a tax notice, remembered seeing the son out at the Silver Tassie. With his woman. Correction, with his expensive woman. Lykke Allborg was nothing, if she was not that.

While straightening up, he found that the missus had made him a cup of coffee, which she proffered with a shyness that caused him to study her long features, the certain hollowness of the cheeks which, he imagined, had increased with age. A perfection? He judged it was.

And in the son's room, when, having found it as empty as a suite in a hotel—"Rose Marie," she had said, "had some things that she wanted to discard. Bedding, blankets, things from Henry's room"—McGarr began patting the pockets of his jacket for his cigarettes, which were gone, she offered him her own, wet from her lips.

Their eyes met fleetingly, but it was enough. Again her hand moved to the hair on her brow, and in a way that was self-conscious and girlish she turned away suddenly. Her hands in her housecoat pockets drew the clinging material tightly around her hips.

Something had changed for her—McGarr could feel it—and from that moment, tasting the dark tobacco, he was unsure if she was following or he was being led.

Into her bedroom and the closet deep and packed with expensive items—sports clothes, suits in a range of colors and styles, dresses, evening clothes, even a kind of ball gown that had been custom-made in Paris on the rue de la Paix; Paquin, Madame Grès, Chanel—only the best and all bagged and hung, as though inventoried according to use. Ski clothes, yes. And several changes. A jogging suit. Some outfits that would look right on a golf course.

Below was an array of shoes. Even the pair of heeled huaraches, in which he had seen her on the day of the murder, was contained in shoe trees.

Noticing a small door at the very back of the closet, McGarr opened it: another smaller and air-cooled closet with furs, a dozen, seventeen, eighteen. A sable coat which, he imagined, reached her ankles, made nineteen. He wondered who—Roche or Craig—was after wanting to make it twenty, but McGarr said nothing, not wanting to spoil her mood. Against his burned and bruised hand the cold fur felt soft and soothing.

In turning he found her next to him again, the warmth of her body—why was he so conscious of it, was his attraction to her unique to him?—giving off a spicy scent, like sandalwood or myrrh, but heavier, deeper than that and slightly musky. And for a moment he thought she would reach for him.

The chiseled upper lip jumped once, as her eyes—hooded —trained down on his. A shoulder curved toward him, that hand coming up from her hip as though she would wrap his there in the darkness among all her precisely filed clothes, which were, he assumed, meant for nothing but mirrors.

And McGarr, in spite of his injuries and exhaustion, still managed to feel the moment. It was real, the feeling between them. Heady, hot, and he imagined something quick and bru- tal, a kind of disorder which would be quickly subsumed by the overall harmony of her world.

The bed. It was plain but swathed in a lacy coverlet.

McGarr wondered if in his exhaustion he was making too much of her orderliness and the way she was using her body, the swing of her shoulders and hips—always toward him—but in the bathroom, stocked with bandages, plasters, prescrip- tion medicines, and surgical equipment worthy of an emergency room (all again contained behind glass and "com- posed"), she finally touched him. A hand on his shoulder, easing him onto a white, enamel stool.

She stared down at his cheek. "Your bandage—it needs changing." Not, You're injured, or, You need care.

And her ministrations, easing the gauze from the burn and applying some soothing salve, her curves soft against his shoulders and back, swaying, the silk sounding like a gentle breeze through rushes, made his eyelids again feel weighted, his limbs leaden and heavy. And did she pull his head and neck into her thighs, when he swayed on the stool? He thought she did, though his body was forcing sleep upon his mind, for she said in a kind of whisper that brushed against his ear like a caress, "The bed is only through that door. I won't bother you. I'll wake you if you are phoned.

"Come. I'll help you off with your jacket. Your shoes."

But no mention of the blast which she had as much as witnessed, as he forced himself to his feet. He fixed his mind on the image of her standing in the blown-out window frame, her dark features made suddenly light and youthful by the flames. And before in the other window after her husband's death.

"Come. I'll help you in." Into the bed with the lacy coverlet. Did she add, "Who's to know?" in French? He thought she had, and, leaning his weight toward the door and the hall, he imagined how it would be to waken in the depths of that woman, her darkness in layers. Her shadows. She appealed to McGarr. Even at that moment after little sleep when, he imagined, his body could feel only pain.

The kitchen. He poured more coffee.

But only in entering the final room did it strike him that his feet were no longer falling on broken glass and wedges of glazing compound, but rather on parquet flooring that was clean in the thin light through the tall windows.

And it was neither cold nor drafty there in her studio. McGarr approached the two windows that faced the garden to find that they had been covered with something clear. Reaching out, he touched his fingertips to clear plastic which had been stretched—he checked the edges—on a frame as tight as a drumhead.

Stepping back, he noted that the frames had been cut to fit the, say, 10-foot by 4-foot windows. And no awkward brace strapped the corners. The joints were slotted—mortised and tenoned—and McGarr marveled at the work.

"I used the plastic to protect my pieces," she said, again at his side and rather close, as if they were lovers or—could it be?—conspirators. But the pride in her voice was undeniable. The tympanum of the windows—what she used to look out on the larger world—had been violated by the blast, breached, stoved in. It had spewed debris everywhere. But she had coped, cleaned up quickly, and sealed off her refuge perhaps more completely than before. She, an artist with a stretcher and another kind of membrane.

"Pierre brought me a roll from Paris. Impressive material, is it not? Strong. Go ahead—feel it."

Roche, her contact with the larger world. Her emissary, her protector as much as Craig had been, but her keeper and censor too, McGarr did not doubt. The Guards at the door had had to turn him back three times since Craig's murder, she having chosen not to see him.

What if, perchance, she had wanted to establish her own connection to the larger world and not just by way of the clothes that McGarr had viewed in the closets and had doubtless been bought by others or by phone? He now turned and looked around the room. No phone. Only in the kitchen, Craig's bedroom, and down in the shop. Two there.

To have left the premises on her own, then, when, say, Rose Marie had taken a day off? No. McGarr remembered the apprehensive look on her face when she answered the flat door for him, and he imagined that she was scarcely able to venture into the shop alone. Yet.

He turned to her. "Do you have a desk?" he asked and noted that in spite of the blast and her most probably sleepless, work-filled night, her large features looked almost fresh.

And now, did she even smile? Yes, he was sure of it, but just the slightest tug at the corners of her mouth. "I don't know what you mean by that?"

"Correspondence. A writing desk."

She merely turned aside, indicating with her chin a corner

of the room near the window which was untouched and looked out into the rubble-strewn lot.

There the neatness obtained as well—pencils, pens, writing paper, and envelopes all contained by made-to-fit cuts of stretcher wood that had been glued to the bottom of the drawer, so that in pulling them open nothing might become misaligned. But either she had had no incoming correspondence or she had thrown it away.

McGarr was about to close the drawer of the desk—Art Deco, like so many of the other appointments in the room—when the care she took with her own objects, her—what was the word? conservation? yes—her conservation of all that she owned overwhelmed him for a moment. Such care was possible only because she had delimited her horizons to one room and what could be seen from those windows.

The box of stationery. It looked new, as did the wood that held it in place. And the ink in the Mont Blanc pen, the large, cigar-shaped model—the "Diplomat"—that would be the correct size for her large hand, had formed a bright, black bubble on the gold nib, as he unscrewed the cap. The window on the side showed that the reservoir was nearly full.

And what did he now think he had heard said about the pen and the paper? And by whom? The maid? "Every penny accounted for, from a box of stationery to a 'Mount' Blanc fountain pen costing half a bleedin' fortune just to write one letter." Yes, by Rose Marie Coyne, who had had her own reasons for so saying, McGarr did not doubt.

He pulled the box of stationery from the drawer and removed the envelopes and notepaper. "Any more around?" he asked.

She eased herself onto the desk, sitting close enough that he was again encompassed by her aura and scent. "What are you doing?"

"Counting," he said. The box said that the one hundred

sheets of notepaper and fifty envelopes had been made in the Republic of Ireland, which made it just about the only Irish product in the room. A cash-register slip inside said that it had been bought in the Eason's shop in Talbot Street, which was across the Liffey, two bridges down from Craig & Son. Six weeks and a day ago.

Forty-nine envelopes. Ninety-eight sheets of paper.

McGarr tried to assess the emphasis. One letter in at least half a dozen years. It couldn't be, but it probably was. He glanced up at her.

"I've always wanted to correspond."

"With whom?"

She only looked away in the manner she had the day before, when he had asked her the questions that mattered.

"They didn't write back."

She dropped her eyes to the radical slope of her chest, the silk deep lilac in the shadows, and brushed a fleck of tobacco from the housecoat. Her nipple, protrusive in the material, quivered.

"If they did, you would have written back."

She drew on the cigarette, her heavy upper lip with the chiseled edge trembling slightly. McGarr waited, watching for the smoke to appear, wondering how much time it would take, again thinking about how she had spent her days, and for decades.

Time. In this, the small world of her own creation, it must have been opprobrious, like a kind of self-inflicted punishment, and she would have watched it, paying out the terms of her penance.

Then why was the Art Deco clock, which Pierre Roche had given her, the only thing in her small world that was out of order and stopped—McGarr did not need to see the hands— at 4:47, the same as the clock in the shop office.

Opening the case, McGarr touched a finger to the pendulum and listened to its tick. It remained steady and strong in the darkness, having been stopped to a purpose.

The darkened showrooms of the antiques shop were cold, and in the office the bezel of the early Georgian, musical, long clock felt almost wet to McGarr's touch. Concealed there he discovered a tight, flat packet, about the size of a children's book, wrapped in clear plastic and tape.

She had followed him there, pausing, looking around tentatively, as at a new world, and again standing too close.

"Will you tell me why?" he asked, turning to her, the old canvas obvious below the plastic.

She only looked off, drawing the lapels of the housecoat over her chest.

17

It was the time of night that in her own house Maisie Edgerton-Jones liked least: half nine, quarter to ten, when her eyes had grown too tired to read or watch telly, and the prospect of a long, perhaps sleepless night seemed bleakest. Anyhow, there she had already read the good books, and the programs on her own box were neither piped nor in color and the screen was only half the size of the one in the McGarrs' den.

And then there were all the arts periodicals that Noreen subscribed to and Maisie had been leafing through showing every class of beautiful thing. Perhaps that was why she felt so different tonight, though she suspected it was just the fact that she had something to do.

The phone. Noreen had said she'd call when she got to the airport, and already once, not more than a half hour earlier, the phone had rung. But by the time she picked it up, whoever was on the other end had either tired of waiting or only listened to the sound of her voice, repeating the number as was only polite, before ringing off. It wouldn't have happened, say, twenty or thirty years ago, when apologies for a wrong number would have been profuse, but, then again, not every bowsie and mot had been on the exchange then. Things had changed so.

She glanced down at what she considered the immensity of her dog, asleep on the carpet in front of the television, its back to the screen and its shortened foreleg, the result of the old injury, raised in a kind of somnolent salute. The wide, black pad was exposed and seemed to be keeping time with each beat of its heart. A bounce, another, and again.

She then scanned the fresh scorches on its coat, again feeling a hollowness in the pit of her stomach at the thought of what might have happened, only to tell herself, as she had a good dozen times in the past day, Sure and he's only a dog, of which she had had dozens when she was hunting, and she could always get another, though never a one that would be at all the same.

And, like the car—her Humber town brougham, which she had gassed up and parked out front, the keys on the plush of the chair by her hand—the dog helped fill her hours, which this stint of having something to do for the McGarrs had made her realize were all too idle. Her best days, of course, had been during the War, when she had been a battlefield nurse with Montgomery's Army in France, working round the clock with not a single day off in four and a half months.

Perhaps she would see about getting something to do, maybe some volunteer work or, better, a little part-time job in a shop, someplace smart like Noreen's. But how to ask without changing things; as neighbors the McGarrs, now there eight years, could not be better and confirmed—Noreen's maiden name being Frenche and all—what had been some of her best hopes for the Republic.

For a moment she was moved to consider, as she had not in many weeks, marriage, and how comforting it might have been to have had somebody else—a life companion—about now, but she put it out of her mind with the sound of the doorbell.

Noreen. She had taken a cab all the way in from Swords.

The old woman shook her head at the expense. A tenner at least.

Nevertheless she glanced at her image in the hall mirror, the careful design of her graying hair and the onyx-and-gold choker that she donned against the trip to the airport. Noreen always looked well turned out, and it would not have done to have had her picked up by a harridan. She had inherited the necklace from an uncle's last wife, who in one of her several preceding marriages had been a marchesa and used to such things. Otherwise, Maisie was wearing a black velvet jacket and slacks with Chinese slippers to match, and she felt rather modish and chic. For her.

But swinging open the heavy Georgian door she found not Noreen but a man standing behind the screen. "Yes?" she asked.

"I beg your pardon, but is this 87 Belgrave Square?"

Maisie, squinting slightly, examined the cut of his clothes, which was odd, and the tint of the lenses of his glasses, which made the skin around his eyes seem jaundiced. And then, she had never cared for anybody who kept his hands in his pockets, especially in weather that was not cold. He was a small, square man with close-cropped, graying, brown hair that was matted and wet in the rain, which since sundown had continued to fall.

"The number on the door, I believe, signifies that."

"The residence of Mr. McGarr?"

Maisie now placed the clothes, the glasses, and the accent. A Frog and untrustworthy, as she had discovered after a brief, poignant affair during the War. "Who, may I ask, is after wanting to know?" She clasped her hands in front of her. It was always best to get a name.

"Monsieur . . . Boisneau, from Liège." A hand came out of the side pocket and reached between the lapels of the raincoat, the other trying the handle of the screen door, which was locked. "I saw an item in the window of his shop, and I was given this address. Perhaps the madame is at home?"

When she said nothing, he added, "I really am in a rush. I'll pay cash. The lady'll do." He removed something from his wallet and again tried the door. "My card?"

"Not necessary. I'll see if she's in." Maisie made as though to turn, then turned back, noting that both hands were again plunged in the raincoat pocket and the man was scanning the street.

"Which item is it?" she asked.

"The Yeats gouache."

"Of the Leopardstown racecourse?"

A pause. The man again faced her squarely. "No, the other one," he said in a way that made his diminutive teeth visible.

"Of?"

"Of . . . his brother, the poet."

"Are you certain you have the right McGarr?" she asked, debating whether she should close the heavy, paneled door. But then, she would have to lock it to be sure, and that would be too much. Perhaps he really was a customer, even if mistaken. "With the shop on Leeson Street?"

"Yes, Leeson Street."

And then with the door open she could keep an eye on him. "I'll see if she's in her office . . ." With a finger she pointed up, as though to indicate the upper floors of the house. She turned and started down the hall toward the stand and the phone there. She did not know what he really wanted, but now she no longer cared. Noreen's shop was on Dawson Street, and Jack Yeats's work did not include a gouache of his brother.

She carried the phone into the darkness of the dining room, where in turning and glancing at the hall mirror, which gave her purchase on the front door, she saw the man take something from his pocket.

And before she could even place a finger in the dial she saw him reach up and draw the instrument—a blade, it flashed—across the screening, which shrieked as it was rent, and then down the side. His other hand reached through the flap and began fumbling with the lock of the screen door.

She dropped the receiver in its yoke and paused, panicking, wondering if she should make a dash for the heavy, paneled door and shut and lock it or run to the pantry and the key to the gun drawer, but already the man was in the house, closing the screen door and looking out to see if he had been noticed.

And with what even then struck her as absurdly foolish calm, she carried the phone back into the hall and placed it on the stand, then turned and began walking toward the kitchen and the pantry, hearing the heavy front door close with a clump in back of her.

The dog. Passing the den, she thought of calling to him, but some fear either of what might happen to him or what he might do kept her from saying anything, and she even considered closing the door. He was asleep on the floor, the television blaring above him with some replay of a Gaelic football match.

Langlois caught her in the pantry, reaching up for the key on the board. One of his hands grasped her chin, raising her neck, the other bringing up the canvas-cutting mat knife.

"I'm sorry," he said in French, "but you're now in the way."

And it was only when he swiped at her that she reacted, jerking up her forearm, which absorbed the searing flash of the knife blade. Once, twice. The third strike clattered across the onyx choker and bit into her cheek and ear, but before the man could lash out again she felt some great power hit them low. It sent them crashing into the cupboards, where her head

214

came up against something hard and she fell, the dog on top of them, tearing at the man, who beat and kicked away at the animal.

Canned goods, glass bottles, and jars fell on them, until the man gained his feet and tried to make the door, where the dog, lunging, it seemed, for his neck, brought him down against the pantry door. She could no longer move, and for her remaining few moments of consciousness, in which she attempted to wrap a tourniquet around her left arm, which was spurting blood, the thrashing and beating continued, the pitch of the dog's growl now a high, angry snarl.

Lying on the floor, the P.M. had felt the vibration of the front door closing. Seeing its mistress pass by the door, however, it had lowered its eyelids once again, only to have heavy footsteps in the hall wake it. A hand with the key ring in it was seen leaving the room but again only vaguely. McGarr? The dog had again closed its eyes, too tired and sore to rise for a greeting. But then a scent became apparent to it, different and heightened. Threatening. A menace.

The blade had fallen, and, when Langlois tried to pick it up, the dog's teeth came down on his hand, grinding through his flesh, cracking the bones—Langlois could hear them—but still he held on to the knife, tugging open the door with his other hand and stumbling out into the hall, pulling the door shut on the hand and the dog.

And how long it lasted he did not know—a few moments or an eternity—feeling the dog's hot breath, it seemed, in the marrow of his bones, breathing pain into him, until at last the grip slackened somewhat and he wrenched it free. He again slammed shut the pantry door, against which the dog now began hurling itself.

Langlois could hardly imagine that the hand was his own, running as it was with his own, the old woman's, and perhaps the dog's blood. Already it was swollen, and he now felt sick, nauseated. He staggered toward the sink and the dish towels that he could see on a rack. Under cold water, the hand felt huge but mercifully numb. He knew it would not last.

If the woman—the young one, the redhead, McGarr—were in the house, the barking, which was furious, was sure to bring her. Turning, he caught the glint of something on the floor by the pantry door, at which the dog was lunging. The blade. He felt great relief, having it in his hand once more, but he nearly blacked out straightening up.

And he noticed something he had not seen before: lights in the rear kitchen window which looked out into the garden, from—he advanced upon it cautiously—the house next door.

Peering out, he saw a burly man with a full beard and fedora carefully negotiating the stile in the wall between the gardens, a torch in his hand.

Langlois spun around, thinking of the keys to the car, which he, standing in the shadows and the rain of the green across the street, had watched the old woman park in front of the house. Had he dropped them, like the mat knife? Worse, had he dropped them in the pantry with the dog? He would need the machine to find the address in Inchicore, especially at this hour and now being injured. Caution had kept him from renting a car.

A beam flashed across the window. "Peter," somebody called. "Noreen?"

He had to reach his other hand around to feel the raincoat pocket on the right side, and it was with a kind of thrill that he found them there, though he was already moving toward the front door.

He paused there listening for some sound above in the house, but he heard none. Well, he had tried. Having silenced her would have made it all so much easier.

He opened the door, pushed the torn screening away, and stepped out onto the front landing. Below him at the curb glistened the rounded lines of the old Humber. The sponge-rubber soles of Langlois's shoes squeaked on the rain-wet slates.

18

Busy still? McGarr wondered who Maisie would be calling and speaking to at such length, given the hour, and if it was Noreen who had rung. But then why? Noreen would not have phoned for a lift. It was too far and the old Humber too slow. More, it was too much to ask of somebody her age.

He pressed the button of the hand-held phone in the police communications van that was parked on Heytesbury Lane, a fashionable street in Dublin's select Ballsbridge, and began dialing the exchange, when he was stopped by Greaves.

"He's on the blower himself, Chief."

McGarr put up the phone and glanced at Tobin's bearded half smile. The Special Branch Chief was wearing a cashmere overcoat with what McGarr guessed was formal attire below. Tobin had made a brilliant marriage to the daughter and only child of a chain-store magnate. She was waiting in a large car parked not far from the van. Tobin shifted uncomfortably on the narrow seat next to the van's bank of electronic circuitry, though his smile remained. He would be the last to suggest that he had other commitments.

"Number?" McGarr asked.

"Same," said the Technical Bureau sergeant who had installed the tap. "The shop on the quays."

McGarr, again thinking of his own house and wife and the telephone call he had gotten from her from Paris, dug into the pocket of his raincoat for a Woodbine.

The technician looked away.

"Janie—why don't she answer the bloody t'ing?" Greaves asked. "She's there, sure. Where the hell else *would* she be?" He then shot out his hands when they heard the number respond and a tentative, "*Oui?*"

Roche responded in French, "Have you completed your preparations?"

There was no answer.

"Please, Louisine, you know how important this is." Then, "Don't make me have to go through it again," as though Roche knew or expected he was being overheard. "It's just for the weekend, but there's so much paperwork to clear up, and William . . ."

Whispered Greaves to McGarr, "Like I said." In an earlier phone call, Roche had seemed to make a point of telling an assistant that he'd be gone for the weekend, maybe a few days longer, even though he had left the man only hours before. "The estate . . . I hope you can understand."

Now, "You know what must happen?"

No reply.

A long wait. "You agree?"

"No."

"*Louisine*"—an exasperated pause—"you are the most difficult person. Must I tell you again?"

McGarr would appreciate that.

"You're there all alone. You haven't even got food, for goodness sake."

Though she had a chef.

"And money? What will you do for that?"

There too, McGarr had been led to understand, she was without any care.

"I can't leave you like this."

Greaves's eyes met McGarr's. Why not, if only for a weekend?

"I'll be there in an hour or so. I'll have the driver honk, as usual, then let myself in."

"I'll be in bed."

Roche sighed, but before he could say anything she rang off.

"The monitor on?" McGarr asked, reaching for a light.

Greaves pointed to a tape recorder, then opened the door for McGarr. "G'luck."

Tobin asked, "Will you be long, Peter?" although his eyes remained fixed on the recorder.

"I hope not, Ray, but, as you know, people are various."

"Just what is it again that you hope to gain from all of this?"

McGarr removed the cigarette from his mouth and stared down at its end. "It's not as though you're here by engraved invitation, now is it?"

Greaves, smiling, turned away.

McGarr stepped out into the dark, wet street, ignoring McKeon and Delaney, who were parked in a car by the curb.

Edwardian Dublin: its bay windows were tall and narrow and manicured hedges led to alcoved front doors. In the shelter of one, McGarr rang a bell and waited. Eventually a light was switched on behind translucent, leaded panes, and a ponderous step made the staircase creak.

The great bulk of Roche's upper body was wrapped in a shiny leather jacket, the short collar of which was raised to the white hair that curled at the back of his neck. And his eyes, beneath the reconstructed ridges of bone and flesh, seemed hostile, until McGarr stepped into the light.

"Ah—Chief Superintendent McGarr. I was expecting you, though, sure not at this late hour."

"Saw your light, Mister Roche. Thought we might have a

chat." Smiling up into the man's horrible face, McGarr removed his wet cap and, stepping past him, began climbing the stairs. "Going out?"

"What makes you say that?" Roche closed the door, though he remained at the bottom of the stairs.

"Your jacket, of course. Unless it's unnaturally cold up here, and"—McGarr turned to the man—"*sure*, it's not. *Luvelly* piped heat. And look—there're your cases, all *five* of them."

"Yes," said Roche, having to use the rail to raise his bulk to the landing, where he paused, breathing heavily. "I thought I'd do a bit of fishing and try to . . . forget for a few days."

"Ah, yes." McGarr advanced into the spacious and austerely furnished flat. "The memory is remorseless at times, is it not?"

The only decoration in the sitting room was a group of paintings in small format, which, instead of having been placed individually, had been set in rows on one wall, which, McGarr imagined, caught the north light: all of Paris in the several seasons.

"How the past can tyrannize," McGarr went on, "delimiting our scope of activity—the choices we make, the things that happen to us, what we choose to do." He sat in a low and softly cushioned armchair and placed his cap on his knee. He stared up at the big man, who stood squarely by a sideboard tall enough for him to place an elbow on.

"It imposes a certain determinism, wouldn't you say? Denying the willed self, as it were, and forcing—because of what happened in the past that now shapes the present—forcing events upon us that otherwise we might avoid. In your case, for instance." He allowed his eyes to take in the man's bulk, the gloves that matched the jacket.

"Really?" Roche cocked his head and smiled slightly. "It's always valuable to hear oneself discussed. A nightcap?"

"Yes, please."

Listening to the conversation in the communications van parked out in the street, Greaves noted that Tobin's smile grew somewhat fuller. Drinking with a suspect was frowned upon by both the Gárda and the courts.

"You were saying?"

"That Pierre Roche could scarcely help himself."

"Which is often the case," Roche replied jocularly, handing McGarr a snifter filled with a fluid, the amber color of which was almost red. "But doubtless you have some particular regard in mind."

"Yes. Certainly." McGarr tasted the liquor. Cognac. "From Segonzac?" he asked Roche, who had returned to the sideboard, against which he now leaned.

"Not far."

"It's very good, and at first the bottle, placed there by the door of the gardener's kip, threw me off, until I realized that Coyne wasn't a clock-watcher and was certainly even less conscious of time drunk than sober. Drunk he would have noticed only darkness and light, and the bottle was just another of the several things that were done—that by Rose Marie Coyne, who was just trying to protect her son—after you, Mr. Roche, ran amok and murdered your partner, William Craig. Or shall we refer to him as Wilhelm Krugger?"

Roche drank off his snifter and poured himself another. On the sideboard were crystal vases that contained sprays of flowers, bowls with dried fruits and nuts. "I'm puzzled. Aren't you planning to caution me?"

"You have the right to—"

Roche held up a hand. "Please—I consider myself cautioned. And Solicitor Glennon, should he be present?"

"If you think him necessary."

"No." Roche shook his head, as he selected a walnut and placed it in the maw of what appeared to be a nutcracker. "I don't think so. That would disrupt your creative flow, and we couldn't have that. I believe I'm in for quite a story. Do continue."

In the van parked out in the street, Tobin folded his hands and lowered his head, as if staring down at the shine of his patent-leather shoes or praying.

"It was an act of passion, certainly," McGarr went on, "but of retribution too."

Roche raised one of his reconstructed eyebrows. He smiled, and for a moment McGarr felt something like pity for him, until he remembered the dead Guard.

"Where to begin?"

"Why, at the beginning, of course, Chief Superintendent. I don't want to be spared a detail."

"And you won't, if I can help it, but it's difficult to choose where to begin, you see. With the arrival of von Behr at the Louvre in 1941, perhaps?"

Roche's head went back.

"Or—to save time—with the crucial event that must have been a matter of no little conjecture to you for these forty-some years? *Who* told him how big a fool you and Louisine Faure had made of him in Paris? Von Behr—the German *Einsatzstab Reichleiter* Rosenberg chief, an aristocrat, an art expert, and evidently a treacherous and ugly man. And you, just two French *blancs-becs* with a palette of paints, a knowledge of conservation techniques, and some old canvases and frames. His outrage knew no bounds, and he reacted with a savagery uncharacteristic even of him.

"Whatever combination of things that he did to her, he managed to crush what was best in her—the joy that's obvious in the paintings above me; for life, for her work and her art, which, I believe, she's only now getting back. She remained for the rest of the War, while you were recovering, content to paint for Krugger and Langlois thirty-eight copies of impressionist series pieces that now hang in the Jeu de Paume, and since then who knows what else?" *Content?* It was a poor choice of word but McGarr could think of no other.

"And from you? Well, from you von Behr and his Gestapo, thinking you dying anyway and as a final, gratuitous act, crushed your"—again McGarr searched for a term—"manhood." McGarr paused while Roche, whose smile had not changed, replaced the metallic instrument in the crystal bowl. "Incredibly, you recovered and not merely physically. You've gone on—with some help, of course—to carve out no small domain in the world. You are now a man of taste, refinement, and wealth."

Roche nodded to him slightly and picked the walnut meat from the shell, placing it on the gleaming surface of the sideboard.

"The memory and doubtless the resentment lingered, as, of course, it would, and you were presented daily with the picture of Louisine living with another German, though at least in his regard for her Krugger had been different.

"But had he been any different from you yourself or from, say, Villanbrecque or Langlois or the others who had dared her and then required her to paint copies of other artists' work? Who had kept her secreted away in some apartment or flat, perpetrating forgeries and then, later, having to keep a close watch on her for fear she wasn't totally committed to the larger conspiracy, the one directed by Krugger and Langlois.

"I don't know how you learned of it, but I can guess. It was either because you and he shared a Strasbourg background or because she got in touch with you, and when you learned of their removal—hers and Krugger's; Langlois, it seems, was left behind—you used that knowledge to secure a share in what they had done and were attempting. Why not? Certainly, you had already paid the price without any benefit at all. But because she had revealed the not-so-little secret once, it was likely that she might fancy doing it again, and I can imagine that the wraps were drawn even tighter about her."

Again McGarr sipped from the glass. "It's that, you know, which finally foiled your plans. She had the illusion of freedom with all the very finest that the rue de la Paix could provide, with what appeared to be control over household funds, with the view of the quays and the Bay and its ships out the window, but with three warders, counting the maid. And how to break that? She thought she knew.

"Rose Marie, I'm sure, dutifully reported the purchase of a box of stationery and a Mont Blanc fountain pen, but she had grown old herself. It came too late, the letter was gone, and suddenly Krugger/Craig had his old partner, Langlois, from whom he had absconded, back again. Or at least he knew he soon would.

"But Langlois, who, incidentally, had been searching for you three for years, had been hurt and was greedy, having had nothing but his civil servant's salary all these years, whatever small royalties his books about impressionism brought him, and the prospect of his pension. And he perceived an opportunity provided him by just that patient, careful research that had up until then yielded little fruit. It was a wedge which, if placed properly between you and Krugger/Craig, would eliminate one of you and get the other to reveal the repository of the thirty-eight genuine Louvre canvases. But how? And the source had to be credible and unimpeachable.

"The son. Krugger's son? Your son? I suppose it doesn't matter, but Langlois who was either informed in Louisine's letter or guessed there was a son, decided to use him to smoke you out. He guessed that the boy would be interested in his real beginnings, and the gift of a painting—a supposed bequest from an uncle—was readied along with the suggestion that his name was not really Craig.

"It proved enough, and in a matter of days after receiving it, Henry Craig was in Paris where Langlois, acting supposedly as a 'disinterested' researcher, filled him in, even allowing him to take away a small entry in the Louvre archives—photocopies wouldn't do, not for this—as proof of Krugger's duplicity, that it had been he who had told von Behr about you and Louisine.

"Did you know this when, by your own admission, you met Henry Craig at the airport? I don't think so. You met him there in an attempt to put a lid on things. If, with his gambling and other debts, he needed money, then you were there to tell him to hang on, the entire"—McGarr remembered McKeon's words—"mini-empire would be his if he'd just relax. He was your sole beneficiary, and he stood to inherit his mother's estate as well.

"Did you tell him more, what other valuables you, Krugger, and his mother held in common? I don't think so, Henry being an intelligent fellow and perhaps putting it together himself. And then, you might not have had the chance, given the news he had for you.

"And how to deal with it—that it had been the 'friend' and partner of over forty years and the man who for all that time had been living with the woman you loved, who had also been the one who had turned you in to the Gestapo, who had nearly had you killed, who had had you taken to von Behr's headquarters and—"

"That's enough," said Roche.

"—had you—"

"I *said*, that's enough."

But McGarr continued, "—as much as castrated."

Out in the van in the street, Tobin glanced at Greaves, who nodded.

"But worse, wasn't it?" McGarr stood and carried his glass to the sideboard.

"How would you know?" The hooded eyes were dark now, the skin of the forehead drawn taut, the nostrils flared.

"I wouldn't, I don't. I have only to look." McGarr reached for the object in the glove, a kind of tongs, but with a rounded, serrated maw for grip. "A souvenir, perhaps? Did you carry these around in your pocket for forty years, or is this their permanent shrine, to be fondled whenever the thought strikes you?

"You took a trip, didn't you? Argentina, by way of France. You couldn't go to Langlois because that might draw him out even more than he was already, but you had to be sure, so you checked yourself in under the name of Briscoe. A coincidence, the name, that of a certain publican on the Enniskerry Road? Not in the least. Documents—you had to show some to get into the files.

"It rankled, didn't it? The knowledge that for all those years Krugger had been having you off the same way you and she had had von Behr off, but worse. Far worse. You were the goat . . ."

McGarr waited while Roche shifted the mass of his body. They were only an arm's length apart. "But not exactly a goat, as it were, Mr. Roche, and you couldn't wait. Even in New York, where you had to change your planes on your return from Argentina, you knew what you were going to do and how. Was it from there that you called Krugger/Craig and told him some story about having to discuss an urgent matter so that you could get back to the Argentinians or whoever you had said immediately? Probably—a direct dial with no record. You wanted him to be ready and waiting, the shop lights on, the door open, dressed to kill"—McGarr did not smile—"as he usually was. And no witnesses but the proper one, up there in the studio window. An early riser.

"The gun. Krugger's own, again with the proper ammunition, there in the desk drawer. Dirty stuff, ugly enough to carry everything away. No doubt you brought that with you.

"A face-off? Of course. You presented the evidence, you cornered and berated him. A beating? No. The contrast between how he looked and how he would look was too much to be ignored, but it wasn't difficult for a man of your size—the bulk that you had gained because of your special difference—to collar an old man with bandy legs, to haul him down the passageway and out into the garden, and through the low, arched door, and into the lot.

"How did you know she'd be watching? Did you call to her or perhaps fire off the gun once? That's immaterial, but she was watching, wasn't she? Otherwise you would have taken him up into the studio itself and killed him there, amn't I right?

"The shot? Low, of course. The groin. What he, not you, had had his pleasure from these many years.

"Then back through the gate, shutting and locking it. The gun? Who knows? You, of course, but it'll surface. You probably have it under the belt of your jacket right now. And did you stay around to hear Bobby Burns's 'When Oft' Through the Glens' chime on the clock in the office, as you told me before? The same clock which on three separate occasions you tried to return to and wind? You had heard that from Rose Marie without a doubt. She told you it wasn't striking, but by then she too could not return . . .

"Had you, you would have found that your witness wasn't as frightened and passive as you thought. She, of course, had begun the whole bloody business, and even if she couldn't bring herself to swear against you, she had another way of drawing our interest."

"You're lying," said Roche.

"Am I?" As McGarr began to reach into his raincoat, Roche's

hand moved toward the bottom of his leather jacket. "Go ahead," said McGarr. "I'd like that. Nothing to hold you on now—the innuendo of dead or missing witnesses, forty years of misplaced passion and convoluted greed. A weapons charge? I'd take it."

Out in the van in the street, Greaves's eyes met those of the Technical Bureau sergeant, and Greaves reached for the radio on his belt.

McGarr tossed the packet, which he had taken from the clock and now from his raincoat pocket, onto the sideboard. "Recognize the plastic, the tape, the—neatness of the wrap? What's below you're even more familiar with. Stopped the clock, it did: 4:47, like the one in the studio. Was that the time that you shot Krugger? To the minute, I'd say, she bringing the hands of the one in the office back so they'd match. Symmetry. An artist, after all."

McGarr reached for the decanter. "Nightcap?"

Roche said nothing. His eyes remained fixed on the packet.

"You shouldn't perhaps. A long drive?" McGarr asked, though he believed he knew better. He drank his off, half wishing he could take the decanter with him. "Good night, Pierre. May I call you that?"

In the van, Tobin was perplexed. "Well—what more does he want?" the young man nearly shouted. "I'll arrest him myself." He reached for the door.

A former stevedore, Greaves dropped his powerful hand on Tobin's wrist.

"Take your hand off me."

"Please, sir, he knows what he's doing."

"Not by half. He's a mucker, and I'll have you up before—"

"Yes, sir—but the pins are in place."

"What pins? His?"

Greaves only looked away.

19

Inchicore: the two dozen short streets that remained from McGarr's childhood were forlorn in the first pale streaks of daylight. Schools and parks had replaced the slums, and the railway works had expanded, biting off more space. A power plant and factories had taken yet more, and then the road southwest to Naas had been widened. Traffic bristling with lorries as much as cut the community in two.

And yet the older, larger, people-filled Inchicore was a cityscape that McGarr still prowled in his dreams. Stepping carefully across the sooty tracks toward the boxcar that Roche had had shunted off on a spur so that it faced Railway Avenue and the back of Rose Marie Coyne's house, he was overwhelmed by a sense of *déjà vu*: that years ago, perhaps, while playing here as a child he had known that one morning at dawn he would again cross the yard with a large, lame dog by his side and the Commissioner of Police and the Chief Superintendent of Special Branch behind him; that because he had known the area so well he had not had to guess how Roche planned to remove his cache of paintings from the site.

"We will load the car ourselves," Roche had told the railway traffic manager, who had wondered how, way out there in the far corner of the yard. "Though he's done it before, you know.

Antiques, that class of thing. A Frenchman. He's a big dealer of that in the city." But more likely automatic weapons, rocket launchers, and gelignite, McGarr had thought, and he had known how it had been accomplished: through a low gate that had once been an entrance to the railway yard before Rose Marie Coyne's house had been built in front of it.

There he now stopped and removed from his pocket a long pick that was attached to his key ring. The railway officials had been unable to find the key, and meanwhile Sinclaire, who was posted in the house across the street from Coyne's, had radioed that Roche had arrived, pulling the car in on the far side of the small park, not far from Maisie Edgerton-Jones's old Humber.

"He's walking fast and straight for the door. A dark-brown leather jacket. A cap to match. Gloves."

And why not? McGarr thought. There was nobody about and speed was now a necessity. Thirty-eight paintings set in air-board cases would take only a half hour to load and seal, and from Coyne's he would phone the station. "Westport is the ultimate destination, though with a single car, like that, it'll take a week," the railway official had said. Westport, where Roche had a holiday house and a sea-going yacht. "All fitted out for a journey, it seems," said a Gárda contact there.

Roche would only then have to go to ground, and with his connections—Tobin now shifted nervously, as McGarr worked what proved to be a well-oiled lock—that would not be hard, were Langlois not awaiting him.

"Nearly there now, Chief. I saw the curtains move, though. He's expected."

Indeed he was, and would Langlois be waiting for him at the door in the narrow hallway that ran the length of the factory mews and would be darkened to the purpose? That too seemed likely, and McGarr was hoping for as much.

"Jesus," said Tobin, "why don't you take them now?"

"It wouldn't be fair," said McGarr, opening the gate door and lowering the volume of the radio in his pocket.

"Fair to whom?" asked Farrell, following McGarr and the dog into the deeply shadowed back garden.

The sky over the top of the house had turned a shade of tourmaline, McGarr noted, which was nearly the shade of his wife's eyes. He again thought of Maisie Edgerton-Jones. "Why, fair to the state which would only have to house those two"—McGarr thought of the word "foreigners," but chose rather the Irish term—"blow-ins, and we're servants of the state, are we not, Ray?

"And then," he directed them to the wall near the back door, lowering his voice to a whisper, "the fella here is after languishing in retirement."

Said Sinclaire over the radio, "The key now, it's in his hand."

As with the pick in McGarr's. "Unless, of course, you'd like to go in there yourselves."

"What are you planning?" asked Farrell, adjusting the fit of the glasses over his watery eyes, worried he might be asked to preside over an indiscretion.

"Right—it's open now. He's looking up the street."

McGarr took the scrap of cloth Noreen had found on the floor of the pantry and held it down to the dog.

"He's stepped in. He's closed the door."

McGarr heard a scuffle from within the house, a low, stifled shout or scream, and then the report of a large-caliber hand-gun. Swirling the pick, his other hand on the knob, he shoved open the door and stepped back for the dog, which padded inside, tentatively first, then with increasing speed, its nose raised, scenting the darkness. McGarr closed the door and stepped back.

The second scream was long and agonized, and followed

by the shrill, angry attack of the dog, which continued, it seemed, for whole minutes. There was a cry for help—desperate, imploring—in French.

McGarr only nudged up the brim of the cap and dug in his jacket pocket. He remembered how he and his childhood friends used to walk the top of the railway-works wall with its four long and dangerous jumps. One friend in falling had been snagged on a spike and had been ripped from belly to forehead, losing an eye. He wondered if back then he had been a different person, more tolerant and less judgmental. And less vengeful.

And he remembered the Coynes living here and even, now, Rose Marie out here in the garden, hanging the wash, a child—could it have been Curtin/Coyne himself?—playing in the gravel by her feet.

"Do something!" Tobin demanded. "It's—"

The dog could still be heard in the hallway.

McGarr drew in a foot. "After you." He opened the door. "Chief."

Tobin did not move.

"Was it really necessary?" Farrell asked, his eyes not wanting to meet McGarr's.

McGarr thought about what Noreen had told him of Maisie Edgerton-Jones and the assistant in Paris. He thought of the young Guard dead out in the alley and of the hapless Curtin/Coyne. And again he thought of his own beginnings here in subproletarian Inchicore, where, perhaps because of Ireland's particular past, calling the police was less acceptable than almost any retribution taken. Yet he doubted it was that which had caused him to loose the dog on Langlois.

He stared down at the glowing head of the cigarette and wondered if perchance he was not simply one person, but rather—like Krugger/Craig, who had acted savagely, only to

233

be called a gentle man by all who knew him afterward—a multiple of identities, and at the moment an atavistic McGarr, who understood a justice that predated the laws of the Oireachtas, had come to the fore.

He glanced up at Farrell. "Most decidedly. And, sure—he's just doing what he's designed for."

The moiling flux of Farrell's eyes moved up over the wall at the end of the backyard.

They found Roche's body crammed into one corner of the hall, the blood from his slit throat pouring, like black ink, down the shiny surface of the leather jacket. Langlois was nearly on top of him, a hand—bloody and swollen—raised as though waving.

But it was Langlois's neck that was most obvious. His head was thrown back, and the area between his chin and his chest was a raw gouge that was still bubbling with the reddest blood, straight from the heart.

The dog hobbled back to McGarr's side, its chest and flews bloody, its ears down and tail between its legs, knowing it had done something wrong.

"It'll have to be destroyed," said Tobin. He turned and began trying the closed doors.

Over an easily dead body, thought McGarr, reaching down for the P.M., when an old voice came to them:

"Take your hand off that knob and step back. And if Peter McGarr is out there, tell him I'd like to have a word."

20

___

"**A**h—there you are and with the mutt again. When I heard the animal I knew you couldn't be far. Savaged him, did it?" In the dawn light, dim through the shrouded windows, McGarr found Rose Marie Coyne sitting at the head of a long table which nearly filled the tiny room. She had something in her hand, which she held toward him. "You'd better take this from me now. Me wrist is achin' from the burden, and enough is enough.

"Who's he?" she asked, as McGarr took the Luger from her hand.

"Tobin. Special Branch," said McGarr.

"And the other one?"

"Farrell, the Commissioner."

"Dignitaries. I'm flattered, but what's needed now is a hand at the kettle. I'm parched after fending off your man with the razor, and then, if I'm to play the tout, I'll play to me own. The water will be hot on the hob."

McGarr turned and glanced at the other two men.

Farrell only placed his hat on the table and sat at the other end. A witness would be needed.

His exasperation plain, Tobin turned and made for the door. In the hallway he could be heard giving orders.

"And then the curtains, Peter, if ye don't mind. The day is for the living, and haven't we both made it through?"

The new daylight through lacy inner drapes mottled the Luger in his hands. He removed the clip, which was fully loaded, and the chamber smelled sour and metallic. The weapon had not been fired in years.

"The mister gave me that. A darlin', a gent. Says he, 'Rose Marie, these paintings have a certain value, and it's not as though we can store them in a vault,' and he cocked his head in a way that said more. 'Your family and your house in Inchicore is known to everybody, I'm led to believe, and . . .' sure, he didn't need to go on. I knew what he wanted, my Tom having been a Fenian hero and martyr, though unsung, and then dead in Brixton Prison but six months.

"Treason, the Brits called it, and they would have hung him anyway, but there wasn't a glom or a smash-and-grab artist in all of Dublin who would've come on the place. And then"— she glared at Farrell and her eyes, like milky agates, swung to the walls—"who'd think of all that beauty being here, of all the places in the world?"

Placing the pistol on the table, McGarr turned to the paintings that were hanging on the wall—a dozen or so of Monet's *Nymphéas*, which he had viewed in the Orangerie many years ago. By every standard—as a particularized study of light in flux; as objects that were at once beautiful and central to the development of modern art—the canvases were attractive. Bathed in early-morning light, their chromatic vibrations were insistent, if restrained, but McGarr was rather more interested in the old woman's appreciation of them.

"They're the only thing for weather like this. So cool and calming, like you're sitting down at the water's edge itself. At other times I might put up some other ones, which are in the closet over there, depending on me mood. But mostly I keep the room shut and locked with the humidifier on, like Mr.

Craig, who paid so much and the current too—God bless his dear, dead heart—told me I should. The women in the neighborhood thought I was just being cagey, like some of them were themselves, and keeping all me good things under plastic in one room that nobody never saw." She glanced at McGarr. "It happens, mind."

He nodded. For women of her generation in that neighborhood, it had probably been the rule not the exception, and he wondered how Krugger could have been privy to such an intimate knowledge of the setting.

"You see, with the kids and all, the lads in the Army took what turns out a pretty sort of pity on me. Because of De Valera and the Special Powers that made them illegal, Enda Briscoe—who I'll never forgive for what he done to my youngest—managed to get himself to Germany, not just England, like me poor hubbie. There, I don't know who he met or what he done, but during the War he'd just show up from time to time, wanting a bed"—she looked away demurely—"and then, near the end of things, he arrived here one night with a woman—the missus—and two satchels.

"One contained them"—on a knobby wrist, her hand crooked to the walls—"all rolled up like so many wads of wallpaper, the other stuffed with money, all of it rubles. The mister followed not long after, and had I not been told otherwise, I would have sworn he was Craig from the North, like he passed himself off as." She shook her head once. "Brilliant he was for the years before Roche arrived." Her features glowered.

"The missus's doing all the way, though she made sure there was no proof. For the mister it was as though he'd seen a ghost, though to give Roche his due, he soon proved himself worth it.

"It was like he was trying to prove something—himself better than the mister, I should imagine, to her—and, of course, she fancied nothing better than to have two men slaverin' over her, getting her this, that, and the other priceless thing, though she maintained otherwise."

Tobin now appeared in the doorway and pointed to the table. A Special Branch detective entered toting a tray that seemed tiny in his beefy hands.

"That bitch, and I use the word"—she raised a bony finger and shook it—"advisedly, can think of nobody but herself. And when she tired of them, she ruin't everything that was supportin' us all, these here valuables that would have kept us in our old age, and, it seems now, even the channel to the boys in the North who'll be after wanting for our help come this fortnight."

Farrell turned to Tobin, who glanced at McGarr and muttered something, then left the room.

Grasping the teacup in both palms, she raised it to her wrinkled lips. Closing her eyes, she took quick, audible sips until it was empty.

McGarr sat and filled it again.

"Where was I?" she asked.

"The son," McGarr suggested.

She raised her chin. "Whose son?" Her head quivered.

"Henry Craig—why him?"

She puffed her lips and expelled some air. "Why not? Another ingrate who could do nothing but run up debt. And would he listen when his father tried to explain?" Again she raised the teacup. "Thrashed off to Paris, stirred up a cloud of venom, and then—like the mother—decided he would wait for everything to fall into his lap.

"And then—who else was there? Roche himself? Who would run things? Or the missus?" She cocked her head, one sallow eyelid closing and her upper lip drawing tight. "I can tell you I wearied my poor, pitiable brain trying to think of some way to make it her, but she had no reason—or so it might seem—for murder, though it was as much she who pulled that trigger as Roche himself.

"And then—like me own son, poor Ned, a weak but dear little one from the start—we were unsure of just how much or little he might say. Later, we found that out, didn't we, running to the Tassie for naught more than the expectation of a drink. The whole situation took us, who'd been away from such stuff for so long, by surprise, I can tell you, and we didn't know which way to turn. Enda"—she stared down into her teacup and shook her head—"turned fool and threw the bomb. He then had no choice but to offer himself up, though it's what he deserves.

"And me?" She glanced up at the walls and the paintings hanging there. "I'm after having lived my life well, all in all, and righteously, given what I hold dear." She reached out and touched the back of his hand. "And, Peter, I hope you can say as much for yourself, come your time."

At the door, McGarr asked, "Westport?"

She smiled slightly. "A shill. The railway car itself would have arrived there all right, but picked cleaner than a bone in an alley. The mister—as you probably know—had been an expert at such things." Lifting the top of the teapot, she peered in.

Out in the shadows of the railway-works wall, a Special Branch squad had broken the seals and stripped some of the crates that could be seen in the open door: Armalite rifles, hand grenades, gelignite that had, McGarr supposed, been packed or transshipped from the shop on the quays. OBJET D'ART. HANDLE WITH CARE, stenciling said. REGISTERED CARGO: ANY INFORMATION LEADING TO THE APPREHENSION AND . . .

Tobin's smile was thin and sickly, his eyes accusatory. "I hope you know what this represents, Peter?" Before McGarr could even begin to guess, he answered his own question. "Months, years of effort, down the drain. Could we have traced the transit of this material . . ." He glanced at Farrell. He shook his head.

"I wonder," Tobin went on, "if Peter has anything to say. Now."

Farrell had looked away, up over the wall where two sea gulls were squabbling over scraps on a nearby roof.

The men in the doorway of the car had stopped their work and were staring down at McGarr.

Puzzled, he reached for a Woodbine. It had been he himself who had discovered the specifics of the weapons transferral, and he rather doubted the wisdom of any policy that assumed any such delivery inevitable. Wasn't it more important to keep weapons out of terrorists' hands than to know into which hands they had been placed?

He turned to Farrell. "Buy you a drink?"

Farrell pivoted, as though the invitation had been long in coming.

Somebody in the railway car chuckled, and Tobin swung his head to him.

Out in the street, Sinclaire was putting the P.M. into the backseat of a Murder Squad car.

A year later—or was it two?—McGarr was being driven down Grafton Street when a singular-looking woman caught his eye. Tall and dark—it was the contrast between wide shoulders, a narrow waist, and definite hips that had caught his eye, along with her rangy gait.

She stopped to watch a chalk artist copying a picture from a postcard on the sidewalk. Giving advice, she indicated something with her toe, and then turned away, smiling slightly.

McGarr's were not the only eyes to follow those legs.